Greek Island Memories

Ian Wilfred

Greek Island Memories
Copyright © 2025 by Ian Wilfred

This is a work of fiction. Names, characters, places and incidents are used fictitiously and any resemblance to persons living or dead, business establishments, events, locations or areas, is entirely coincidental.

No part of this work may be used or reproduced in any manner without written permission of the author, except for brief quotations and segments used for promotion or in reviews.

ISBN: 9798311236782

Cover Design: Avalon Graphics
Editing: Laura McCallen
Proofreading: Maureen Vincent-Northam
Formatting: Rebecca Emin
All rights reserved

Greek Island Memories is dedicated to four special author friends that I share so many happy memories with: Rosie Hendry, Jenni Keer, Clare Marchant and Heidi Swain.

Acknowledgements

There are a few people I'd like to thank for getting *Greek Island Memories* out into the world.

The fabulous Rebecca Emin for organising everything for me and who also produced both kindle and paperback books. Laura McCallen for all the time and effort she spent editing the book, Maureen Vincent-Northam for proofreading, and the very talented Cathy Helms at Avalon Graphics for producing the terrific cover.

For my late mum who is always with me in everything I do.

Finally to Ron who has had to live with me talking about these characters for the last six months.

Chapter 1
Vekianos, 1st January

Helena was nervous, anxious, and scared. Today was the day she had been dreading for years and she wasn't yet sure how she would react when she sat down with her mum Evangelina and brother Filippos. Thankfully, she was meeting up with Filippos first to discuss why their mum might have called them together. She had her suspicions but assumed her brother likely wouldn't believe her; after all, it seemed impossible to fathom that their mother might finally be stepping down! But if she was right at least they would both go into the meeting forewarned.

She left her little bungalow, situated just across the courtyard from the family hotel, and took all the shortcuts down into Vekianos harbour, which was one of her favourite places on this gorgeous Greek island where she had lived all of her life. The first thing that hit her as she entered the harbour was how very quiet it was, but then, it was early morning on the first day of a new year, and all the tourist businesses had been closed since the season ended back in the middle of October. It would be a very different story come late March or early April, when the gorgeous Greek island would start to slowly come back to life again.

The few businesses that did stay open during the winter months were all closed today as it was New Year's Day, and everyone was at home recovering from last night's celebrations, aside from a few of the older locals who were out walking their dogs and getting a little fresh air.

She waited at the end of the harbour wall for

Filippos to arrive, knowing he would probably be late as he had been out celebrating last night with his wife Nadia. Looking out to sea Helena realised this really was her happy place and had been for all her fifty years. There was nowhere else in the world she would want to be. She wasn't like her sister Voula, who embraced change and had fled the island at the first opportunity. Knowing her own life was likely about to change, and that there was nothing she could do to stop it, made her concerned and nervous.

'Hello, Aunt Helena, you're out and about early.'

'Hi, Marios, happy new year!' she greeted her beloved nephew. 'Give your old aunt a hug.'

Marios was her pride and joy, and their bond had been solid since the day he was born twenty-five years ago. She had, for lack of a better word, been part of the 'team' bringing him up, looking after him when his parents were both working. They were the happiest times of her life.

'Yes, I'm waiting for your dad. We've got a family meeting with your grandma. What's your excuse for being up early today of all days? I expect you're on your way home from a party? If so, I hope you had a good time.'

'You're spot on and yes, I had a lovely time, thanks. But I'm now off to bed ... unless you need me at the meeting? Do you know what it's about? I ask because something strange happened the week before Christmas with Grandma. Do you remember when I spent the day with her, moving furniture and boxes around so she could clean behind and underneath things?'

'She was probably having a good sort out before the season starts again,' offered Helena, a bit glad to hear that she wasn't the only one who thought Evangelina was acting odd.

'Maybe, but she said something odd when I moved a big chest of drawers back into place. She was quietly talking to herself and she said, "That's perfect, and there's plenty of drawer space for someone to fill." But why would she say that when it's her drawers?'

'I don't know, but this big clear out she's been working on has been going on since the hotel closed in October, and it's clearly more than just her normal end of season deep clean.'

'Hopefully you find out today what's really going on. I'd best be off though as I need to get some sleep before going out again tonight.' He smiled cheekily and Helena couldn't help but laugh and pull him in for a hug.

'Make the most of it while you can, Marios! We're into a new year now and before we know it the holiday makers will be starting to arrive, putting a stop to your partying.'

'Exactly! See you later.'

She smiled as Marios left. He was a good lad who worked really hard, she was so proud of him. Looking back out to sea she noticed there was not a boat in sight; everything was still quiet and peaceful, apart from the racing thoughts inside her head. She just knew today wasn't going to be like any other. Hearing footsteps she turned around, spotting Filippos walking towards her. He was early, and that was certainly a first!

'Good morning, Filippos, happy new year! Did you have a nice night?'

'We did, thanks, quite quiet really, and we were home by one-thirty. How about you?'

'I was happily fast asleep by ten-thirty but that was probably a mistake as I've been awake since four this morning. I saw Marios just now, and he seems to have enjoyed ringing in the new year with his friends.' She laughed.

'I remember those days,' said Filippos, a bit wistfully. 'Where have the years gone?' Before

Helena could answer he continued. 'Now, what's so urgent that you needed to see me before we go up to chat with Mum in the hotel?'

'I think today's the day Mum is going to tell us she's retiring.'

Filippos laughed. 'That's not going to happen! She's been threatening to retire for years but she never goes through with it. She'll never willingly hand over the running of her hotel to anyone else. What would she do with herself? How would she fill her days?'

'I think you're wrong. She's been different these last few months, ever since Uncle Zois died. She's been slowly clearing her office out and throwing things away, as though she's packing up to go somewhere.'

'Ok, say you're right. Even if she *is* retiring, there shouldn't be anything for us to worry about. You've been basically running the hotel for the best part of your adult life and you're more than capable of doing it on your own.'

'True, but all the major decisions have been made by Mum. Think about it, how many times in your life have you heard her say: "I'm Evangelina Aetos and as I own and run this ten-bedroom hotel, so *I* make the rules."?'

'Too many to count! Those words take me right back to when we were children. If I had a euro for every time I've heard that I would be rich! But that's part of why I'm convinced she'll never give up running the hotel. Think back to when Dad died, and Voula came back thinking she could help but then tried changing everything. It wasn't long before Mum put her foot down and Voula left again. I really think you're worrying over nothing, but if you're right, just know that you're more than capable of running the hotel standing on your head, with your hands tied behind your back. There's only one way to find out though, so let's head up the road and see what this family meeting is all about.'

Helena wished she had her brother's confidence that she would be capable of being the boss and taking over from their mum.

'What made you decide to quit working in the hotel once you were an adult?' she asked Filippos. 'If you had stayed on you would have been Mum's perfect replacement given you're so good with people, and especially the holiday makers that come to the island.'

'If the hotel had been bigger perhaps I might have, but given its size and the fact that you and Mum cleaned the rooms while Dad did the bartending and ran the restaurant, all that would have been left for me to do was cook the food, and I had no interest in that. I also think it would have been difficult to work with Mum and Dad. Mum was – and still is – set in her ways, and we likely would have come to blows because I would have wanted to modernise the place. I think Voula felt the same way and that's why she took off when she could. That's something else to consider – if this meeting is about Mum retiring, surely Voula should be here with us as it would impact the whole family?'

Helena thought over what her brother had said. He was right, the main reason she and her mum got on so well working together was because she never answered back or disagreed. He was also probably right about Voula's absence suggesting this wasn't a meeting about their mum retiring. The only thing she knew for sure was that they would know one way or the other in the next hour or so.

'Come on, there's nothing whatsoever to worry about. I promise it's all going to be fine.'

Helena still had her doubts as they stepped into the hotel and greeted their mum.

'Come into the kitchen so we can sit at the table,'

Evangelina said, motioning for them to follow her.

The siblings exchanged a startled glance before following her. Only the most serious of conversations required them all to be sat around the kitchen table.

'Help yourselves to a drink before you sit down. This shouldn't take long.'

As Filippos opened a can of fizzy drink Helena got herself a bottle of water. She could see her mum was building herself up to something and the sooner it was out in the open the better.

'I will get right to the point,' Evangelina began. 'I'm retiring, and before either of you say anything, please let me explain. I know that I've threatened this before but this time I mean it, and because I know I would be tempted to keep interfering with everything if I stayed, I have made the decision to leave Vekianos altogether.' She held up a hand to silence the siblings as they both went to protest at the same time. 'I'm going over to the mainland to live with my sister Dora in Parga. Since your Uncle Zois died last year she has been very lonely, and we will be good for each other. Of course, I will come back and visit often, but as a guest.'

'But, Mum, your home is here with me, Nadia, Marios, and Helena.'

'Please, Filippos, let me finish. I'm only going to be a boat ride away and during the holiday season you'll be going to and fro several times a week. This is the right step for me and is coming at the right time. Besides, it's only natural that I pass on the running of the hotel now as you three children will be inheriting it when I pass. Which leads me on to my final point: I haven't yet told your sister my plans. I invited her here today – well, to be precise, I asked if she wanted to come for Christmas and New Year's – but she said she was too busy so I will call her later and explain.'

'I doubt she'll be concerned,' said Filippos with a

roll of his eyes. 'We all know Voula has no time for this island because it's far too small for her. I'm sure she'll be more than happy for Helena to run the hotel.'

'I think you're wrong. Without me here on the island interfering and getting on her nerves, I think Voula might be keen to come back and assume the helm of running the hotel. She tried it once before, after your father died, though that only lasted a short time as we both had our own ideas about how to run the hotel. She wanted full control then, and I wouldn't let her have it, but now I'm no longer an obstacle.'

There was silence as they all processed the possibility of Voula's return. Helena didn't mind taking orders from her mum but to have her sister bossing her around was a different matter. The only way she could avoid that was to leave and get a new job, but that would mean securing a new home as well because her little bungalow behind the hotel would be needed for whomever replaced her. Helena had gone from secure within the status quo to a completely uncertain future in just a matter of minutes!

Chapter 2
England, 1st January

Jenny was awake early, which was a surprise as she had been out the night before. But saying that, it wasn't as if she had drunk a lot, and if she was honest with herself, she hadn't really had that much fun. She had just been going through the New Year's Eve motions to keep her friends happy. What she had really been looking forward to was kicking off the first day of the year with her dad, and she hoped they would be able to have a nice walk down along the river later on.

As she lay in bed, she thought about how both their lives had changed since her mum and dad's divorce. This was going to be the year they could both really move on with their lives. But first she had to talk to him about the big decision she had made. She knew he would support her no matter what, but she was still a bit nervous as she got up and started to get ready for the day.

Greeting her dad in the kitchen a few minutes later she couldn't help but notice the surprised look on his face. 'I know, can you believe I'm up so early on New Year's Day?'

'I didn't say a thing!' Her dad laughed. 'Did you have a nice evening? I know you weren't entirely looking forward to it.'

'It was ok. I smiled and said yes and no in the right places, but I also kept looking at the time and counted down to the moment I could head home.'

'Go into the lounge while I make you a coffee. And how about a nice bacon sandwich to kick start the day? Actually, not just the day but the whole new year!'

'Coffee and a sandwich sound perfect. Do you need a hand?'

'No, I'm fine. You go in and get warm. I'll bring your drink in while the bacon is cooking.'

As Jenny plonked herself down on the sofa, she couldn't help but smile and feel a little proud of herself. She had designed the decor for her and her dad's new apartment, with his input of course, and seeing it all done up was a reminder of how well he'd been coping since her mum had left him and they sold the old family home. It was nice to see him picking himself up and moving on with his life.

'There you go, darling,' her dad said, handing her a mug. 'The sandwich won't be long.'

As she waited she flicked through her phone and her social media accounts, something that didn't interest her so much these days.

'Here you are, one New Year's Day sandwich. I bought the ketchup for you to put on yourself.'

'Oh, thank you! That smells and looks lovely.'

'While you get stuck into that I'm just going to clear up in the kitchen.'

As Jenny ate she thought about the fact that now she'd made the biggest decision so far in her life, it was time to plan her future ... though what that entailed she hadn't a clue.

'Another coffee?' her dad called from the kitchen.

'Yes, please.'

'I'm going to grab a shower but I was hoping we might have a chat later today,' her dad said as he refilled her mug. 'There's something I'd like to talk to you about as your thoughts and advice would be valuable.'

'Of course, Dad. I'll be here whenever you're ready.'

Jenny was curious what her dad might want to talk about, but not overly worried. Over the last year they'd come to rely on one another and were comfortable being very honest. And that was all down to her mum leaving. It had been difficult, but ultimately it was best for their family, and they were all happier these days.

Jenny took her plate and mug back into the kitchen when she was done eating and took some minced beef out of the freezer to thaw. She would make them a cottage pie for dinner tonight after their walk. For lunch they'd head to the River Boat Inn to enjoy a drink and a ploughman's while they chatted.

Paul turned to Jenny as they set out on their walk a while later. 'This is lovely, and I know it's cold but it's nice to be outdoors and it's dry. Thank you for suggesting it.'

'Of course! Now, what was it you wanted to have my thoughts on? You have me intrigued!'

'Retirement. I know we've talked about it, but I've been having second thoughts. My original plan was to stay on in the civil service even though I'm eligible for retirement next month, but now I'm wondering if I should. I don't need the money as my pension will more than cover everything I need, and maybe it wouldn't be such a bad idea to have a fresh start. What do you think?'

'You already know my views on that, Dad. I know you keep saying you're only fifty-five, but they will take every ounce of energy out of you if you let them and I'd hate to see you worn down right when you should be making the most out of the life you've built for yourself. No, you need to slow down and enjoy your newfound freedom. Also, I know you're concerned that you'll be bored, but like I've been saying for the last year: you could do some voluntary work a couple of days a week, or even get a part-time job if you wanted. You've given your whole working life to the government but now it's time to say, "goodbye and thank you for the lump sum and the pension".'

'Not all my working life, technically, as my first job – which I did for a few years – was working on the Greek island of Vekianos. Gosh, that was over thirty years ago now, and yet it seems like yesterday.'

'Yes, and now you're actually allowed to talk about that time. Mum would never let you mention it; I think she was envious of that part of your life.'

'Which was so silly as I didn't even know her then, and it was very much in my past by the time I met her.'

'Perhaps you could go back for a holiday or something else you weren't allowed to do while you were with Mum?'

'That's not a bad idea,' said Paul as they reached the pub. 'You find a seat while I get the drinks. What would you like?'

'A glass of white wine, please.'

Jenny found a seat in the corner near to the open fire and took her coat off to settle in. She was pleased her dad was retiring and she was confident he would find a way to fill his time.

'There you go,' her dad said as he placed her wine glass on the table and settled in across from her. 'Today's the day you make your big choice, isn't it? You've had two months to think everything through so what will it be? Will you be relocating to your company's new offices or will you take the redundancy?'

Jenny took a deep breath. 'I'm taking the money, and I am one hundred percent happy with the decision I've made. It's been a good company to work for, and I've been happy for the seven years I've been there, but I don't want to move over a hundred miles away. I know they're doing the right thing as it will help them to grow, but I just wouldn't be able to afford my own home up there, even with the bigger wage they've offered me. To be honest, even before all this came up I was starting to get a bit bored with the job. There's a lot more to life than helping people with their finances and investments!'

'I'm behind you all the way.'

'Thank you, Dad. I know I'm doing the right thing. It does mean that tomorrow is going to be a big day for both of us. Who would have thought we'd both be returning from our Christmas holiday only to submit our one months' notice?'

'It's funny how that's worked out! But the world is our oyster now.'

'That's the scary thing – figuring out what to do next!'

Chapter 3
Rhodes, 1st January

It was ten-thirty in the morning and Voula had only just got up. Walking from her bedroom into the lounge she spotted the two empty wine bottles and her head pounded, reminding her that she had managed to drink both herself, plus have a few gins beforehand. But why shouldn't she celebrate the new year the way she wanted? She had decided against taking anyone up on the offer to go partying, and told everyone she wouldn't be staying on Rhodes for the holiday. Thanks to her little white lie, her friends believed her to be back on Vekianos with her family, but the truth was she had been in hiding, not wanting to go out in case she bumped into her ex, Elias. It would have been a disaster on an already emotional evening like New Year's Eve.

The downside to her lie was that she would have to stay in her apartment until at least tomorrow if she didn't want to be spotted by anyone she knew. But given the way her head was feeling after all the alcohol, it wasn't like she wanted to be going anywhere anyway. A quiet day recovering was exactly what was needed to kick off the new year. The previous year had been horrendous, and she found herself wondering – once again – how she had let everything go so wrong. Well, technically she did know that answer – she broke her one rule and had a relationship with a colleague. Though there had been a few occasions in her working career when she had been very tempted, she had never let it happen ... until now.

But in her defence, she and Elias had been in a relationship for two very happy years before he started working with her. The owner of the hotel she managed had offered Elias a role as the food and beverage manager, and though Voula had been hesitant about seeing her personal and professional lives intersect, she had wanted to be supportive of Elias. But it started to go wrong almost immediately. Elias wasn't keen on her being his boss, and she soon saw a different side to him, a side she hadn't known about before. What made it worse was that a lot of her best staff, who had supported her for many years, didn't like him, and the more they came into conflict with Elias, the more it affected her relationship with them. She had hoped to regain her friendships and improve those relationships over the last two months, since she and Elias had split up, but sadly that hadn't happened, and she felt more alone every day. The whole situation was a mess, but she was determined that this new year would be a chance to start over, and to do so she had to focus on the future – *her* future.

After a nice long shower and a hearty breakfast her headache had gone, and she even surprised herself with how well and positive she was feeling. Sat at her desk, she found herself doing something she hadn't done for over twenty years: looking for a new job. She didn't really want to leave her managerial position at the hotel, but it was getting increasingly difficult to see Elias at work every day, and given how many bridges had been burned because of her relationship with him, it felt as though the only way to get her life back on track was to move on and seek out a fresh start.

Thankfully, this kind of task was when she was at her best. She was a methodical person and so it was easy for her to switch off from her emotions and focus on the task at hand. She had decided to first concentrate the job search on hotel management jobs available here on the island of Rhodes. But she wasn't naïve enough to think there would be that many to choose from, so she planned to broaden her search to other Greek islands next. The last thing she wanted to do was have to look for jobs back in Athens, the place where she'd trained and worked for many years, as she preferred island life, but she might have to if there were no alternatives.

Throughout the day her phone beeped with new year's wishes but she didn't reply to any of them. The last thing she needed was to have her concentration interrupted. Her initial suspicions that it would be difficult to find the right position on Rhodes had been proven correct, but on the positive side, the other islands had lots of opportunities that interested her. She made herself a spreadsheet with all the hotels she wanted to apply to and then started to go through the list, investigating each one. She began by finding out who owned them, and then looked at size (based on how many rooms they held), and the facilities each hotel offered.

She finished up and switched the laptop off around seven-thirty that night, then went and poured herself a glass of wine to enjoy while she decided what she wanted to eat. A quick look in her refrigerator and freezer told her that her only option would be something with pasta, but that would do. She set the water to boil then made herself comfortable on the sofa and grabbed the remote. Before she could turn the TV on though, her phone rang with a call from her mum. She knew she couldn't – and shouldn't – avoid it, but she wasn't looking forward to lying, which she'd have to as she'd told her mother she would have to work over the new year period, in order to avoid going home for the holidays.

She took a deep breath before answering. 'Hi, Mum. Happy New Year! Did you have a nice night out? You mentioned you might go down to the harbour with Helena and Filippos – was it busy? And what have you been up to today?'

'Stop and take a breath for goodness' sake, Voula!' Her mother laughed on the other end of the line. 'I had a quiet night in by myself, which I was more than happy with as it meant I was in bed early. Just before I turned the light off I gave you a call to wish you a happy new year, but as your phone was switched off I called your hotel instead. You can imagine my surprise, then, when the security guard informed me that the hotel was closed for the Christmas and New Year period! You obviously had your reasons for not wanting to come home to celebrate and that's perfectly fine – you're an adult, after all, and have the right to make your own choices! Anyway, I want to be clear that that's not why I'm calling, and we can move on.'

Oh dear. Voula felt uncomfortable being caught out by her mum but still wasn't ready to tell her that the real reason she had wanted to spend the holidays alone was because she had split up with Elias and was feeling very sorry for herself. She wasn't one to show weakness to anyone, not even her family, and she didn't want to spoil the confident, in control, successful business woman façade she'd worked so hard to create.

'I don't want to take up all of your evening so I will get straight to the point of my call. Voula, I'm retiring from the hotel once and for all, and moving over to Parga to live with your Aunt Dora.'

Voula wasn't exactly shocked, per se, given her mother had been talking about retiring for some time now, but she also didn't know quite what to say. So, she remained silent.

'I suspect you have thoughts on the matter so please don't be afraid to share them. Based on their reactions, it's come as a surprise to your brother and sister, but Helena is more than capable of running the hotel and I think she'll thrive with me not looking over her shoulder all the time. To be clear, this doesn't affect your stake in the hotel, and I've made it clear in my will that the three of you will own equal shares, and can do with it as you please.'

There was a short silence, and Voula knew she needed to say something.

'I think it will be good for you to have a break from the hotel, Mum. You've worked so hard for so many years, and especially since Dad died, and with Parga only a short boat ride away you'll be nearby if Helena needs any help. And, of course, you can pop to and fro if you're missing it or you want to see the family.'

'Oh no, that's not happening. I'm making a clean break and if your sister needs help it won't be coming from me. I don't mean that in a horrible and unkind way, it's just that if I don't cut myself off completely from it, I know I will end up doing more and more, unable to truly let go. Now, why don't I let you get on with your evening? I just wanted to make sure you knew what was happening, though my news won't really affect you given that this little hotel is only a small fry compared to your big fancy hotel! Still, it would be nice to see you back on Vekianos before I leave so we can have a proper family send-off.'

'That sounds like a great idea. I promise I'll be there,' said Voula before they exchanged goodbyes and rang off.

Voula put down the phone and walked to the kitchen to pour another glass of wine.

Half an hour later any thoughts of her mum retiring had gone from her head, her focus back on finding a job. It was obvious now that it wouldn't be here on Rhodes, but the big question was which island it *would* be on. As she glanced over the spreadsheet with all the available positions, her phone rang with a call from her boss, Lois, the owner of the hotel.

'Hi, Lois, happy New Year! Is everything ok?'

'Happy new year to you, too! I'm sorry to disturb you while you're on holiday at home with your family, but the thing is ... I have a problem that indirectly concerns you.'

'Oh? How can I help?'

'The manager of the hotel I own on the island of Kos has had a heart attack and won't be returning to work, so I need to find a permanent replacement.'

Was Lois going to ask her to go and take over the role? The hotel on Kos was only a quarter of the size of the one she was running here on Rhodes, so it would be a huge step down professionally. Voula needed to be very careful in her approach here...

'That's very sad. Dysmas is a lovely chap, and he's always been devoted to the hotel and the staff.'

'Yes, I agree. I've got a plan of action though, and I wanted to run it by you. I'm thinking of asking Charis to go over and run it as he knows the hotel very well, having worked there for many years before coming over to be your deputy.'

'I think he'd be the perfect person for the job and he's so ready to be running things on his own. He's been such an asset for me, and he'll be missed, but this is a great opportunity for him and he's going to be overjoyed.'

'I'm glad to hear you say that, but it does leave us in need of a new assistant manager here on Rhodes. An obvious choice has popped into my head – someone already working for the company who is very keen to make a name for themselves, and who I think would be perfect in the role.'

'Who are you thinking of?' asked Voula, feeling wary.

'Elias.'

'Sorry, Lois, did I hear you right? Did you say Elias? He's good as a food and beverage manager, sure, but do you really think he's ready to step up into the assistant general manager position?'

'I'm sorry, Voula. I understand why you might be a bit reluctant to work so closely with him, but I need to do what's best for the hotel. It's not up for further discussion; I will be offering Elias the vacant position.'

Chapter 4

Helena hadn't slept well after yesterday's announcement from her mum. It wasn't that she doubted that her mum would go through with it – after all, she had sensed for several months it was going to happen – and if she was honest, she wasn't nervous about taking over the running of the hotel as she knew she could do the job inside out. She also knew that Filippos and her sister-in-law, Nadia, would be there to support her one hundred percent. No, the concern that was buzzing around inside her head was Voula. What would she have to say about this whole situation? It would be one thing if Evangelina was going to be staying and living at the hotel, on hand to navigate any sibling conflicts that arose, but it was a completely different story with her being across the water in Parga.

Knowing she could take total control might tempt Voula to come back and try again, and given that her last attempt to run the hotel and undertake changes had been a disaster, this time she might just have something to prove. Helena thought back to the time around her dad's death and the way Voula had acted. The family had been grieving and so they hadn't been fully aware of what Voula was planning until she sat everyone down and told them she would be taking over their father's duties. What she hadn't banked on was her and Evangelina disagreeing over everything, and after many – many! – arguments, Voula had left in a huff.

To try and clear her head and think things through, Helena would do what she always did when she was trying to figure things out – she would go for a walk. Also, she needed to buy some food, which she could get on the way back. But before she left, she knew she'd best pop across the courtyard to the hotel and see if her mum needed anything.

'Hi, Mum,' she called out as she let herself into the lobby. 'I'm just nipping out and I wondered if you needed any food shopping picked up?'

'I don't think so, Helena, but thank you. I thought this afternoon I might go down to the harbour and see a few friends, and I can grab anything I need then. I should probably start to tell people my plans sooner rather than later as the last thing we need is for the locals to start gossiping and getting everything wrong and mixed up. And talking of my plans and the future of the hotel ... have you had any thoughts on what I said?'

'You're right, of course. I *can* take on the running of the hotel and I know both you and Filippos will be there to support me if I need it. I'm not saying it's going to be easy, but every year brings its own challenges and you retiring just means that this next season will challenge me in a new way.'

'That's the right way to look at it.' Her mum smiled kindly. 'I suspect that your brother will get more involved once I'm gone and I know that the two of you will make a very good team. If your dad was still here, he would be very proud of you both.'

'Thank you, that's a lovely thing for you to say. I just hope I can live up to both your expectations.'

Looking at her mum Helena could tell there was something else she wanted to say, but it looked like she was giving it some thought before putting it into words. That could only mean one thing: it was about Voula.

'By the way,' her mum finally continued, 'I spoke to your sister yesterday evening and I told her my news.'

Helena tried to give the impression that she wasn't that concerned, but her mum wasn't silly, and she would likely know what was on Helena's mind.

'It must have come as a big shock to her,' Helena hedged.

'To be honest, I don't really know. You can never tell with Voula. She puts on that act of being confident and in control.'

'But she *is* confident and in control. She would never be as successful as she is without that control.'

'Ok, I'll give you the in control bit, but as for confidence ... well, I've long suspected it's all an act and we haven't seen the real Voula for years. And saying that, I thought you should know I caught her out last night, and I got the impression that not all is good in her life at the moment.'

'You've lost me. What do you mean you "caught her out"?'

Evangelina explained how Voula had lied about working over the holidays, when in truth her hotel was closed.

'I suspect she just wanted to stay and have Christmas with Elias rather than come back here to Vekianos,' Helena said with a shrug.

'Yes, that's what I thought, too, up until this morning when I got a little unexpected insight into the situation. Take a look at what came in the post today – it's a letter from Elias that was mailed before Christmas.'

Helena took the letter out of the envelope and started to read it, shocked to discover that her sister and Elias had split up! He said he was sorry for what had happened and hoped he would still be welcomed at the family hotel.

'That's so sad. I thought they were very happy and they seemed great together the last time they visited us here. I wonder what went wrong. At least it explains why she didn't come back here for Christmas; it would have been very awkward for her to have to explain, and she probably wanted to avoid feeling pitied.'

'Yes, you could be right, but I also think there could be a lot more to it. Now, you go and have your walk. You need to enjoy the next few months of peace and quiet before the season starts again. But remember, Helena, you will be just fine because you know the job as well as I do. I'm confident that life around here will carry on like it always has done.'

Helena smiled, unsure what to say. Because things *would* be different, not having her mum at the hotel. Whether it would be a good thing or a bad thing, only time would tell.

As she walked down the little streets and alleyways towards the harbour it crossed her mind that in just a few weeks lots of the shop and restaurant owners would start preparing for the new season ahead, and her little town would start to come alive again, ready for the busy summer months ahead.

Once down by the sea wall she spent a few minutes looking out to sea, soaking in the calm. She was feeling more relaxed and for the first time since her mum had told them about her retirement plans, Helena started to let thoughts of the future filter through her mind. She considered what she might like to change in and around the building, and thought that the bedrooms and bathrooms would need to take priority. If she was honest, thoughts of upgrades had been in her head for many years now, the seventies pine wardrobes and beds, and the terracotta walls, looking more dated with the arrival of each new summer season.

The idea of making changes and freshening the place up were exciting, but they also made her feel sad because so much of the hotel's design reminded her of her dad. She could still remember the day he took delivery of all that pine furniture; he was so proud and happy that he had been able to afford to refurbish the hotel, and shared with anyone who would listen that his was one of the most modern holiday accommodations in Vekianos. Sadly, now it was one of the most dated, and if they wanted to keep up with the competition, change was necessary. Still, any thought of modernising the hotel had to wait until October, when it closed again for the winter, so there was plenty of time to appreciate the memories it evoked. For now, she needed to focus on getting through her first season as 'the boss'.

As she walked along by the harbour wall, moving away from all the closed restaurants, her memories of her dad led to memories of her first days working in the hotel after she'd left school all those decades ago. So many of her friends had been excited to head off to work on other islands, or in Athens, like Voula had, but Helena had never felt the urge to escape. Why would she when she lived in paradise? No, all she'd ever wanted was to grow old here on Vekianos. Would she have liked to have a loving husband and some children? Of course! But sadly that had never happened for her.

There had been a time in her life when she really thought she had found love, and believed that her future would include a happy life with a loving husband and children, but it wasn't to be. Though she'd believed that Sotirios loved her the way she loved him, she had come to realise that she was just a stopgap, a way for him to entertain himself until someone or something better came along. The heartbreak had nearly broken her, and even today the hurt was still there in some ways. It had made it impossible to trust or move on with someone else. Thankfully, she had had some escape from the devastation of Sotirios leaving, and that was the joy of seeing her nephew, Marios, growing up into a good, loving, and caring young man. He was the light of her life.

Twenty minutes later the town was behind her and she had reached the narrow coastal path. After decades of wandering this way, she knew every twist and bend in the path. Come to that, she probably knew every stone and rock she passed as well! This was her happy place – the place where she'd walked and thought ever since she was a child – and the place she came to time and again to clear her head and think things through. It was also where she did her dreaming. Though most of her dreams had never come true, she was happy to keep dreaming them as they provided a welcome respite from the day-to-day stresses of life.

Approaching her favourite place to sit – a rock that was on a bend in the path, allowing you to sit and look back at where you'd come from, or look out to sea – she could see someone sitting on her rock – yes, it was *her* rock – and started to get annoyed, but then she recognised the person as Marios. That was fine then. After all, she had been the one who introduced him to her special spot in the first place, and it was kind of nice that from that day on it had become his happy place as well.

'Great minds think alike!' she called out to her nephew. 'What brings you here today? Or should I say, what do you need to think through?'

'I'm not sure why I'm here, to be honest,' he said with a shrug. He shifted over on the rock to make room for Helena. 'I suppose I'm a bit unsettled now that everything is changing. It doesn't seem that long ago since Grandad died, and now Grandma is going to live over in Parga, which is a huge shock to me. To be honest, it had never crossed my mind that she might leave the hotel. How are we supposed to go on without her? I also worry she won't be happy having to move away from the place and people she loves. I know she shouldn't have to be working at her age, of course, and I get that if she was still living at the hotel she wouldn't be able to stop herself from getting involved, but it's just so sad to think of seeing her go.'

Marios had voiced everything that Helena had been avoiding thinking about so she had to agree with him. But, ultimately, they had to go along with Evangelina's wishes. Not wanting to upset Marios or get into a conversation about such a loaded topic, she decided to change the subject.

'Your dad tells me you'll start on preparing the boat next week, readying it for the season ahead. Last year you two painted the outside so does that mean this year it's the inside's turn?'

'Yes, we're planning to do lots of painting on the top deck, and Mum's been busy all winter making new seat pads, so it should look fresh and new by the time we're open for business. It'll be a busy few months ahead to get everything done but I'm ready to get stuck in. These past three months labouring on the building site has been hard and I can't wait to get back on the boat.'

'But you've had a good winter with your friends, haven't you? And you've had some time to relax and have a bit of fun?'

'I've had better winters, to be honest, but it's ok and all that's behind me now. It's time to move on.'

'Sounds to me like there's something or someone that you want to move on from. Could that someone be Natalia?' She nudged him gently with her shoulder and watched as a blush touched his cheeks.

'Yes. She's told me she won't be coming back to Vekianos once her winter job in the French Alps has finished.'

'Oh dear. Did she say why?'

'She was honest, I'll give her that – a bit *too* honest if you ask me – and said she thought our relationship had run its course and we both needed to move on.'

'I'm so sorry, I know how much you thought of her and that the summers you've been together have been very special to you.'

She felt a bit choked up, wanting to say more but the words would not come out. She wished she hadn't come here today because now memories from over twenty years ago had come flooding back; things that she really didn't want to think about or remember.

'Are you ok, Aunt Helena? Is there something wrong?' asked Marios.

'Oh, don't you worry, I'm fine. Well ... actually I'm not... You see, I know how you feel because the same thing happened to me. Many years ago I was seeing a lad and thought we had something really special, but then, one summer, he just didn't come back. In my case he didn't explain why, which hurt, but just like I did, you will move on, and life will continue. I promise that though it hurts now, things *will* get better, and someone else will come along, the right person, who makes you want to let down the drawbridge and let them in. Just ... please promise me you won't be like me and keep that drawbridge closed, because I can tell you from experience that it's a big mistake to do so, and will leave you feeling so alone.'

Chapter 5

The Christmas and New Year holidays were over, and it was back to work for Paul and Jenny. Although they were both off to do the same thing – telling their employers that they were leaving their jobs – their days couldn't have been more different. Whereas Paul merely had to sit at his desk and send an email to the relevant people to tell them he would not be staying on after he had reached retirement age, Jenny had to sit down for a face-to-face meeting with her boss, Shirley, who had first employed her seven years ago and had become a very close friend and her main support in the company in the meantime. Today was going to be difficult, but Jenny knew she was making the right choice for her future.

But before that difficult conversation took place later on, Jenny had a pile of files to go through first. Just because she would be leaving in a month's time, it didn't mean she would allow her work output to suffer or slow down.

Her first job was to sort out her to-do list for the rest of the week. She had kept on top of her emails while she had been off for the Christmas break – something that she hadn't needed to do, but she'd wanted to as she always liked to be ahead with everything – so thankfully there would be no surprises. As she sat going through everything and planning out her schedule, her mind kept drifting to her dad. This was a far bigger day for him as saying goodbye after all those years working for the civil service would not be easy, especially coming on the heels of such a difficult year when his whole life had been turned upside down and inside out by the divorce and the move. Jenny was so impressed at how he was coping, but there was no denying that he had been one of the big factors in her decision not to move up to the midlands with the company. Deep down she knew he would be ok, but she'd still worried that her leaving would be a step too much for him.

It was nearly three-thirty and so almost time to sit down with Shirley and tender her resignation. As Jenny walked along the corridor she smiled sadly to herself, knowing how much she'd miss this place. She knew every part of the building and had spent time in many different offices over the years while she climbed the ladder in the company. She was pleased with how hard she had worked to earn all the promotions over the years, and though it was always tough to say goodbye, it was time. The one thing she hadn't done just yet was think about her future, though she wasn't sure if that was because she'd just been too busy or if she was scared to face up to the unknown.

As she reached Shirley's office she hesitated for a brief second before knocking on the door. Was she really doing the right thing? But then she thought of her dad. She nodded to herself, and then knocked.

'Come in, Jenny, take a seat. You know James, don't you?'

Jenny was a bit thrown as she walked in and sat down. Why was the company's CEO sat beside Shirley? She hadn't even realised that he was in the building today as normally he worked from home. Perhaps this meeting wouldn't be as straightforward as she had thought...

'Don't look so worried!' James said, as if reading her mind. 'I just thought I'd sit in. Pretend I'm not even here,' he added before miming locking his lips and throwing away the key.

'Thank you, James,' said Shirley, looking a little out of sorts. 'Now, where to start... Jenny, you know better than anyone else how this move to the midlands is the best thing for the company. The merging of several offices into one big modern unit won't just help to make everything more efficient and streamlined, it will also lead to more substantial growth for the business. It's an exciting step forward and will help to make us one of the big players in the industry. Isn't that right, James?'

James replied, 'Yes, definitely, and we're not going to beat around the bush, Jenny: we want you to be a key part of this exciting new chapter. You've played a big part over the years getting us to where we are now, and we need you to continue contributing to our growing success.'

Jenny was a bit taken aback by their declarations, and though she was extremely flattered, there was ultimately nothing they could say or offer that would change her mind.

'Jenny, we have worked so closely together for so many years and I'm proud that what we have is so much more than a working relationship, so let me get to the point. It's not just the company that needs you, it's also me and the team. I know that the past year has seen a lot of change and disruption in your personal life, and I suspect that you asked for this meeting today to tell me that you want to take the redundancy money rather than moving with the company. I also know that you won't have made the decision lightly. So, James and I have been talking at great lengths about it, and we would like to offer you an enticing reason to stay.'

Shirley pulled a piece of paper out of the file in front of her and slid it across the table to Jenny.

'This is the wage we would be willing to offer you to stay on with the company and come and collaborate with us in the midlands. We need you, and the company is willing to pay generously to keep you.'

Jenny sat there flabbergasted as she looked down at the sheet of paper on the desk in front of her. They were offering her an additional ten thousand pounds a year. It was a lot of money, and would definitely make a difference in her life, but it could have been double that and she still wouldn't change her mind. She wasn't willing to put a price on her dad's happiness.

'Thank you,' she finally whispered. 'That's a very generous pay raise.'

'Yes, but we also acknowledge that you may need some time to think this through, so we've come up with a plan. What you could do, if you'd like, is leave this offer on the table for the next six months. You could use that time to switch off from the company and your work, to be with your dad and maybe take a holiday or two. I think a break is just what you need as your life has been all about this company for the last seven years. Have some Jenny time and come back to the new office, with your new salary, and start fresh. What do you think?'

She honestly didn't know what to say and couldn't think straight. She had always been made to feel valued, and recognised she was a key player in the business, but she hadn't realised just how much they needed her – or wanted her, come to that.

'I'm sorry, I'm a bit lost for words. This generous offer really is so kind of you.'

'As Shirley said, we want you to take your time making this decision, so rest assured neither of us are expecting you to give us an answer today. But Jenny, I want you to know that we really do need you. You have helped us get where we are today, and it would be such a shame for you to not be part of the next chapter in our journey. Now, is there anything you would like to ask us before we wrap up here?'

Not knowing what to say, Jenny simply shook her head, and after a few pleasantries and smiles she headed back to her office, thankful the day was nearly over and she could soon go home.

As she pulled into the apartment's car park she realised she couldn't remember any of the journey she had just taken. One minute she was leaving the office, and seemingly the next she had arrived home. Looking across she could see her dad's car parked in his usual spot. Boy did she have a lot to tell him! And then she remembered what he had also done today, and wondered if his boss had persuaded him to stay on for another couple of years.

'I'm home!' she called as she let herself into the flat a few minutes later.

'Hello, darling, how did it go?'

'Ok, thanks. Let me just go and get changed and then I'll tell you all about it.'

Paul found he was nervous, and it was no wonder; Jenny had been on his mind all day as he anxiously waited to hear how her resignation meeting had gone. He hoped the company hadn't bullied her into something she wasn't happy with as he knew she had given two hundred percent to that job over many years and deserved more than a complicated ending. He recalled the couple of boyfriends she'd had over the years, who had always taken second place to her job, dealing with Jenny cancelling holidays and weekends away at the last minute because of her work. In hindsight, it was understandable why the lads had eventually ended the relationships. He appreciated her commitment and work ethic, but it was one thing wanting to succeed in a career, and another thing entirely giving up all the best bits in life to achieve it. He hoped that leaving the job and making a start somewhere new would give her her life back, and create time for some fun. No, make that lots of fun. She deserved it more than anyone!

'I poured you a glass of wine,' he said once she returned. She'd changed into a t-shirt and leggings and already looked more relaxed. 'Now you can tell me about your meeting with Shirley. How was it?'

'No, you go first, Dad. What happened once you sent your email?'

'I received one back from HR. They said that the date I gave for getting my pension was correct and informed me about the holiday I have due to me, and that was it! My immediate boss did call to say he was sad to see me go but it was primarily to make an appointment to hand over everything I'm currently working on. It just proves that what I've been saying for years is true: just like everyone else, I'm just a number.'

'How are you feeling now you've done it?'

'Great, thank you. My pension should more than cover my living expenses and I'm looking forward to slowing down. Now it's your turn.'

'Mine was ... not as straightforward. When I went to see Shirley, James was in the meeting!'

'The CEO? I'll bet that was a surprise. They didn't bully you into staying, did they?' Paul asked with a frown.

'Nothing like that. They did offer me a huge pay raise though, and six months to make up my mind.'

'That's wonderful, darling! It must be gratifying to know how much they want you to stay. Of course you'll take the job.'

'Well... Yes, I was very flattered, in one way, but in another I'm not surprised, and I don't mean that in a smug, over-confident way. To be honest, I think I would have been shocked and disappointed if they *didn't* try and persuade me to stay on with the company. Ok, I didn't think the pay raise would be as good as what they've offered, but a part of me assumed there would be a carrot dangled somewhere along the line.'

'I sense by the tone of your voice that you aren't happy? No, that's not the right word... Not ... excited? That's it! I meant you don't sound excited about the offer.'

'I'm happy for the company overall. It's been great to see them achieve so much and I'm very proud that I was one of a team that helped them get there, but I just know that once in the new office life is only going to get harder, with longer days and more pressure, and that's not what I want. No, I think it's a good time to leave. Better to do it while I'm on top, rather than burned out.'

'I can understand that. So, what happens now?'

'I work my one month's notice and then after that ... I haven't a clue. The only thing I do know is that it will be something that I can switch off from once the day has come to an end. No more twelve and fourteen-hour days for me. Now, do you think we should get dinner started? I was thinking pork chops and mashed potatoes. Sound good?'

Paul nodded and as Jenny headed off to prepare dinner he marvelled over how well his daughter was dealing with her tough career decisions. He really was very proud of her, and he hoped she would stick to her guns and find a job that didn't take up all her time.

And as for him? He found he was a bit scared not knowing what the future held for him. Filling those forty hours a week he used to spend sat behind a desk would not be an easy task, and it would be odd to not have work to think about. Yes, scared was definitely the word that came to mind.

Chapter 6

It had been three days since Voula had been told about Elias' promotion, and today was the day she would hand in her notice. She knew she should be feeling nervous, but strangely, she wasn't. In fact, she felt relieved.

She was at her desk early that morning, the only other members of staff on duty the night manager and the porters. Her first job was to pack up all her personal belongings from her office and as she took the last box to her car she saw that the breakfast staff and day receptionists were starting to arrive for the morning shift, the hotel slowly coming to life.

Switching on her computer she checked to see how much holiday she was due, unsurprised to find that there were quite a few weeks owed to her because she never really took time away from the hotel. She planned to use those days as her 'get out of jail free' card so that she wouldn't have to stay on any longer than she needed to.

After a couple of hours of planning and drafting emails to the relevant people, including the owner of the company, the board of directors, and the HR department, it was time to press send. She had decided against giving the real reason for her resignation, not wanting to admit that it had anything to do with Elias, and instead said it was to do with her mum retiring and her being needed back at the family hotel.

Task completed, it was time to wait for all the responses to arrive. And while she waited, she had a hotel to run. She was determined that today would be a positive one, and that the staff would see her at her best; on fine form as the caring and efficient manager she was.

As she kicked off her shoes at home after work that night, and then went to the fridge to pour a glass of wine, she was thankful to have finished for the day. It had been a stressful one, but she knew that no one ever would have guessed as all they'd seen was a boss that was in total control of everything. If only they knew the truth.

After a shower and another few glasses of wine she returned to her job search. Picking up her laptop she opened the spreadsheet she'd created. As she began her research she quickly crossed off over half a dozen jobs for various reasons – the salary wasn't high enough, or the hotel had dreadful reviews, or it just wasn't the type of business she knew she would be happy working in. She worried she was too old to be starting over again, and that she would never find such good employers, but she also felt like she had no choice but to leave her current role. Oh, why did Elias have to get himself promoted? Come to that, why was he even still working at the hotel? Surely the right thing for him to do would have been to resign after their break-up and seek employment elsewhere?

She looked at the clock, surprised to find it was way past midnight, and was frustrated that she hadn't really achieved anything apart from figuring out where she *didn't* want to work. Turning the light off and heading to the bedroom she felt defeated. She didn't want to experience another day like today so perhaps she should be looking at this career move in a different way. Could it be that her time running hotels was over? Everyone knew it was ultimately a young person's game, so maybe it was time for her to try her hand at something else. But what? She pondered if there was anything else she might like to do. Did she even have a dream job? She'd never really thought about it before.

As she got into bed her phone beeped with an incoming email. Opening it she found it was an advert for a new hotel opening on the island of Mykonos. Clicking on the link to the website she was greeted with professional images of a gorgeous and very chic hotel with a stunning pool area and outside space, and a fabulous looking indoor/outdoor restaurant. She clicked through to view the rooms, surprised to find it didn't have many bedrooms and suites, but that was actually what made it special. This was really top end luxury, and exactly the type of business venture she would love to be part of. Sadly, it didn't look like this actual hotel had any vacancies as the website showed images of all the management and staff. But perhaps this was a sign, and this was the direction she should pursue in her career? If she could get in at the beginning with this sort of project, she could help to build its success right from the start, which would be so rewarding. Suddenly feeling very awake, she opened her browser and started researching new hotels being built and existing businesses that were being refurbed to this standard.

Her heart started to race and the phone fell out of her hand and onto the bed as a thought struck her and she realised that the answer to all her problems was right in front of her. How had she not seen it before? Picking up the phone and looking at the Mykonos hotel photos again a vision formed in her head, a vision of the family hotel on Vekianos transformed into the most exclusive luxury hotel retreat on the island, and the premier offering anywhere in the Greek islands.

Chapter 7
Vekianos, 1st February

It had been a month to the day since Helena had sat down with her mum and brother and talked about her taking over running the hotel, and in that time a lot had happened. For a start, Evangelina had been ruthless in getting rid of her belongings; everything from clothes to furniture had been given the boot. As the space had been cleared out, Helena had grappled with whether to move out of her little bungalow and into her mum's apartment in the hotel. Her initial reaction was a no, as she loved where she was living, but on a practical level she knew she probably *should* move into the hotel because the apartment was a lot bigger and she would have more room to move around, plus space for an office.

To put off making a decision, she had concentrated on all the things she wanted to change around the hotel to modernise it, things she knew could and would improve it. The first job would be decluttering the bedrooms as she knew the guests didn't want all the knick-knacks in the rooms. Experience had shown her that almost every single time customers checked out she would inevitably find the tops of the wardrobes full of all the things they had put there to create space for their own belongings. Of course, her mum and dad – and especially her dad when he was still alive – could never understand why they would do that, no matter how many times she tried to explain that they needed clear surfaces to put their possessions on, or gently suggested that they didn't need or want ornaments cluttering up the place.

Yes, decluttering would be top of her list before

the season started. The other thing she would love to do – and something she would need to discuss with Filippos, and her sister-in-law Nadia – was get rid of all the dated flowery curtains and terracotta-coloured walls. She hated the colour after living with it for so many years, and the rooms needed to be made brighter and airier and ... 'fresher' was the word she was looking for. But then she felt panicky again. How many times in the last month had she felt like this? Every time she stopped to think about what would happen when her mum sailed over to Parga, the whole situation seemed so vast and very scary. There were just so many unknowns.

As she left her little bungalow and headed across the courtyard to the hotel, she tried to put out of her mind all the thoughts of changing things. These months before her mum left to live over in Parga should be all about keeping things normal, not rocking the boat.

'I can't believe February has arrived already!' she said after greeting her mum. 'What happened to January? It flew by way too fast.'

'Do you think so?' Evangelina asked, looking thoughtful. 'It feels like it's been dragging for me, but I suppose that's because of all the anticipation of moving. Still, I've managed to achieve a lot and am starting to feel ready for the big day. I can't believe how much stuff I have collected over the years though! Well, not just me as a lot of it was your father's. I know I should have got rid of most of it after he died but it just felt too difficult to face at the time.'

'That's understandable,' Helena said kindly. 'Remember that you don't need to clear away or get rid of things you don't want to, Mum. There's lots of space in the garages to store things you might want in years to come.'

'I know, but it makes sense to do it now and get

it over with once and for all. Shall we have a coffee and a chat while you're here? ... Oh, I think that's the door. Hello?' she called.

'It's only me!' Nadia replied, walking into the kitchen.

'You have perfect timing, as always. We were just going to stop and have a coffee. Join us?' asked Helena.

'Yes, please, that would be nice. Filippos is working with Marios on the boat, and I was wondering if you needed a hand with anything, so I thought I'd pop over.'

'That's so kind of you,' said Evangelina warmly. 'Have a seat and I'll make the drinks.'

As they settled around the kitchen table Helena was happy her sister-in-law had joined them. Nadia always brought lightness to any conversation because she was always so positive and practical. They chatted about Vekianos and bits of gossip they'd heard over the last few days before Helena asked after the boat's progress.

'Filippos is happy with everything and they're already well ahead of where they need to be, to be ready for the start of the season.'

'That's great news! How about that nephew of mine? Has he moved on from Natalia yet?'

'He says he has, but I admit I'm not so sure. I think once we get into the season and the holiday makers arrive back on the island he'll be fine as the work will keep him busy and occupied. Filippos is just waiting to see if Sara is coming back to join them for the season. If not, they'll have to find someone else to help with the boat as they won't be able to manage it between just the two of them, but we have quite a few weeks before the trips will start so there's time to find a replacement if necessary.'

'It won't be long before we have the first guests checking in ourselves,' Helena said with a glance across at her mum.

'No, Helena, *you* will have customers here, not me. I will be over in Parga enjoying my retirement with your aunt.'

'About that, Marios and I were thinking we should have a party before you go,' said Nadia.

'Thank you but there will be no party. The last thing I want is everyone here on Vekianos coming to say goodbye and eating and drinking us out of house and home in the process.'

Helena relied, 'Mum, you just can't leave without doing something to mark the occasion. It's not right.'

'Yes, I can. I'm going to pick up my case, get on your brother's boat, and set sail. Simple as that.'

There was an awkward silence, Helena and Nadia knowing there was little point in arguing because what Evangelina said goes.

Eventually Nadia offered, 'Ok then, if you don't want a party for all your friends here on the island, that's fine, but we should at least have a family meal, don't you agree, Helena? Perhaps Voula will come back for a couple of days to join us. Surely that would be ok?'

Evangelina appeared to think it over before she spoke.

'You know what? That would be nice. Yes, I think I would really enjoy that; thank you, Nadia. Just family though. Perhaps Dora would even like to come over from Parga given that she worked here at the hotel for many years.'

'As long as you're sure, Mum?'

Helena had a sudden thought, but wondered if she should say something, or if it might push the conversation back to not having any celebration. She decided she had nothing to lose and went for it.

'Could I suggest something?' she asked her mum. 'And please remember it's only a suggestion, but ... every year you send half a dozen Christmas cards to people who have worked here over the years, some who you've known for over thirty years.'

'Yes, but what's that got to do with my retirement?' asked Evangelina.

'I was just thinking, why don't we invite them to join us? We could give them accommodation here at the hotel as the rooms are empty before the season starts, and you could reminisce over all the years you've worked here with the people who shared the time and the work with you. What do you think?'

There was a loaded silence and Helena worried she had said the wrong thing. She was just about to take it back and say it was just a silly idea, but before she could Evangelina started to talk.

'I suspect you are expecting me to say no, but I actually think that is a lovely idea. Of course, they don't all know each other because they were here at different times over many years, but it would be nice to have everyone back here before I say goodbye. Let me just go and get my address book.'

As Evangelina went off Helena and Nadia shared a smile, knowing this was already turning into much more than a simple family meal. No, this would be something very special – that is, as long as Evangelina's old employees accepted the invitation.

'Here we go! Now, let me see ... I think there are only four or five that I usually hear back from. First is James, who was one of the first people we employed who we didn't already know. He could turn his hand to anything: cooking breakfast, cleaning the bedrooms, and of course working in the bar. I had a Christmas card back from him in December and he mentioned he's working in the Netherlands right now. Then there's Stepanie, a nice girl and another good worker. She always puts a little letter in with her Christmas card giving an update on her and her grown-up daughter's lives. She's a devoted single mum and a lovely woman. Then there's Emma, who was always a very quiet girl who just got on with things, no drama – unlike a lot of the other staff! But then there's a reason I don't keep in contact with everyone; there are quite a few I would like to forget!'

Helena laughed. 'I remember lots of young female employees who fell for the charm of the Greek waiters and then had their hearts broken. They were lucky you were there to pick up the pieces.'

'Yes, there's no denying that the lads we employed were a lot easier to handle. Of course, my favourite member of staff has always been Paul, and I'm glad to say that I still hear from him. He's married with an adult daughter.'

'So that's who you'd like to invite? Paul, Emma, Stepanie, and James?'

'Yes, but also Sandra. She was loud and full of fun when she worked for us – I think it was for three or four seasons – and she still always sends me a birthday card.'

Nadia said, 'Evangelina, your face lights up when you talk about these people; it's lovely! I remember some of them myself and it reminds me that we really have had a lot of good times here at the hotel.' She took a deep breath, as if preparing herself for battle. 'Look, I have to say it: are you *sure* you're doing the right thing by retiring? I know for a fact that Filippos will support you if you want to change your mind, and I'm sure Helena feels the same.'

'Nadia's right,' said Helena, nodding. 'It's also worth saying that if you do go ahead with the retirement but then find you don't get on with Dora, you can still come back. You'll always have a home here.'

'That's very kind of you girls but I have made my decision. It's time to hand the baton over. Now, enough of this talk, you two have a party to organise and invitations to send out. I know this will come as a huge shock to both of you, but I'm now actually quite excited about the idea of marking the end with a lovely reunion.'

Six hours later Helena was sat in her little bungalow with a notebook, making plans for the party. The names of those who had worked at the hotel over many decades had brought back lots of good memories of so many happy and fun times. But there was no denying that she had felt sad when her mum had talked about those people all having families and partners, as it was what she'd always wanted for herself. But then she felt bad for feeling sorry for herself and tried to shake off the melancholy. She had no reason to feel sad because she had a wonderful life here on Vekianos, and though she didn't have children of her own, she had Marios, who was like a son to her in all the ways that mattered. Thinking ahead to the party to try and distract herself from her bad mood, she hoped the old staff her mum wanted to invite would be able to come back to visit. She was also very aware that there was one other person that needed to be invited – her sister Voula – and that she'd had a fallout with Paul when she had come back from Athens all those years ago. She had used him to get back at one of the Greek lads that she had been seeing, and when she headed back to her job in Athens Paul was left sad and looking very silly. Perhaps Paul shouldn't be invited as a means of avoiding any potential drama? But no, that seemed unfair to Paul, and the truth was that Helena would sooner have Paul at the party than Voula.

A couple of hours later, and lots of notes made, Helena was still thinking about Paul. About the happy times they'd shared working together, but also the times they'd spent socialising together. He'd always brought a smile to her face, even during the difficult times when Sotirios was away and she was on her own. Then her mind went to what could possibly have happened between her and Paul if she hadn't been in a relationship. Would their friendship have turned into something else? Perhaps even the happy ending she had always dreamed of? There was no denying that Paul had looked at her in a way that suggested he was interested, and he had taken every opportunity to help her with her chores, even when he shouldn't have been on duty.

But then she remembered that there had been two sides to him, and she always saw the other side when Sotirios returned. Sotirios had made it clear that he didn't like them giggling away together, so Paul had often disappeared or avoided her during those periods, giving her the cold shoulder. If only she'd known then that she was choosing to spend her time with the wrong man...

Chapter 8

Jenny was home from work before her dad, which was unusual. As she walked into the apartment block she checked the post box, finding a letter for her dad with a stamp saying it was from Greece. As she put her bag down she unlocked her phone and texted her dad to make sure he was ok. Within seconds he replied to say he had stopped to see someone but would be home within the hour. After changing out of her work suit, she made a cup of tea and looked in the fridge to see what they could eat tonight. She saw her dad had taken two chicken breasts out of the freezer to thaw, and she decided she would put them in a casserole dish with leeks, carrots, onions, parsnips, and peas.

By the time Paul walked through the door the dinner was in progress and Jenny was on her second cup of tea.

'Dinner's in the oven!' Jenny called out to him. 'I've put the kettle on and just as soon as the tea is ready you can tell me about your day.'

'Sounds perfect,' said Paul before going to change.

Returning a few moments later he said, 'Sorry I'm late but I popped in to see Mark, who I used to work with. He retired last year and he messaged me to say he'd heard I'd given my notice. The long and the short of it is that he is so happy he retired and he's still keeping busy as he has a part-time job. He joked that he doesn't know how he even has the time to go to work. He also has a new puppy that takes up a lot of time, and has thrown himself into redesigning his garden.'

Getting a dog and working in the garden were

both out of the question for her dad as he was in an apartment and wasn't allowed animals, so she zeroed in on the one part he *could* accomplish.

'Does this mean you're thinking about taking on a little job to keep you occupied a few days a week?'

'Yes, I think I'll need something, but I'm also going to look at joining a group or two. I quite fancy a walking group – not for big, long hikes, but morning strolls. Something easy. We'll see though. How about you? Good day?'

'Yeah, it was fine. A couple of the departments have now moved to the new building in the midlands, so the office is feeling a little empty with more and more rooms with no desks or filing cabinets. Shirley has asked if I might be able to stay on a few weeks longer to go up and see how I feel working in the new place. They said they'll book me into a hotel and cover any travel expenses. I know that this is their way of trying to persuade me to stay on, but I think it would be silly not to go and at least take a look.'

'I agree. You never know how you're going to feel about something until you try it. Do you want help finishing up dinner?'

'No, you're fine. You enjoy your tea while I go and peel some potatoes. I'm going to serve them mashed with lots of butter tonight, I think.'

'That sounds good to me, darling.'

Jenny knew her dad was worried she would never find as good a job as the one she had now, but as far as she was concerned, that was a worry for another day. For now, her priority was getting him through the early days of retirement. Once she could see he was settling into his new normal and building a new life for himself, then she would think about her career.

As she went back to the kitchen she realised she hadn't given him the post that came earlier so she took it back into the lounge.

'It looks like it's from your friend in Greece,' she said as she handed it over. 'Gosh, could you imagine if I had said that when we were with Mum? I can hear her shouting, "Oh yes, Greece – home to the best years of your father's life."'

'I suspect you're right. I wonder what it is,' he said, ripping the envelope open.

'Dinner should be ready any moment so bring it to the table. You can have a read while I serve everything up.'

As they were eating Jenny could see her dad was deep in thought but she left him be.

'This is very tasty, and the mash is so creamy. Perhaps I should let you get home from work first every night?' joked Paul.

'I'm more than happy to let that happen. By the way, what was your letter about? Not bad news, I hope?'

'No, not bad news. It was from the family I used to work for in Greece. The mum – Evangelina – is retiring from the hotel, and her children are having a party for her and have invited some of the people who used to work for them.'

'How great is that? You can make a holiday of it! That would be the perfect start to your retired life and a lovely way to celebrate finishing work.'

'You're not wrong, but I don't think I'm going to go. It's really not my type of thing and given that it was thirty years ago when I worked for them, I'm sure I won't know anyone else who's there.'

'You will though – what about the family members you worked with?'

'No, I suspect it will be people who I've never met. People like me who spent time there for a couple of summers and then moved on. When I was there I was the only one working at the hotel apart from the family and a few locals, and to be honest,

I'm not sure I can remember a lot of them. There was an uncle and an aunt, and of course Evangelina and her husband, but I know he died several years ago.'

'But you said they had children?'

'Yes, three. Their son, Filippos, worked on a tourist boat and he was dating a lovely girl that worked at the hotel, Nadia. They eventually got married, which I know because Evangelina mentioned it in one of the notes she always sends with the Christmas cards. Then there were two daughters: Helena, who worked at the hotel – a lovely, sweet girl – and Voula, who worked in Athens.'

'I get the impression by the way you said Voula's name you weren't keen on her?'

'A long story there. Can I finish off the mash?'

'Yes, and while you're eating it you can tell me the long story. I'm intrigued.'

'It seems very silly now, all these years later, but Voula sort of made a fool of me. I was young and very naïve and shy when it came to girls, and when Voula first came back for a visit with her family I found her a little scary and intimidating. To be honest, for the first week she hardly acknowledged me, but then something happened one evening when she was down at the harbour, and the following day she was friendly towards me – almost flirty, in fact – which was something I definitely wasn't used to ... from *any* girl. Of course, I was flattered that this beautiful girl was showing me so much attention. She invited me out one evening and though I was nervous, I agreed. But as the evening went on, she showed me less and less attention, and as we chatted, I came to realise that she wasn't really looking at or listening to me, too focused on what was happening around us.'

'She was using you, Dad, wasn't she? ... Sorry, am I jumping ahead?'

'Yes, you are!' Paul laughed. 'But you're right, she was, and I was silly not to see it coming. In the end, I asked her what was wrong and said I would leave if she wanted me to. She said she was waiting to see someone and then, all of a sudden, her demeanour changed. After basically ignoring me for the whole evening, she was suddenly all over me, smiling and then kissing me. At that point I noticed a nearby lad staring at us, and the penny dropped: she was using me to make him jealous. Later on, Filippos explained that she had been going out with this other lad when they were teenagers but he'd called the relationship off and so she was using her visit as a chance to get some revenge. I guess I was the best tool to accomplish her goal.'

'Oh dear, poor you!'

'It's funny thinking back to it now, but at the time it really hurt me, and I think that was when I truly started to grow up.'

'Did you ever see her again? I would have wanted to get my own back on her.'

'No, she never came back to visit while I was there.'

'I really think you should take them up on the invitation. It will be a nice break, and it seems like you got on well with the brother and the mum. How about the other sister?'

'Helena was a completely different story. She was quiet and shy but very friendly once you got to know her, and I enjoyed spending time at work with her. Her boyfriend, Sotirios, didn't like that Helena and myself got on so well with each other though, so I often had to make myself scarce when he came around. She seemed really in love with him, and they made a lovely couple.'

'You were all quite young then though. What makes you think she loved him?'

'She was always trying to make him happy,

though I suspect she never really succeeded. From my vantage point on the outside, it was definitely a one-way relationship...' He looked thoughtful for a moment and then shook his head. 'I don't think I will take them up on the invitation after all. I don't know how any of their lives have turned out and I don't know that I need to.'

'That's exactly why you should go though, to catch up with them and find out what's been happening there over the last thirty years.'

'Well, I already know that Helena didn't get the happy ending she deserved as she and Sotirios split up. He left the island at the end of a season and never returned, and from what I can gather from all the cards over the years, she is still single, which is such a shame as she would have been a lovely wife and mum.'

'It sounds to me like you were picked up by the wrong sister, Dad. I really think you must go. The holiday will be so special for you and I'm sure you'll enjoy catching up with the family. And you never know ... you might be able to get your own back on that Voula woman.' Jenny winked and Paul laughed.

'Ok, ok, I'll go! But under one condition: that you come with me. You know you need a holiday just as much as I do and it would be fun to take you back to the place I think I was happiest. My favourite place with my favourite person – what more could I ask for?'

Chapter 9

As Voula stepped onto the boat to take her over to the island of Vekianos, she knew this was the start of her new adventure, even if it felt as though she was about to be living on a knife edge with no job, no income, and no assets other than her apartment on Rhodes. Her focus over the next few days had to be on creating a secure future for herself, though she had no plans to discuss it with anyone. Oh no, her master plan was staying firmly in her head at the moment. That's why her family thought she was visiting – to tell them about her break-up and to talk about Evangelina's impending retirement and move. The actual goal of her trip was to undertake secret research to figure out if her ideas for turning the family hotel into an exclusive resort were achievable.

As she glanced over the side of the boat she spotted Vekianos in the distance, and for once she felt her body freeze. It was a place she never thought she'd live again, but if her plan worked it would be her new home. But she was getting ahead of herself. For now, she need only focus on putting on the act that everyone knew – the confident, in control Voula persona she had perfected. There would be no letting her guard down in front of her family, and this four-day visit would need to be just like any other if she was to succeed.

Once off the boat she walked the long way up to the hotel as she knew she needed to take in what it looked like from the harbour. She knew all ten guest bedrooms had a gorgeous sea view, but what was the impression people looking up at it got? As she walked alongside the harbour wall she realised she hadn't actually looked up at it for years because she'd never needed to know before now. It had always just been the family home, the place she came back to visit, nothing more, but this time it was completely different. This time was about the potential business she could build from the existing shell.

As she pulled to a stop and looked up to the hotel, the only word that came to mind was 'disaster'. It looked so dated and she knew instantly that it would take a lot of money to make it look ultra-modern and stand out. Continuing on up the hill, she thought about what was awaiting her – the dated rooms, the crumbling exterior, and the glaring lack of a swimming pool for guests to enjoy. She would need mega money to create her dream.

Approaching the gate, she knew it was showtime. But Voula was ready to perform. Time to get the interrogation over with so she could concentrate on her secret plans.

As she got to the main door, she found her mum and brother waiting to greet her with big smiles.

'Welcome back, Voula! Did you have a good journey? It's so lovely to have you here, isn't it, Filippos?' Evangelina said in a rush. 'Your sister just popped down to the bakery for your favourite pastries and should be back any moment. Why don't you let Filippos take your case to one of the hotel bedrooms and I will make the coffee.'

Voula felt a bit thrown. This warm welcome was very odd, and she wasn't sure why her mum was being so over friendly. She was acting as if she was welcoming holiday guests, not her daughter. No, nothing about this felt normal.

'Here, sis, let me take that,' Filippos said as he grabbed her suitcase.

'Thank you?' she said to his quickly retreating figure. She turned to her mother, still confused by the effusive welcome. 'It's nice to be back and I'm looking forward to hearing all the news, especially your plans for your new life in Parga.'

The two women went into the kitchen, which was just as Voula remembered it. The only changes that had been made over the decades were the electrical fittings that had been replaced over the years when the old ones had worn out. For a moment she thought back to being a child at this very table and how happy she had felt surrounded by her family. It was like she had been a different person then, not consumed by ambition and more than happy to just plod on with island life. Her mum was talking but she had missed what Evangelina had said, too lost in her memories.

'Sorry, Mum, I didn't catch that.'

'Coffee?'

'Yes, please, black no sugar.'

'Coming right up. Sit yourself down... Oh, sounds like Helena's back.'

Helena walked into the kitchen with her guard already up. Voula would likely already be in control and no doubt there would be questions about the fate of the hotel and what was going to be happening once Evangelina left. She spoke first, eager to get the upper hand.

'Welcome back! You're looking well. I like your hair in that style; it really suits you.'

'Thank you. I thought as I was getting older it was time to have it shorter. My days of competing with the thirty-year-olds are over and I have to face up to the fact that I'm fifty now, which means shorter hair and hopefully fewer worries!'

'I know exactly what you mean, Voula. We're all getting older and it's time to start making changes. That's why I'm giving up the hotel – I realised it was time to hand over the keys to Helena so – as you youngsters say – she can put a "new twist" on the business,' said Evangelina.

With that Filippos appeared in the doorway, laughing his head off. 'Youngsters, Mum? The three of us haven't been young for a long time, and to be honest, I wouldn't want to go back to those days. Life for youngsters is so hard these days, what with all the technology and everyone knowing each other's business. No thank you! I was happier when I didn't know what was going on in the world, and I can't imagine spending my youth focused on social media likes and online battles.'

There was an awkward silence as Evangelina and her three adult children settled in around the kitchen table – the scene of so many family meals in the past. Each seemed to be realising that with Evangelina going away this wouldn't be the family kitchen anymore. Helena found herself wishing someone would speak to break the silence.

'I suppose I should explain why I'm here,' Voula finally began. 'Elias and I have split up. The relationship ran its course and though we were still cordial, he was promoted to assistant manager and it became impossible for us to continue working together.'

Helena and Evangelina exchanged a glance, surprised that Voula was being so open.

'I'm sorry to hear that, Voula,' said Evangelina. 'Just to clarify, does that mean you aren't working together any longer?'

'Yes, I've left the company and am taking a little break before starting another job. So, Mum, have you made any plans for the few days I'm here? I thought perhaps we could have a family meal.'

Evangelina looked a bit thrown by the sudden change of topic but went along with it, as though sensing that Voula had opened up as much as she was able to for now.

'Of course! The plan was to have a sit-down tomorrow evening, just the six of us, if that's ok with you? Filippos was going to take me food shopping in the morning but you could come as well, if you like?'

'The meal sounds good to me but I don't think I'll come shopping as I have some loose ends to tie up. I have my laptop so will try and get it done while you're out, so it's out of the way. How are things with the boat?' Voula asked her brother. 'Are you ready for the new season?'

'Yes, nearly ready,' said Filippos, filling Voula in on all the work they'd been doing.

In no time at all the coffee was gone and the pastries had been eaten, and they'd had a nice time chit chatting about different people they knew on the island. Filippos got to his feet saying that he had to get going, and though part of Helena wanted to escape as well, she felt it would be rude to leave at the same time.

Once the three women were alone, Evangelina turned to her daughters with a serious expression. 'There's something I need you to do while you're here, Voula. As I mentioned last time we spoke, I've been having a big clear out and both your brother and sister have done their bit and taken the few things that are theirs. I've put all your things into boxes as well and I'd appreciate if you'd go through them and decide what to keep and what to toss.'

'What sort of things?'

'There are clothes, old school things, even some toys from your childhood.'

'You can just throw it all away. I'm sure there's nothing of any importance as I didn't even realise I still had things here.'

'It's fine if you want to throw them away, but I would prefer it if you did it yourself as it's been hard enough getting rid of my own possessions.'

'Sorry, I didn't mean I expected you to do it, I just meant that I don't think there will be anything I need in the boxes. Of course I'll sort through it.

Actually, why don't I go and get it done now? Where are the boxes?'

'Up in the apartment, in your and Helena's old bedroom.'

'It shouldn't take long at all. See you in a bit,' she called over her shoulder as she headed out of the kitchen.

As Voula walked up the back stairs to the apartment lots of memories came flooding back. How many thousands of times had she been up and down these stairs?

Heading in through the main door of the apartment she glanced out the window to the main road. Their family's living space was located on the opposite side of the building to the guest rooms, so none of the windows faced out to sea. She was a bit shocked as she entered the living room, finding it practically empty. Her mum really *had* had a major clear out. For the first time she felt sad at the thought of her mum moving away, and although this apartment was a big part of her plan for the hotel, she couldn't let herself think about that now. That was the future, and she owed it to herself to first say goodbye to the past, just like her mum had been doing these last few months.

Walking into the bedroom she'd once shared with her sister it felt so big, which was a first, because all that was in there were her boxes, six of them in total. Kneeling on the floor to look inside, she could see why it must have been so difficult for her mum to go through all her things. One box was all clothes, mostly things that she'd left here years ago when she was working in Athens. By leaving clothes at home, she was able to travel back and forth without any luggage. The next box was old school books. There was another box with books and one with toys and games. How was there still so much of her stuff here and why had her mum and dad not got rid of it decades ago? One box was left and she could see that it was full of photographs, some in albums, some in packets, and others loose. She knew that this was the point when some people would get upset and full of nostalgia, but not Voula. For her they just proved how far she had moved on from this island, making a real success of herself out in the world.

She knew she couldn't throw them away just yet, so she set them to one side and readied everything else to go to the charity shop. Taking the first box of clothes down the stairs to put by the door, she stopped in her tracks, realising this was a full circle moment. She might be taking boxes of her childhood mementos out of the apartment now, but very soon she would be bringing boxes into this space from her life in other parts of Greece. Had she made the right decision to return to Vekianos? She didn't know just yet, but one thing she was certain of was that she had no other choice.

Chapter 10

Voula was awake early, but she knew there was no point in going down to get a coffee just yet as her mum would already be up, and she wasn't ready to get into any uncomfortable conversations this early in the morning. Having dropped the twin bombshells yesterday that she didn't have a job or a man in her life, she knew her mum would have a lot to say once the two of them were alone, and she suspected that one of her first questions would be whether or not Voula would be coming back to help Helena run the hotel. The answer to that question would need to be different to the answer in her head as she wasn't ready to share her plans just yet.

To delay going downstairs she took a good look around the hotel room she had slept in. One of the few good things the hotel already had going for it was that all ten bedrooms were around the same size, and each had that same fabulous view out to sea.

Opening the little balcony doors, the first thing that hit her were the old-fashioned columns of the balustrade, which were about three feet tall. They would be replaced by glass so that when the guests sat outside there was nothing interrupting their view. Turning to look back into the room, she realised that the bed was in the wrong place, and would have to be moved from the side wall to the back wall, so that guests could sit in bed looking out to sea at the start and end of their day. Of course, she already knew that all the existing furniture in the rooms would have to go and the carpets replaced with wooden floors. They'd also need to update the technology, adding a huge TV and lots of LED lighting to each room. In terms of design, her plan was to take inspiration from the new hotel on Mykonos, as she had learned over the years that the best route to success was to be inspired by other successful businesses. Let them do all the expensive market research and spend money making mistakes before coming up with a fabulous finished product. She would take inspiration from everything they did right and apply it to her hotel in a way that made sense for this particular building in this particular setting.

Now back to the task in hand. From the bedroom she walked into the bathroom and decided immediately that everything had to go. Because the bathrooms weren't small, once the old baths were removed there would be enough space to have quite a big walk-in shower, and she knew she could do something really fun with the design in here.

After about an hour of looking at inspiration images on her iPad and seeing what might work where, it was time to head down to the kitchen. This was her opportunity to talk to her mum alone and find out if her sister was ready to take over running the business on her own, or if Voula might be able to convince the family to let her take charge.

'Good morning, did you sleep well?' Evangelina asked.

'I did, thank you. It was lovely to wake up to that view and I really appreciated it today. Aren't you worried you'll miss it when you move to Parga?'

'Of course I'll miss it! In fact, there's so much I'll miss, but Parga is lovely, and I'll be happy there. I know you all think I'm silly going and leaving my home here, but Helena is more than ready to take over.'

'As long as you're sure you're going to be happy. That's all that matters.'

'I will and I'm only a boat ride away. It will

probably be a bit odd to be a visitor to begin with, but I'm sure I'll adapt quickly to the situation.'

'How about Helena? Is she excited about becoming the boss? It will be a lot different for her as you were always the one who made the decisions, and she's been the one who has carried them out.'

'To be honest, she hasn't said a lot about how she feels, but I know she's preparing. In the weeks since I told you all about my plans she's asked thousands of questions and made loads of notes, and I know Nadia has promised to be here on a daily basis in the beginning to help out. And Filippos will support her in any way he can. I think she will be just fine and a month after I'm gone it will be as if I never was here, everything ticking along nicely.'

Voula wasn't sure that was the answer she'd wanted to hear and she realised she had to take Helena's role into consideration. If Voula was to go ahead with her plans for the newly refurbished hotel she would need to get Helena onboard, because if she wasn't there would be a big backlash from their mum and brother. She needed to make her sister feel important, so perhaps she could create a job for her with a fancy title? She'd have to think on that...

'I know that you will support your sister along the way, and especially now that you haven't got a job to keep you away. Perhaps you could both work together here? You did it once before, after your father died.'

'Yes and look how that ended up.' Voula couldn't help but roll her eyes. 'You and I fell out as we both wanted different things for the business, and Helena avoided us both.'

'But it would be different this time around because I wouldn't be here. There would be no clashes between us and your sister wouldn't be stuck in the middle.'

'Of course I will help Helena in any way I can,'

offered Voula, choosing her words carefully so as not to give her plans away or make her mum suspicious.

'Good morning! Did I hear my name?'

'Yes, I was just saying that I will support you when you take over from Mum.'

'Thank you, but really it should be the other way around. You're the big hotel manager so you should be coming back and managing the place while I carry on as I am. The timing is perfect as you don't have a job and I know you would be good at it.'

Helena wasn't sure what had made her say it, but now it was out there, there was no taking it back.

'Don't be silly, Helena! Your sister wouldn't want to be back here in this little hotel; it's far too small and she would be bored to tears in no time. No, Voula likes the big, two hundred bedroom hotels with all the glitz and the glamour, not a traditional Greek family hotel that has withstood time. We offer guests what they want when they come to our little island: old Greece style and comfort. At the end of the day, we will always be Vekianos, never chic Mykonos or Rhodes. Isn't that right, Voula?'

For the first time since her return, Voula was feeling so very uncomfortable. Her mum had summed up everything that Voula wanted to change about the hotel, so how could she avoid agreeing with her? Thankfully, they all heard Filippos pull up in his car outside just then, giving her an excuse to avoid answering.

'That sounds like your brother. Are you ready, Helena? If you take the bags, I have the list. And are you sure you don't want to come with us, Voula?'

'No, I'm fine, thank you. I'm going to make another coffee and get on with some work up in my room. What time do you think you'll be back?'

'I'm not sure. It depends how many people we bump into for a chat!' Evangelina laughed. 'We'll see you when we get back.'

'But will that be in an hour? Two hours? Longer?'

Helena was confused. Why was her sister insisting on knowing exactly how long they were going to be? Voula was up to something. What was she hiding? Could it be the real reason she'd decided to visit for a few days? It seemed obvious now that she'd returned to continue whatever it was she had planned to do all those years ago, and this time there would be no one to stop her.

'Ready to get going?' Filippos asked as he stepped inside, cutting the tension that had been building.

'Have a nice time,' Voula said with forced cheer. 'I'll just get another coffee and take it back to my room.'

As they walked out to the car Helena wished she could stay and spy on her sister in order to figure out what she was up to. Was someone coming to visit her? Or perhaps she was popping out but wanted to be back before them? Whatever it was, she was playing her cards very close to her chest.

Voula had to work fast. First on her list was taking photos of the restaurant. It was dated and faded, just like the bedrooms, but it was a good size and having only ten rooms there was plenty of space, even if all the rooms wanted to eat at the same time. She was happy with what she found and concluded that this would likely be the easy part of the project, needing just some new lighting, decorating, and furniture.

Next was the outdoors, which would be the biggest and most expensive part of the whole refurb. It was also the thing that concerned and frightened her the most. As she made her way around the front of the hotel to the patio area where the guests could sit and enjoy the view, she made a mental note that she needed to see which side of the hotel might be best to relocate the patio to. There was more room to the left of the building and if a part of the garden were taken away it would be perfect. And by moving the patio she could get to the main event, the thing that if she couldn't pull it off she could jeopardise the whole project – the swimming pool.

She could vividly remember standing here on the patio with her dad and telling him – over and over again through the years – that the hotel needed a pool. And every time her dad had asked why they needed a pool when there were so many gorgeous beaches around the island, with beautiful, clear blue sea to dive into. Of course, he was right – the beaches *were* spectacular, she couldn't disagree with that – but this wouldn't be a luxury, five-star retreat hotel without an infinity pool. In the high-end market she was hoping to break into it was not just desired, but also expected.

Taking some photos of the area before getting the tape measure out of her pocket, she hurried to get the measurements jotted down, knowing she still had the family apartment to go up to. Her initial evaluation told her that the pool would be quite narrow, but could go the whole length of the hotel so would be a good size overall. She was excited to picture it but that excitement soon faded once she turned around and looked at the hotel's exterior. Oh dear, it was so very Greek and traditional. Nothing about it gave the impression that this was a place with modern, high class, bouquet glamour.

As she was standing there taking it all in, she saw a movement out the corner of her eye. She wondered if her mum and siblings had returned early from shopping but realised she hadn't heard the car return. Turning towards the disruption she came face-to-face with her nephew.

'Marios! You made me jump.' She hastily tucked the measuring tape into her bag and reached out to hug him.

How long had he been standing there? Had he seen her with the tape measure? The last thing she needed was the family to find out her plans before she had thought it all through, worked out how much it was going to cost, and figured out how she was going to present it to them to get them on board.

'Sorry, I didn't mean to startle you,' said Marios as he turned to look up at the hotel with her. 'I suspect you're probably thinking the same as me.'

'Oh? And what would that be?'

'I was thinking how tired the building is looking. It needs a good coat of paint to freshen it up, especially the little columns on the balconies. But I have to say it's still one of the loveliest buildings here on Vekianos. It's a bit iconic, really. Did you know that if you Google search images of the island so many are of this old hotel?'

'Perhaps when Helena is running it, she will get the exterior changed.'

'I don't think anything needs changing, really. A couple of coats of paint should sort it.'

Voula found she was a bit shocked that someone Marios' age actually liked the old look of the building.

'Don't you think it would be nice to see it modernised a little with, say, glass balconies?' she probed.

'Oh no, buildings with features like this one are what is so special about the islands. The modern new builds are ok, but we wouldn't want the whole island to look like that. If visitors to Greece want the chic holiday experience they can go to some of the big commercial islands. Visitors to Vekianos appreciate its charm.'

Oh, how she hated the word 'charm'! She needed to change the conversation quickly.

'Your grandmother has gone shopping with your

dad and aunt. Was there something you wanted?'

'Yes, I wanted to talk to you without anyone else around. It's about the party I'm helping Helena organise. I stupidly offered to take control of most of it, and to be honest, I'm out of my depth. I don't want to admit it to anyone though because they have enough to do with getting the hotel ready for the season. I thought, what with you being so successful at running huge events, you might give me some advice.'

'Of course! I'm happy to help you but I can't promise I'll be here for the party itself as I'm looking for a job at the moment and I'm not sure where in Greece I'll be at that point. First things first, where are you going to have the party? In the restaurant, or out here on the patio? Once you decide, you then need to find out how many people are coming so that you can work out how much food and drink you need to prepare. Why don't we put a plan of action together over the next few days?'

'Thank you, Aunt Voula, it's very kind of you to help.'

'No problem at all. Did you have any questions you wanted to ask now, to get you started?'

'Only one, and it's nothing to do with the party. Why were you measuring the patio when I arrived?'

So he had seen her after all, and now she had to think quickly and give him an answer.

'It's like this, I know everything will be daunting for Helena when she takes over so I just thought I could help by making a list of things she might want to consider once she's in charge. Like we both said, the hotel needs a coat of paint, and I thought if I could get quotes for her it would be one less thing for her to have to think about. Oh, here comes your dad,' she said, effectively ending the conversation. She could only hope Marios had believed her.

Chapter 11

Voula woke up very early. She hadn't really slept well as last night's family meal had been very stressful and she had been on the edge of her seat all night, worried that Marios would say something about seeing her measuring the patio. Thankfully, he hadn't, but she wasn't stupid enough to think he had believed her hastily prepared excuse. No, he would have guessed she was lying, and would likely be curious to figure out what she was actually doing. She suspected he hadn't said anything because he needed her to help him arrange the party, so hopefully she could distract him with the planning and make him forget what he'd seen.

Apart from that, the evening had been ok. There had been a lot of shared memories from when they were children, each telling stories about their father and the things they'd all done together when they were young. She'd got the impression that her mum really enjoyed the evening, and of course Marios found it all intriguing and teased his dad about all the adolescent adventures his aunts had brought to light.

She was glad she had no more secret things to do behind the family's backs now that she had all the measurements and photos she needed. The next task would be to price everything up when she got back to Rhodes, and of course come up with a way to convince her brother and sister that her plans to transform the hotel would be the right thing to make it successful.

'Good morning, Mum, is that coffee I can smell?' asked Voula.

'Take a seat and I'll pour you a cup.'

'Thank you. Last night was lovely, wasn't it? You really seemed to enjoy it.'

'I did. It was wonderful to hear you kids talk about your father and to be reminded of so many wonderful stories that I had forgotten about. When I went to bed it hit me how I'm so much happier thinking about the past. I'm not saying I'm not looking forward to moving over and living with Dora, but I suppose it's because it's a sort of return to the past as well because we grew up together in the same house. Some people would say it's a full circle moment.'

Voula had to agree. There was something alluring about the past and no denying that life had been a lot simpler when she was younger, back in the days before she constantly had to put on the mask of confidence and pretend she was in control every day, which she had been doing now for far too many years. She could also appreciate what it meant to come full circle now she was back on Vekianos.

'Marios has grown into a fine young man, hasn't he?' she said, trying to distract her mum and herself from their gloomy thoughts. 'I see so much of Filippos in him but he also has Nadia's sensitivity. It's a shame Natalia isn't coming back, it really seems to have upset him.'

'Yes, but both Nadia and I are happy about it as that girl used him and it was never an equal relationship. He's still young and he needs to have some fun before settling down. I'd hate to see him hurt the same way Helena was, with her throwing everything into her relationship with Sotirios only for him to leave at the end of a season and never come back. She closed herself off after that, and sadly she's still on her own even all these years later. I don't want the same fate for Marios.'

'I've always thought she was happy on her own. Do you not think that's the case?'

'I don't know, and that's the difference between you and your sister. You, I could read like a book from the beginning. If I ever said anything that you disagreed with you would tell me in no uncertain words how you felt, but Helena has always taken the path of least resistance and just agreed with others. I suspect I could say that the sea out there was yellow with pink spots and she would agree with me.'

'Perhaps, but I don't think you should beat yourself up about it. I honestly get the impression she is happy as she is, although I do know I make her nervous. No, nervous isn't the right word... She seems ... suspicious, I guess? Of me.'

'Well, you did come back here and try to change everything after your father died, so she would have cause to be suspicious of your motives now you're back again. Are you thinking of coming back for good and working in the hotel?' Evangelina asked, hope shining in her eyes. 'You're more than capable of doing it and now you have the bonus of me not being here to get in your way. This could be a big opportunity to carry on with what you planned all those years ago and I suspect life would be a lot easier for Helena if you were here sharing the load. I'm not expecting you to answer right now, of course, but would you at least think about it, and maybe talk to your sister?'

Voula nodded uncertainly and Evangelina walked out of the kitchen with a satisfied smile on her face. Her mum was the head of the family and had her finger on the pulse, and it seemed she had thought of every possible scenario for the future of the hotel. Oh yes, Evangelina was one step ahead of all of them.

Two hours later Voula was down in the harbour and had been staring up at the hotel for over fifteen minutes. Looking at it now, compared to yesterday, she was more convinced that all that was needed was the removal of all the columned railings on all the balconies, and the installation of glass replacements. Also, if the walls were all rendered to a perfect flat paint finish, it could look very modern and chic, the perfect high-end holiday retreat.

As she walked along the sea front she noted that nearly all the restaurants and shops were still closed. It would be another few weeks before they opened their doors, but thankfully she knew of one place that would be open for a coffee and a pastry. It would also be full of locals so a good place to listen in on the chit chat about Vekianos.

As she went up through one of the little lanes she spotted Filippos coming towards her.

'You off to the boat?' she asked after greeting him.

'I am indeed. How come you're up and out so early? I thought you'd have a lie-in after last night.'

'I just fancied a walk and a coffee. Want to join me for a little brother and sister chat?'

'That sounds nice,' he said, falling into step beside her.

They arrived at the restaurant and Filippos went inside to order while Voula grabbed a table outside. It wasn't overly warm this early in the year, but it was a nice day and they'd agreed they wanted to enjoy the feel of the sunshine.

'How are you feeling about all the big changes?' she asked when her brother returned, keen to keep the conversation off of Marios and what he had seen her doing.

'I support Mum completely, but I do worry about this move. Vekianos is her home and has been for over seventy years. This is where all her family and friends are! Yes, she knows Parga well and has lots of friends there too, but it's just such a drastic change combined with her retirement.'

'I sort of agree that she would be happier staying here on the island, but all we can do now is support her decision. Anything else bothering you?'

'I don't think Helena will cope by herself running the hotel,' he rushed out, then immediately looked ashamed. 'Nadia disagrees with me and thinks she will step up to the mark and love everything about being the boss, but she's my sister and I worry that the pressure will be too much.'

'I think we'll just have to wait and see what happens, and make sure she knows in the meantime that she's not alone.'

'Yes, but if she were to fail... I just... I've always felt a bit sorry for Helena. I look at my life with my gorgeous wife and my wonderful son, whereas all Helena has is the hotel. I find that very sad.'

'But you could say the same for me because what do I have?'

'You're different from our sister though. You have a fabulous career and a busy, exciting life. You can't compare your high-flying existence to Helena's.'

Before Voula had a chance to reply, two elderly ladies who they both knew came up to chat. Voula fixed a polite smile on her face but let Filippos do the talking. She was too preoccupied with thinking over what her brother had just said. He was wrong because she didn't have a fabulous life, but she wasn't going to tell him that. She couldn't. It wasn't in her to show that level of vulnerability.

Once the ladies left, Voula turned the conversation back to their mum.

'I think we'll be able to tell after a few months if she's enjoying living in Parga, and if it seems like she isn't then we should suggest she move back. She wouldn't have to live at the hotel if she didn't want to; she could buy a little house, perhaps down here on the flat in the harbour.'

'I think you're right that we should give her time to adjust and see how she likes it. And by then Helena will probably be into a routine so Mum returning wouldn't have much impact on the business side of things. I'm probably just overthinking everything. Nadia's always saying I just don't like change, and she's right. That's why I appreciated last night so much, being sat around the table all together again made it feel just like old times. I enjoyed myself very much. I suspect you're already ready to return to Rhodes though, aren't you. Nothing ever happens here on Vekianos so no one can blame you if you're itching to get back to the excitement of your life as soon as you can.'

She wanted to shout and scream and tell Filippos the truth – that her life was a mess, she was at rock bottom, and she was ready to return to the island and create her dream hotel. But she couldn't, so they quietly finished their coffee and Filippos headed down to his boat. She walked part of the way with him and then decided to walk a little further alongside the sea.

She wanted to make sure she hadn't missed anything while gathering what she needed to start to price out the renovation and work up the budget. The money side was the biggest worry. She knew she could get a good price for her apartment on Rhodes, and that any number of banks would be more than happy to lend her money because of the value of the hotel, but loan repayments were costly, and as she was now out of work every single cent mattered even more than usual.

Just as she got to the end of the sea wall and moved onto the coastal path she ran into her sister. It was the first time since her return that they would be alone together, and Voula knew she had to be very careful with what she said. If possible, it would be best if the hotel wasn't mentioned.

'Great minds think alike!' she said to Helena. 'I've just had coffee with Filippos so it seems I'm destined to spend some quality time with both of my siblings today. Are you heading back up to the hotel? I could turn around and walk with you.'

She could see Helena was building herself up to say something, and she panicked for a moment, wondering if Marios had said something to her.

'That's a good idea. It will give you time to tell me about your plans for the hotel,' said Helena, coldly. 'Or were you planning on waiting until Mum is gone and then surprising us all?'

Voula sighed, her suspicion sadly confirmed. 'I take it you spoke to Marios?'

Helena nodded tersely.

'I promise that Marios has got it all wrong.'

Helena stopped and turned, staring Voula down as she spoke slowly and clearly. 'If Marios has got it all wrong, perhaps you should explain what he did see.'

'He saw me measuring the patio. Listen, it's no secret to either of us that the hotel needs modernising, and I just thought that with Mum going it would be the perfect time to do it.'

'But why are you so concerned about the hotel? Your life is on Rhodes, not here, unless...' Helena looked wary. 'Unless you've decided to move back.'

'I just thought that we could do some refurbishment to the place and then work together, making it an even bigger success than it already is ... and perhaps take it in another direction, one that's a little more glamorous and upmarket.'

'And when were you going to mention all of this?'

'I was going to wait until I'd pulled together some plans and numbers. I still haven't thought everything through, but I guess now you've brought it up we might as well talk about it. So, what do you think?'

'I'm not interested in your plans for the building, I'm interested in how you see us working together in this new "upmarket" hotel you're envisioning. Who would be doing what? I've been working with Mum for years and know this hotel better than anyone, but I suppose you're now expecting to sweep in and take over, with me answering to you? Not bloody likely!'

'I have no intention of bulldozing you, Helena. I thought I could concentrate on the paperwork and booking side of the business, and you could throw yourself into the practical things.'

'Practical. By that do you mean the cleaning and waitressing?'

Voula could see what her sister was getting at, and she was right, Voula *had* envisioned Helena taking care of the hands-on tasks. But that clearly wasn't what Helena wanted.

'You know what? Why don't I make everything easy. You take the hotel and I'll find a job somewhere else on the island. It's one thing taking orders from Mum, but quite another taking them from my high and mighty sister. In short, it's not happening.'

'But ... but you can't leave! I need you and the hotel is your life and your home. What will you do? Where will you go?'

'You don't actually care about me, Voula. And don't worry, you'll soon find another cleaner. Because that's all I am to you. And I suspect that's all I ever was.'

'You can't leave like this. Mum will be furious and accuse me of kicking you out.'

'I'm not giving you the chance to kick me out. I'm leaving of my own accord before that happens. I'll do you one last favour though, I won't say anything about this until after Mum has left to live with Dora. You've won, Voula. The hotel is yours to do with what you like.' And with that, Helena turned on her heel and stormed off, leaving Voula standing speechless.

Chapter 12
Thursday 5th April

'Look, there are two seats over there with a view of the departures board. Do you fancy another coffee? Or perhaps a beer?' Jenny asked her dad.

'Just coffee please. It's far too early for a boozy drink so I will wait until we're on the plane for that I think.'

Jenny went off to get the drinks and as she stood in the long queue, waiting to be served, she tried to get her head around everything. It didn't seem like five minutes since she was last at an airport with both her mum and dad, heading off on holiday, and now it was just her and her dad. It felt very odd as they'd never been away together without her mum, but something about this trip made her feel warm inside. For one thing, there would be none of the usual nagging from her mum, something she did all the time on holidays, always looking for the downside of any trip and finding things to complain about.

As Paul waited for Jenny to come back with the coffee the reality of their impending holiday was sinking in. Though he was looking forward to seeing Evangelina and spending time with Filippos and Nadia, he felt nervous about going back to Vekianos ... and especially about seeing Helena after all these years. If he was honest with himself, she had been the reason he hadn't returned for another season on the island back in the day. It had upset him, seeing her give her all to her relationship with Sotirios only to be treated badly by him. He was interrupted from his complicated thoughts by Jenny returning with the drinks.

'I also grabbed a pack of biscuits,' she said as she handed everything over and sat down next to him.

'Good plan. Airport biscuits are traditionally one of the most difficult things to get into, so you'd best hold my coffee while I try to rip the plastic open.'

'No, you hold the drinks, and I'll show you how to get into them. You just need to use your teeth.' She had the package open in a matter of seconds and they laughed as she handed it over.

Jenny glanced at the departures board and saw that they had about an hour and a half before take-off.

'I can't believe we're in April already. It seems like only yesterday that we both handed in our notices and now here we are, both unemployed and jetting off to the Greek islands. And this isn't going to be just any old holiday; we have a party to look forward to as well!' Jenny enthused.

'That's not strictly true as you have a job to come back to if you want it. You have to admit that you did really enjoy those few weeks you did at the new office.'

'But that had a lot to do with the fact that they put me up in a very nice hotel with gorgeous food.'

'Perhaps so, but you did say you got a real buzz being surrounded by all the different departments that have been brought together in the new communal office space.'

'Yes, but it wasn't enough to convince me to change my mind. Now that's it, Dad, no more UK chat until after the holiday is over. We're off to the lovely Greek island where you had the time of your life and there's so much to look forward to, what with the big retirement party halfway through our trip. Have you found out anything about who else will be there? Are you likely to know anyone?'

'All I know is that Helena was happy for you to join me and has reserved two rooms for us. I know I was a little apprehensive in the beginning about going, but now I'm really looking forward to it. I can't wait to catch up with Filippos and see Evangelina.'

'Yes, and then there are the sisters, which should be interesting ... for me, at least!' She laughed good-naturedly. 'Do you think the one that used you to make the lad jealous will mention it?'

'I don't care if she does. That was so far back in the past it's best forgotten. The thing that I'm looking forward to the most about the whole trip is showing you around the island, exploring all the lovely beaches, and wandering through the harbour with all the shops and restaurants. The season won't have really started yet but hopefully the weather will be good, and we'll be able to get in a swim or two. It will be an adventure for both of us.'

Settling into their seats and a comfortable silence, they checked the departures board every now and then, in between people watching. Jenny could tell her dad was in deep thought, but whether it was about his past or his future she wasn't quite sure. One thing she did know was that they were about to have a lovely holiday together, and that was what mattered most.

Once on the plane they got their books out, and when the drinks trolley arrived Jenny ordered them two miniature bottles of champagne before Paul could say anything.

'What's all this for?' Paul asked once the flight attendant had moved on to the next row.

'We need to start our celebrations off in the right way,' said Jenny, matter-of-factly.

'Celebrations? What are we celebrating?'

'Everything! But most of all, happiness. We're both in a good place and we need to mark that. Here is to two weeks of sunshine, laughter, lots of gorgeous food and wine, and anything else I can add to the list.'

'My daughter is bonkers.'

'Oh yes, and you wouldn't want me any other way.'

The rest of the flight was spent reading and when the captain announced that they would be landing in Corfu in half an hour, Jenny put her book away and pulled up a map of the island she'd screenshotted on her phone. She wanted to know where they were staying.

'Now, Dad, talk me through the island of Vekianos. Where is the hotel on this map?'

'Gosh, it's been years since I've seen the island laid out like this! The hotel is just here,' he pointed, 'on the hill above the harbour, with great views out to sea. Over here is Keriaphos, which is just around the coast – it's a lovely town with nice restaurants – and that there is Thagistri,' he said, drawing his finger along the map to point out the areas to Jenny. 'Thagistri has one of my favourite beaches and there's a great little beach bar – and to be clear, I say that very loosely as it was little more than a shack that sold drinks and some food. I always thought one puff of wind and it would get blown down!' He laughed. 'But I loved it there; it's a very special beach. You know, thinking about it, there really isn't anywhere on the island I disliked.'

'It all sounds amazing. In terms of getting there, we have to get the boat from Corfu to Vekianos, correct?' Paul nodded. 'I'm really looking forward to that part. It just seems like the perfect way to arrive on an island, and will probably feel so romantic.'

'Does that mean my daughter is looking for love on this holiday?' teased Paul.

'Very funny. No, that's the last thing on my mind, and I can assure you I won't be falling for any Greek charm. The last thing I need in my life at the moment is a man so the only romance I'll be looking for is from the scenic boat ride.'

After collecting their suitcases from the conveyor belt in the baggage hall, they headed outside the airport and got a taxi to take them to the harbour. For the first time Jenny noticed her dad had an odd look on his face. He was smiling and trying hard to make conversation, but she could tell he was in a different space. Was he remembering taking this journey thirty years ago? Or was there something else going on in his head? She decided she wasn't going to ask because it was his time to reminisce, not hers.

They had about an hour's wait for the next boat and spent the time soaking in the brilliant weather and watching the sea, and once they'd boarded and left the harbour behind, Paul pointed out the islands they passed.

'Here we are, Jenny, sailing on the wide-open sea. Is this as romantic as you were expecting?'

'Yes, exactly, and I know that once I see Vekianos getting closer that's when the magic will begin.'

'So it's not just romance? You're expecting magic as well?' he teased.

'What can I say? My expectations are high! How about you, Dad? How are you feeling about everything?'

'I'm ok. I think I had a moment back in the taxi; I was thinking about the last time I arrived in Corfu. It's hard to believe I'm taking this journey again all these years later.'

Not knowing the right words, Jenny settled for giving her dad a hug, which he seemed to appreciate.

'I can see land in the distance! Is that Vekianos already?' she asked.

'Yep, that's our home away from home for the next two weeks.'

'Will we need to get a taxi from the harbour to the hotel?'

'No, it's only a short walk so we should be fine to manage it with the suitcases.'

Once they left the boat Paul led the way through the cobbled streets. They were not the best for pulling suitcases along but there was no rush and they stopped often for Paul to point out sights and share his memories. He told her how so much had changed – the crumbling buildings he remembered having been updated and changed into little houses and shops.

'I was so worried the charm of the island would have gone, but to be honest, it's the complete opposite. The changes have only added to it, which makes me happy. Right, now to face the hill. The hotel is at the top so not much further to go.'

Jenny was happy to see her dad so enthusiastic about Vekianos. It reminded her of the enthusiasm he showed for everything when she was a child and they would do things together. As an adult now, she could appreciate her father's joy so much more, and it warmed her heart.

At the top of the hill her dad stopped at the gate to the hotel and as Jenny caught up, she spotted a sign pointing the way to the reception.

'Is it just as you remembered, Dad?'

'Yes and no. It's looking a little tired and could do with a lick of paint, but I'm so glad it hasn't changed. Look, I have goosebumps! Let's ring the bell. They should be expecting us as I told Helena roughly what time we would be arriving.'

Paul rang the bell but before anyone answered Jenny heard someone say her dad's name. As they both turned towards the sound of the voice, she saw an elderly lady coming out of a side door.

'Oh my goodness, Paul, you've not changed a bit

since I saw you last! Still the handsome young man that worked so hard for us.'

'Flattery will get you *everywhere,* Evangelina!' Paul laughed. 'But I have definitely changed. After all, it's been thirty years since I last walked up that hill, even though it feels like it was only yesterday. I'm glad to see you're looking so well, and what is all this I hear about you retiring? I can't believe it.'

'It's true, I'm afraid,' she said, before turning to Jenny with a warm and welcoming smile. 'You must be Paul's daughter. I'm so happy you were able to join us!'

'Thank you, it was so very kind of you to invite me. I've heard so much – and over many years – about this hotel and your wonderful family.'

'You are very welcome! Now come inside. I will just find Helena and she can show you to your rooms. Once you're settled we can sit down with a drink to celebrate your dad's return.'

'I'm behind you, Mum,' said Helena as she stepped outside. 'Hello and welcome back, Paul. Mum's right, you haven't changed a bit.'

Butterflies took flight in Paul's stomach. It felt just like yesterday that Helena had last smiled at him, and he realised that coming back to Vekianos was the best decision he'd made in a long time. He was so pleased Jenny had persuaded him to come.

'Neither have you,' he countered, leaning forward to kiss Helena's cheek. 'It's so lovely to be back on the island and I'm excited to catch up with you and Filippos, and reminisce about all the fun times we had. I'm sorry, Evangelia, but I suspect most of those stories won't be for your ears.'

They all laughed.

'You can't shock me, especially where my son is concerned,' Evangelina said ruefully. 'I knew more about what he was up to back in the day than he ever could have guessed! But he's a good lad and I'm very proud of the husband and father he's become. Talking of my grandson, can you call Marios and ask him to pop up to see me?' she asked her daughter. 'Tell him it's urgent.'

'What's so urgent that I can't sort it out?' asked Helena.

'Never you mind. Please just message him and then show Paul and his beautiful daughter up to their rooms.'

Helena had learned long ago there was little point asking questions when her mother's mind was set on something, so she simply did as she was told and sent the text.

Sorry to bother you but your gran asked if you could pop up to the hotel. She says it's urgent but I haven't a clue what she's up to H xx

'Shall we all meet down on the terrace in half an hour for a few drinks, some snacks and a chat?' Evangelina suggested.

Helena realised exactly what her mum was up to, and the urgent need for Marios' presence made sense. Laughing quietly to herself at Evangelina's matchmaking efforts, she showed Paul and Jenny to their rooms.

Once back down in the kitchen, Helena got a tray of glasses ready and grabbed a bottle each of red and white wine. After taking it all out onto the patio, she nipped to one of the cupboards to fetch some cushions for the chairs, wiped the table down, and then raced back into the kitchen for some bowls of crisps and nibbles.

'Everything is sorted, Mum,' she said as Evangelina wandered into the kitchen. 'If you could just take these couple of bowls out, I'll bring the rest.'

'Ok. Is Marios here yet?'

'No, and you need to be careful.'

'Careful of what? All I'm doing is inviting my grandson up for a drink with our guests. You worry too much, Helena. Sometimes you just need to relax, sit back, and go with the flow.'

Jenny knocked on Paul's door to see if he was ready, and then they headed down the stairs together.

'The view out of the bedroom window is to die for, Dad! I could happily sit on that balcony for hours taking in the sun on the water and the boats in the distance. How did you ever manage to leave a place like this? If I was living and working here, I would never want to leave.'

'I know what you mean, but it's such a short tourist season and once it ends the work dries right up.'

Stepping out onto the patio, Paul waved to Evangelina, whispering to Jenny as they walked over, 'They've picked the best corner, tucked away from the sea breeze but still with a great view.'

'How are your rooms?' asked Evangelina. 'If there's anything you need just let us know. You sit there, Paul, and Jenny over there,' she said as she pointed them into the chairs she wanted them in. 'Red or white?'

'Red for me, please,' said Paul, 'and I expect Jenny will have the same.'

'Yes, please.'

'That sounds like the door,' said Evangelina. 'It must be my grandson. He is a good young man and I'm sure you will like him, Jenny. Out here, Marios, we're on the terrace!' She shouted that last bit, making Jenny flinch.

'I got here as quick as I could. What's so urgent, Gran?' asked Marios, sounding out of breath.

'Do you know, I have completely forgotten what it was I wanted you for!' Evangelina laughed heartily. 'While I try to think what it was, why don't you take a seat next to Jenny there. This is Paul, who worked for us for many years, and his lovely daughter,

Jenny, who must be around the same age as you. Helena, pour Marios a wine, please.'

'I'm twenty-five,' Jenny offered.

'Exactly the same age as my grandson! What a coincidence.'

Jenny realised then why Evangelina had asked her grandson to pop by, but she found she didn't much mind the matchmaking because Marios was *very* good looking; tall, dark, and very handsome, with the most gorgeous eyes. She was more than happy to be sat next to him.

As the group chatted about what had changed since Paul was last on Vekianos, Helena explained that they were the first to arrive and more guests were due over the next couple of days.

'My children have insisted on me having a party before I leave, though I didn't really want a lot of fuss. Marios is planning everything, aren't you?' she said proudly.

'I am. I think it will be nice for you to meet up again with the people who worked with you and Grandad over the years. It will be a nice way to say goodbye.'

'Yes, nice for me and all the old staff, but likely very boring for you and Jenny. The last thing you youngsters need is to be bored to tears hearing stories about the past. I know, why don't you show Jenny around the island instead? You have your bike, or I'm sure your dad would lend you the car. I'm sure you'd have much more fun, just the two of you.'

As Evangelina and Helena headed indoors to grab some more drinks from the kitchen, Marios turned to Jenny.

'I'm sorry about that. I think my gran is trying to do a little matchmaking. You don't have to spend time with me if you don't want to.'

Jenny smiled. 'Who said I don't want to? I think

it'll be nice to see the island with you, especially on the back of a bike. Pick the day and I'll be ready.'

Chapter 13

It had been several weeks since Voula had visited Vekianos and her life on Rhodes was busy. She had spent days getting quotes for work on the Vekianos project and also hours going through hundreds of websites looking for fixtures and fittings.

She was more determined than ever to transform the family hotel, even after the disastrous conversation with Helena, who had thankfully kept her promise by not saying anything to anyone. But top of Voula's list was to find a way to rebuild her relationship with her sister. She really didn't want her to leave the hotel when instead they could team up and work together, and both have a lovely, rewarding life.

Today she was off on a research trip as she had booked one night in the luxury hotel on Mykonos that was serving as the inspiration for her refurbishment of the family hotel. It wasn't a cheap trip, but she knew she would get a lot out of it as getting a hands-on feel for the place would give her more information than all the photos put together ever could. She took one last look at her emails and then made the short drive to Rhodes airport. She was ready to breathe the atmosphere of Mykonos, and hopefully bottle the essence of luxury it had so she could take it to Vekianos and make the hotel the best it could be.

She looked through online pictures of the hotel she was going to stay at as she waited in the departures lounge for the short flight, and for the first time she felt a bit nervous. Everything up to this point had been facts and figures on a computer screen, but now it was beginning to feel real, and for once she wondered if she was dreaming too big. It wouldn't be the first time as the whole of her working career had been about her always wanting more. She was just the type of person who was determined to always be at the top of their game, and this was her biggest dream so far.

She had only brought hand luggage so she was out of the airport almost immediately after landing and into a taxi. It was a very short journey to the hotel and her excitement grew as the taxi pulled up outside the big gates. She smiled because it was the same set-up as the hotel back on Vekianos, the entrance at the rear and all the guest rooms on the other side of the building, taking in the no doubt magnificent view.

She was greeted at the gate by a very smartly dressed young man who smiled and took her bag.

'Welcome! If you would like to follow me, we'll get you checked in and then I can show you your room.'

'Thank you.'

As he led the way she looked around in wonder. Having spent hours scrutinising photos of the hotel's layout and design, the space felt intimately familiar, almost as if she had been there before.

The receptionist greeted her warmly and guided her to a chair. 'If you would like to take a seat, I will just get the details up on the computer... Here we go. I see you'll be with us for one night, Miss Aetos.'

She was shocked that they already knew her name without her telling them.

The receptionist smiled. 'We try to ensure we always know exactly who will be arriving at what time so we are prepared to welcome you.'

'That's a lovely touch,' she said, approvingly.

'Just a few things to point out. Firstly, we are a very small hotel, so you shouldn't get lost.' They both laughed. 'The restaurant, bar and pool are just through there,' she pointed, 'and the gym, sauna, steam room, and spa treatment rooms are on the floor below. The lift to the bedrooms is just in the corner over there. Do you have any questions?'

'No, that's all very clear.'

'Great! If you'd like to follow the bellman, he'll show you to your room.'

Voula nodded her thanks and stood to follow the man who had greeted her at the gate, and who still held her case.

This was the bit she had been looking forward to most: a closer look at the fixtures, fittings, and the bathroom in her room.

They took the elevator up two floors and the young man led her along a short corridor with just four doors. Hers was the last one and he took the key card and opened the door for her, holding it so she could go in first.

'This is lovely, thank you.'

'If you need anything at all the phone is over there. We hope you have a lovely stay.'

Once he was gone she went out onto the balcony, looking down to the pool and the terrace below. She was a bit disappointed to find that these balconies were over twice the size of the ones at the hotel in Vekianos, and were much more private. Enhancing the privacy of the balconies was something she would need to look into. Back in the room her first stop was the bathroom, where she was pleased to see the size was about the same to the ones on Vekianos, and the shower similar to what she had envisioned. The bedroom itself was gorgeous and slightly smaller than the ones she would be working with, so creating a similar look would be easy. She was impressed with the way the fridge and coffee station had been designed to be tucked out of the way and hidden behind a door, which made the room look less like a hotel room. It was a great idea and definitely something she was keen to look into for her redesign.

It was eleven-thirty so she quickly changed her clothes and headed back downstairs to see what else this unique hotel had to offer. Her plan was to grab a sun lounger by the infinity pool and check out what type of guests stayed here, and what type of vibe there was.

As she got out the lift she peeked into the bar and could immediately tell that no expense had been spared. The space was lovely and very modern, with high-end fittings that were glamorous and also likely quite expensive, which made her a bit nervous. Continuing through onto the terrace, which was equally impressive, the magnificent view stopped her in her tracks. The pool had been placed half a dozen steps down from the terrace so it wasn't blocking the view if you were having a drink at the bar, which was genius, and she got her phone out to make some notes, wondering if something similar might be possible on Vekianos. She would need structural reports so added that to her to-do list.

There were only four or five guests around the pool so she had her choice of loungers, and as she settled in she wondered if the hotel was empty or if the guests had just all gone out for the day. Given the amount of money that had been spent to create this luxury paradise, she knew they'd need every room filled every night.

She had the perfect spot to the side of the pool, which allowed her to see everything, and she started making notes about the details of the plants and the type of pots they were in, and the furniture in and around the pool area.

An older and very glamorous woman appeared on the terrace, catching Voula's eye, and she noted that one of the staff was carrying the woman's handbag for her. Once he had pulled out her seat and helped her get comfortable, he went back to the bar and returned with what looked like a champagne bottle in an ice bucket. This impressed Voula. If guests were so happy and relaxed that they were drinking champagne before lunch, that was a very good sign, and something to aspire to. Then she noticed the barman walking towards her.

'Good morning, madam, can I get you anything? Would you like to see the cocktail menu?'

'I'll just have a coffee, please, black no sugar, but I will still take a look at the menu.'

'Of course. There you go,' he said, handing it over. 'I'll be right back with your coffee. I won't be a moment.'

The bar menu hadn't been on the hotel website so she photographed the four pages. It was an impressive menu and she liked the diversity of the offerings. She could imagine lots of cocktails being made before the guests went in to dinner.

As the waiter returned with her coffee, she noticed the glamorous woman was staring at her. Perhaps she was staying here by herself and was lonely? Voula made a mental note that when she walked back up the terrace steps for some lunch in the restaurant, she would walk the other side of the pool to avoid having to get into conversation with her. She was on a research mission and couldn't afford to lose time getting caught up in small talk with strangers.

Over the next hour or so more couples came and had a swim and lay on the loungers. The guests were a mixed bag of ages, but it seemed to work. The main thing that struck Voula was how calm and peaceful the space was, with no music blaring, no children running around, and every movement by the staff executed in a slow, graceful way. She was impressed. The only thing she wasn't comfortable about was the woman looking at her. Did she know this woman? Or did the woman know her? Maybe she was a former guest of Voula's hotel?

She avoided eye contact as she left her lounger and headed towards the restaurant. Voula had already decided to have a Greek salad, a little bread, and a glass of white wine for lunch, and she planned to sit inside rather than on the terrace as she wanted to take in every detail of the restaurant. She was also hoping to overhear some of the servers' conversations, as it might give her some insight about the inner workings of the hotel.

She ordered her salad and then watched the swing door into the kitchen. She realised instantly that there would be no picking up on the servers' conversation as there wasn't one. They were so professional and barely interacted with one another, too focused on the guests to have time for idle chit chat. It made her think about staffing the refurbed hotel. From what she knew about the existing part-time staff, they likely wouldn't be at all suitable for what she was envisioning, so she'd have to let them go. That would probably be a huge problem for her mum as they had supported the family business for many years. No, she had to switch off from that. Those thoughts were for another time. Today and this evening were all about getting a feel for this place.

The waitress came to clear her bowl away and asked, 'Was everything ok with your lunch? Can I get you anything else? A desert or coffee?'

'Everything was lovely but nothing else for me, thank you. This is such a special place; you must really enjoy working in such a modern, deluxe hotel.'

The girl nodded but looked nervous, not nearly as relaxed as when Voula had first come in and asked for a table. Then it clicked. The girl's discomfort must have something to do with the older lady, who was now in earshot.

'Thank you again. I think I'll spend a few more hours in the sunshine, and after that delicious lunch I'm so looking forward to dinner later.'

'I hope you have a lovely afternoon. We'll see you this evening.'

As Voula got up, she realised she needed the bathroom before going back to the pool, but that would mean walking past the woman who was staring at her. Needs must, so she would do what she always did in these situations: put on a big smile and say a friendly hello, but keep walking so there would be no chance of having to stop and chat. She fiddled with her bag as a means of stalling because, just to be on the safe side, she wanted to walk by just as the other woman took a bite of her meal.

Her plan worked and Voula was in and out of the bathroom and back by the pool in no time.

After making a few more notes on her phone she turned the lounger a little towards the sun, preparing to switch off and relax for the rest of the afternoon, something she rarely got time to do.

She didn't plan to fall asleep, so she was surprised to jolt awake some time later and she laughed aloud. She couldn't remember the last time that had happened! It just showed how relaxed she must be feeling; that, or how worn out and tired she was. As she turned to get her phone out of her bag, she could see the lady was back in her chair after her lunch, but this time she was chatting to a man. Looking at the time, Voula found it was five-thirty and she pondered whether she should go for a swim or head up to her room and sit on her balcony. She chose to go back to her room; it would be a good chance to make more notes before going down to dinner.

After getting her things together she headed back up the terrace steps, hearing raised voices between the glamorous older woman and the younger man. They stopped talking when they spotted her and both smiled as she walked past, but she couldn't help overhearing the woman hiss 'you have responsibilities' just as she got to the lift. She thought she recognised the man, but where from she wasn't sure.

Back in the room she called down to reception and reserved a table in the restaurant for eight-thirty. That would give her time to sit in the bar first and have a cocktail or two, and observe the guests and staff.

After a shower she poured herself a glass of water and took it out onto the balcony, sitting down to take in the view of the wide-open sea in front of her. The view was something the hotel really had going for it, but she thought to herself smugly that the view from the family hotel was slightly better as you could see bits of land in the distance, which she felt gave it more interest.

She checked over the list she had been making over the last couple of weeks to see if everything she wanted to research here was done, then got dressed and ready to head down for a cocktail before dinner.

After one last look in the mirror she headed out, opting to take the stairs as it was one area hotels normally forgot to incorporate into the design. This stairwell was great though, with lovely artwork on the walls and a couple of windows showcasing the view, which made it feel in tune with the rest of the hotel.

As she passed reception there were a few staff walking around and she smiled at those she passed. She had stayed in top hotels all over the world where the staff were trained to be friendly and make conversation, always checking the guests had everything they required, but here they only spoke when spoken to, which was lovely. She knew they were there if needed, but they weren't constantly checking on her, which could quickly become irritating.

Entering the bar, she spotted a little table outside that would give her a view into the restaurant as well, so she scooted over to it and sat down.

'Good evening, can I get you something to drink?' asked the waiter who had silently appeared beside her.

'Yes, please, a cocktail I think – the "Mykonos special".'

'Of course. Would you care to look at the dinner menu while you're waiting for your drink?'

'That would be great.'

The waiter handed her the menu and though she made a point of flipping through it in case anyone was watching, it was already familiar to her, given she knew it inside out from researching the hotel. She was more interested in what was going on around her. There was a little bit of calming music in the background, just enough to add to the atmosphere without taking anything away from the surroundings, and looking around she could see most guests were in pairs, sitting, chatting, and looking at the dinner menu. Over in the restaurant she could see half a dozen tables being served, which was a good sign as it suggested that most of the hotel's guests had chosen to stay in and eat here, rather than go into the town.

'Here you are. I hope you enjoy your cocktail and I'll be just over there if you need anything else.'

'Thank you, that's great.'

She sipped her cocktail and as the time of her reservation inched closer, she realised she was actually quite hungry. Spotting the lady from earlier today heading towards her, Voula wondered if she should get up and head into the restaurant early, both to feed her growling stomach and avoid becoming entangled in potentially painful small talk with a stranger.

Too late.

'Good evening, would you mind if I join you?'

Before Voula could say or do anything the waiter had pulled the chair back for the woman to sit down. The young man looked very nervous, and it made her wonder: who was this woman?

Thankfully, Voula had been in situations like this many times in her life and she knew from experience that it paid to be in control of the conversation.

'Not at all. I was just admiring this lovely hotel.'

'That's very kind of you. I spent many years dreaming it up in my head and to see my vision come to life has been very rewarding. By the way, I'm Athena,' she said, extending her hand for Voula to shake.

So, she wasn't just a glamorous guest – she was the owner!

'It's a very special place,' said Voula. 'You really should be so proud.'

'Thank you. Now, I think I should cut to the chase. Are you a journalist here to do a review? Or competition here on the island, about to copy what I have created? I've had my eye on you today and you certainly don't act like our usual guests.'

Voula felt uncomfortable but she had to smile at how similar this woman's approach was to her own. No messing around, just straight to the point.

'I'm neither, but I will be very honest with you – I wanted to see what you've built here, with a view to using the best bits as inspiration for my own hotel on another Greek island.'

'I like your honesty and I'm very flattered that you've come to research us. I would think something like this would go down well on Rhodes.'

Voula was impressed that the woman had clearly

looked up her details. She quickly decided not to correct her assumption that the hotel was on Rhodes, suspecting it was better to keep the truth to herself for now. As the man she had seen with Athena earlier today walked into the bar – looking a lot smarter now – she noticed he was avoiding coming over and the way Athena's face had changed when she saw him.

Then it clicked how Voula knew him – she had seen his photo on the hotel website.

'I take it that's the manager,' she said to Athena.

'Yes, and he's late again. This is the price I pay for employing my son. He's the one thing that lets my dream and vision for the hotel down. Would you excuse me? It was nice meeting you, Miss Aetos.'

With that Athena caught her son's eye and pointed to a table in the corner of the bar. No doubt he was in for another telling off.

Chapter 14
Friday 13th April

It was the first full day of the holiday and Jenny was excited to find the sun shining when she opened her bedroom curtains. She was off out with Marios for the day, all thanks to Evangelina setting them up, and she had twenty minutes before she had to meet her dad downstairs for breakfast, which was just enough time to grab a shower and sort an outfit for her day out.

'You beat me down to breakfast,' she said as she gave her dad a hug a short while later.

'I've been up for hours, and have already taken a walk down to the harbour and back.'

'I wish I had known that as I would have gone with you. Next time, be sure to knock on my door.'

'Good morning! Did you both sleep well?' asked Helena as she joined them.

Jenny and Paul nodded in unison and shared their delight about the beautiful weather for their first full day.

'I've got a pot of coffee and some juice to get you started while you have a think about what you'd like to eat. We have toast and pastries, also eggs, bacon, and sausages... I also wanted to say I'm so sorry about yesterday, Jenny. My mum shouldn't have stuck her oar in and tried setting you up with Marios. It was wrong of her to put you both in that position, and of course you don't have to spend the day together if you don't want to.'

'Oh no, it's fine,' said Jenny, a blush staining her cheeks. 'I'm actually really looking forward to seeing the island and spending time with Marios. He seems a lovely chap and I'm sure it will be a great day.'

'Phew! I'm glad to hear that. I've not seen my nephew with a smile on his face like that for a long time.' Helena smiled warmly at the younger woman and Jenny's blush deepened.

Sensing his daughter's discomfort, Paul interrupted and asked, 'Helena, do you think it's possible to have an omelette for breakfast? Your mum's omelettes are the best in the world and they were one of the things I missed the most when I went back to England.'

As if summoned, Evangelina appeared from the kitchen with a smile and a hearty 'Good morning!' Hearing that Paul was in the mood for an omelette, her smile widened and she said that of course they could make it happen. 'What would you like in the omelettes? To tell the truth, I can't remember when I last cooked one as Nadia took over as the breakfast chef some time ago. But seeing as it's just the two of you here at the moment, we thought it would be a bit pointless her coming over as Helena and I are more than capable of looking after you.'

'I would like an Evangelina special omelette, please.' Paul grinned.

'What's in a "special" omelette, Dad?'

'Everything! That's why it's special, isn't that right, Evangelina?'

'You've put me on the spot now!' Evangelina laughed. 'Would you like one as well, Jenny? It would set you up for a lovely day out with my grandson.'

'Ok then, yes please.'

Helena followed her mum back into the kitchen and Jenny poured the coffee.

'I can see how, as the weeks go on and the temperature rises, this terrace would be the perfect place to sit all day. Every time I look up the view is changing with the little fishing boats going back and forth, and the yachts passing by. You would never get bored.'

'It's very special, isn't it. I'm so happy you persuaded me to come back. I was always happy here on Vekianos, but now it's even better because I can share it with you.'

'I agree. I think a lot of the joy comes from the family. Evangelina is wickedly funny and Marios seems really sweet. I'm looking forward to the day out with him. Helena is harder to read. I get the impression she works day and night, but she seems happy with where she's at.'

'Between you and me, she isn't the same Helena I once knew. Ok, we're all a lot older now, and many decades have passed since we were last running around the island together, but she used to be so fun. She seems on edge now, and the only time I've seen her relaxed so far is when she was talking to Marios. It's clear she's very proud of her nephew.'

With that Helena walked towards them with two plates.

'Here they come!' Paul said, excitement clear in his voice. 'I've dreamed about this smell for years! Thank you, Helena.'

'Enjoy. Can I get you more coffee?' she asked Jenny.

'Yes, please, how about you, Dad?'

'Thank you, please.'

Jenny couldn't get over how excited her dad was just seeing a plate of food. As this was only the start of the holiday, something told her he was going to have a wonderful couple of weeks reliving happy memories and creating new ones. It made her so happy, especially as she was going to get to be part of those new Greek island memories.

'What have you planned for today, Dad? You don't mind me heading off for the day with Marios, do you?' she asked as they finished eating, feeling worried.

'Of course not! Evangelina said Filippos is coming over later on today and we'll be completely engrossed catching up and sharing old stories – the ones that can be talked about in front of him mum and sister, that is! We were a little wild at times...' He broke off as laughter overcame him. It made him look ten years younger and it made Jenny's smile even brighter to see it.

'You're meant to be wild when you're young,' she said, supportively.

'So, did my omelettes live up to your expectations?' Evangelina asked as she and Helena pulled out chairs to join them.

'Oh yes, and more. How was yours, Jenny?' asked Paul.

'I can now see why my dad got so excited over them; they were delicious! When I first saw the plate, I was sure I wouldn't be able to finish it, but oh my goodness, it was so light and fluffy, and before I knew it, I was done! Like you predicted, it's really set me up for the day. I suspect I won't need anything else to eat until tonight.'

'I'm pleased you both enjoyed it, and I know you will have a nice day with my grandson. It will be just the ticket to snap himself out of being miserable.'

When Paul and Jenny looked at her blankly, she rushed to explain.

'He was seeing a girl who comes to the island to work every year – Natalia – but she has called the relationship off and left him heartbroken. Secretly, his mum and I are very happy she isn't coming back as she wasn't good for Marios, but that's another story.'

Jenny had thought Marios saw their day out the same way she did – as a bit of fun – but now, knowing he was feeling a bit fragile, she worried about sending mixed messages and making him more confused or hurt. She'd have to tread carefully today.

'I'd best go and get ready as Marios will be here in fifteen minutes. Thank you again for the lovely breakfast. I will pop back down to say goodbye before I go, Dad,' said Jenny, giving her father a hug before bounding across the terrace and into the hotel.

'What a lovely daughter you have, Paul. You should be so proud. It's like you're best friends rather than a dad and daughter, just like I am with Helena and Filippos. Sadly, it's not the same story with Voula. I think we're just too much alike.'

'I really don't know how I would have got through the last year if it hadn't been for Jenny. I didn't mention it in my Christmas card, but my wife and I split up' – Evangelina and Helena exchanged a surprised look – 'and I've retired. It's been nothing but huge change in my life for months, but I've now got out the other side. I'm a little battered but I'm ok, and that's largely thanks to Jenny's unwavering support. You'll know all about change though, Evangelina. Looking forward to your move?'

'I am. Ever since my brother-in-law died, I've been worried about my sister. Moving over to Parga will allow us to grow old together gracefully, and will give Helena the space she needs to put her stamp on the hotel.'

'I can understand if you're feeling a bit apprehensive, Helena, as you have big shoes to step into, but you know the hotel as well as your mum and you're going to do a terrific job,' said Paul, supportively.

'I couldn't have put it any better myself! I have a few things to sort out before Filippos arrives, so I will leave you two youngsters here to chat,' said Evangelina.

Helena felt a little awkward, left alone with Paul, but she didn't know why. Paul had been one of her best friends once upon a time, and they'd spent a lot of time together at work and socialising.

'It's so lovely to be back. I left it far too long,' said Paul, sounding a bit wistful.

'We thought you might have come back when Nadia and Filippos got married. He would have loved you to be here ... the whole family would have.'

'Yes, I should have been here for that, but my wife wouldn't let me come. I know it sounds stupid now, but I was never allowed to talk about my time here on Vekianos. She hated the thought of me working here even though it was years before we met.'

'How strange. Why was that, do you think?'

'Probably because she knew my summers here were the happiest times of my life, and she was jealous. Thankfully, we realised we were better off apart and all of that is now well in the past.'

There was silence as Helena thought back to those years. They really had been happy times.

'You know you don't need to be nervous about things when your mum leaves, right? You will be brilliant. Even after the few hours we spent chatting last night it was so obvious that you're the backbone to this hotel. Your mum might be the face, but it's you that keeps it ticking over day in and day out.'

'Can I tell you something? But please don't say anything as no one here knows yet.' Paul nodded. 'I won't be staying at the hotel. I'm leaving, too.'

'I don't understand. Are you going to Parga with your mum? But if that's the case she would already know, surely?'

'Voula is coming back to Vekianos to run the hotel. She's planning a big refurb to turn the place into a five-star, glitzy, glamour retreat hotel for the rich and famous, with no expense spared.'

'No way!' Paul's shock was clear on his face. 'But it's perfect as it is. Ok, a lick of fresh paint here and there wouldn't go amiss, but to totally overhaul it? Are you sure you've got that right?'

'Yes, but she's not planning on saying anything until Mum has gone and settled into her new home with Aunt Dora.'

'So she's, what ... kicking you out?' He looked aghast.

'She did offer me a job – no, that's wrong, she actually suggested we run it together – but her vision has me doing all the actual labour while she flits about taking the credit. I refuse to take orders from her so I have to walk away.'

'So, what are you going to do?'

'I'm not sure, but I know I can stay with Filippos and Nadia until I figure it out.'

'So, you'll lose your home as well? Are you still in the bungalow?'

'Yes, but I don't mind that. It's never been the same since Sotirios left. It's now just somewhere to live.'

'Can I ask you something about Sotirios?'

'Yeah, I don't mind talking about him. To be honest, it might actually be nice because I never do. For decades now everyone has tiptoed around the topic of him and me, so he's basically never mentioned. I'm left portrayed as poor dumped Helena. Ok, it's true that I was dumped, but I don't need anyone's pity.'

'Of course you don't,' Paul said.

'I promise I'm happy with my lot.'

'I've believed everything you've said up until now, but that I'm not so sure I believe. You aren't truly happy, Helena. I can see it in your eyes that the hopeful, happy girl I once knew is long gone. I hope it's ok to be honest – and I really don't mean to be rude! – but I think you've given up on yourself, and that's part of why you aren't fighting Voula to keep your job and your home.'

Helena was shocked. It was like Paul was looking right into her heart and soul, and she could feel her eyes fill and the tears rolling down her cheeks. Because the truth of the matter was that Voula wasn't the only sister who had been putting on an act all these years.

'Please excuse me, Paul.'

As Helena went back indoors Paul's heart was racing. All he wanted to do was put his arms around her and make her feel safe, but more than that he wanted to help her to believe in herself again and not give in to her sister. This was Helena's hotel, and no one should take it away from her.

It appeared that the feelings he'd had for Helena all those years ago were back.

Chapter 15

With one last look in the mirror Jenny was ready to go. As she walked down the stairs into the reception area she found Evangelina on the phone. She smiled and waved silently, then went out the front door to wait for Marios. After a couple of minutes, the door opened behind her and Evangelina stuck her head out.

'Excited to see the island?' she asked.

'Very! Since we decided to visit my dad hasn't stopped talking about Vekianos and all it has to offer. I can tell how happy he was working here and after everything he's been through these last few years, he deserves to be reminded of the places and people he's loved in his life.'

'I'm so pleased to hear that. Paul may be at retirement age but he's still a young man in my eyes, and it's wonderful to have him back here with us, even if it's only temporarily. That sounds like Marios' bike coming up the hill, so I'll let you get on. He's a good lad and though he might come across as a little shy at first, I know you'll bring him out of his shell.' With a wink she was gone.

As Marios parked and got off the bike Jenny felt herself blush, realising she wasn't dressed for getting on the back of a bike.

'I think I'd best go and change, Marios,' she called over to him.

'Don't do that! You look lovely and you'll be just fine. Now, what would you like to see on the island? Do you have a preference on where you want to go first?'

'Why don't you surprise me?'

Marios looked a bit nervous, and thinking about

how she'd have to manoeuvre herself onto the back of the bike and wrap her arms around his waist, Jenny knew they needed to break the tension and make them both feel a bit more comfortable and at ease with each other. And then she came up with an answer.

'You know what? I would love to look around the harbour. We could go and see your dad's boat, and stop for a coffee or some lunch, and we could probably do all of that on foot. What do you say?'

His relief was instantaneous and he smiled.

'Of course we can walk down. As for the boat ... I think you'll find that very boring as it's just a tourist boat, nothing special.'

'I will be the judge of that,' she said, affecting an imperious tone and causing them both to laugh. 'Why don't you hop off your bike and lead the way? I'm counting on you to be the perfect tour guild, so I'll need you to point out the famous places and buildings – and I don't mean little alleyways where you had your first kiss! – and, of course, fill me in on the island's history.'

He smiled and she knew the ice was broken for good and they were in for a nice day. He took the bike and parked it under a tree and then walked back towards her, laughing.

'What's so funny?' she asked.

'I was just thinking that I need one of those flags that tour guides have in Athens, so no one in the group gets lost.'

She giggled. 'I don't think we need to go to quite that length. Now, lead the way and show me all the places that made my dad fall in love with this island.'

It was nice to make the walk to the harbour as it was downhill and she wasn't burdened with a suitcase and a big bag this time around. As they fell into a silence Jenny realised she would have to take the lead in the conversation, but she had plenty of questions lined up.

'I think that this is the way my dad and I came up to the hotel,' she began. 'This is gorgeous, all the bougainvillea. It's just like you see in all the photos of the Greek islands,' she added as they turned a corner onto a new road.

'Probably because this *is* a Greek island?' said Marios. 'Sorry, that sounded a bit sarcastic and it wasn't meant to.'

'No, my observation was silly. I suppose what I meant was that it's wonderful to see it in person. What's next on this tour, Marios? I'm hoping it might involve a coffee.'

'No problem at all. Would you prefer to sit inside or outside? Or we could even grab a takeaway coffee and continue walking. I'm up for anything.'

'If you were by yourself where would your coffee come from?'

'That's easy. There's a great little place on the other side of the harbour, near to where my dad's boat is moored. It will take about twenty minutes to walk over. Can you wait that long?'

'I can.'

Jenny's head was on a swivel as they walked down to the sea wall, trying to take it all in.

'To live and work here with that view out to sea... You are a very lucky man, Marios.'

'Yes, and I don't take it for granted. I realised I haven't asked, what do you do for a living?'

'Nothing at the moment. The company I worked for have relocated to another part of England and though I could have gone with them, I didn't want to move that far away from my dad, so I took the redundancy money they offered. They've been very kind about it, saying there's still a job with them if I change my mind, but I don't think I will.'

'Sounds like you're a valuable member of the team,' said Marios, making Jenny blush and look away, nodding silently.

'We just need to go up here for the coffee.' He pointed and they turned the corner. 'If you like, we can get it to take away and then go down to the boat.'

'Fine by me.'

'Ok, I'd best get my dad one as well.'

'I'm looking forward to meeting him as my dad's talked a lot about him.'

'Here we are. It's the tour guide's treat so how do you like your coffee?'

'That's very kind and will absolutely be reflected in the star rating of your review. I take it white with one sugar.'

'So, you're giving me stars? What do I have to do to get full marks on your scoresheet?' he teased, then coughed, looking a bit embarrassed. 'That didn't sound right, did it? I'm going to shut up now and get the coffee.'

As Marios went inside Jenny smiled to herself. Because the answer to his question would be that if he looked into her eyes and gave her a kiss, he would get ten out of ten. She could feel herself blushing just thinking about it.

'There you go,' said Marios, handing her her drink. 'It's really hot so be careful. Shall we head down to the boat? I have to explain before we get there that it's probably not at all like you will be imagining. It's old and held together with years and years' worth of paint, but visitors seem to like it, and it does the job.'

Jenny wasn't sure what to expect as she followed Marios down one of the lanes until they got to the sea wall. They carried on walking beside it towards what looked like three or four boats moored up ahead. They all looked old and about the same size.

'Which one is yours?' she asked as they got closer. 'They look almost romantic, and so full of character.'

'It's the far one. It's odd how people often say these old boats are full of romance. I don't see it myself, beyond the fact that they're from the past and they provoke a kind of nostalgia.'

'Oh, Marios, you're such a man.' She laughed. 'Women look at things differently and can see the love and romance in something like a boat. It makes me think of a lone female standing in the harbour waiting for the boat to return after being at sea for months. The way her eyes might light up as she spots her true love heaving in the sails and preparing to weigh anchor, the thrill of their impending reunion after the long separation they endured while he's been at sea...' She sighed happily, and then was broken out of her daydream by the sound of Marios snorting with laughter.

'I think you've either been reading too many books or watching far too many films!' he teased. 'This old boat sees very little romance but lots of holiday visitors, sailing off to Paxos or Parga, depending on what day of the week it is, for a few hours before sailing back to Vekianos in the evening.'

'That's still romantic!' she argued. 'Think of all the honeymooners and people celebrating milestone anniversaries that have stepped foot onto your boat. Now, come on, Mr Tour Guide, if we don't pick up the pace your dad's coffee will go cold.'

'This way. Watch your step as we've not got the plank across. If you let me go first I can take your coffee and then help you on. Hi, Dad!' he called out. 'We have a visitor.'

She handed him her coffee and waited while he put the drinks on the boat before taking her hand to balance her as she jumped the couple of feet from the jetty to the deck. She enjoyed the sensation of his strong grip and held on just a bit longer than was necessary, not ready to let the feeling go.

'Hello, you must be Jenny!' a friendly voice

greeted them.

'It's nice to meet you, Filippos, my dad's talked a lot about you over the last few weeks, sharing stories from when you were both younger.'

'Somehow I don't think he's told you all of them as some definitely need forgetting, but yes, we had a great couple of summers together. I'm actually going up to the hotel in a bit to have some lunch with him and catch up on old times. What brings you and this lovely young lady to the boat today?' he asked his son. 'I thought you were off around the island on a grand tour.'

'I wanted to see it,' admitted Jenny, 'and the harbour and the town. I have two weeks to see the best of the island so there's no rush. This boat is fabulous, by the way, and not a bit like I thought ... although I don't know exactly what I was expecting. My tour guide has promised to tell me all about it.' She winked at Marios.

'This particular visitor is full of questions and is expecting a VIP tour of Vekianos, which apparently includes the boat,' Marios mock whispered to his dad.

'Well, son, I hope you don't disappoint.'

'Oh, I'm sure he won't.' Jenny grinned as Marios blushed and Filippos smiled.

'Well, I will leave the two of you to continue your day and I will head up to see your dad. Oh, by the way, if you want a job while you're here, I have one going on the boat.'

'What? What job?' asked Marios, looking confused.

'Sara called me earlier to say she's not coming back for the new season, so we need to find another crew member. Now, time for some food, beers, and a long overdue chat with Paul. Catch you both later.'

The young people waved him off then turned to one another.

'If we take our coffees up the other end of the boat it's a better view,' said Marios.

'Sounds great! Your dad's really nice and I can see why he and my dad get on so well. I'm sure over the next couple of weeks there will be many drinking sessions, so it's a good job your boat trips haven't started yet. Plus, you need a new crew member. Will that be a problem?'

'No, not really, as the job doesn't involve the actual sailing of the boat.'

'But if the third crew member doesn't sail the boat, what do they do?'

'Lots. They serve water and supply suntan lotion to people who forget theirs, and generally make sure all of the guests are happy and keep an eye on everything while my dad and I deal with the sailing. Once we're back in port, they sit here on the boat in the evening and sell the tickets to the passing tourists. The last girl that was here, the one not coming back, was great at that, and we had a good camaraderie between the three of us so it worked well. It's not a huge surprise, if I'm honest, as we sort of knew she might not be back because her boyfriend lined up a good summer job on another island, and it makes sense that they'd want to be together.'

'So, a girl can do the job?'

'Anyone can. The main thing is selling trip tickets, so as long as the person is personable they'll be just fine. Why, would you like the job?'

'Yes, please! A summer working on a Greek island, going out to sea every day, getting a tan... What's not to like about that? No, I'm only joking. I'm headed back to England in two weeks' time.'

'Two weeks, you say?'

'Yes, why?'

'Because that gives me two weeks to persuade you to stay. That sounds like my phone, excuse me.'

Jenny was shocked at the turnaround in Marios

from earlier. He'd started as such a shy lad but here he was slowly coming out of his shell. She had to admit she was enjoying it.

'Sorry, that was my Aunt Helena wanting to tell me my grandmother is cooking for everyone tonight and she expects us to be there. Is that ok? It's not really what I had planned...'

'That's totally fine. I'm sure it'll be a nice evening. But is it going to mess things up for you? You said you had something planned?'

'No, nothing really, I thought it would be just the two of us tonight, that's all.'

'At least we still have the rest of the day together.'

'True. So, what would you like to do next? Take a walk out and around the rocks to the headland?'

'That sounds good, but first I would quite like it if you kissed me.'

She could see his face light up, all traces of shyness gone, and with that he leaned towards her and did just as she'd asked. And that made her very happy indeed.

Chapter 16

As Jenny got out of the shower, she still couldn't believe the day she had just had. A holiday romance was the last thing on her mind when she and her dad had decided to come here for the two weeks, but saying that, all she and Marios had done so far was kiss. Could that be called a romance? Maybe, but either way, the day wasn't over yet, and she was looking forward to spending the evening with him and his family.

Looking at the time, she saw she had another half an hour before she needed to be downstairs for dinner, so she took her glass of wine out onto the balcony. Yet again she was blown away by the magnificent view. She had always just considered Vekianos a place her dad had worked when he was young, but now, being here, she realised how very special it was to him. It made her so happy to see her dad relaxed and enjoying himself so much. Also, from the way that Evangelina talked about how much he had done for them when he worked here, it was obvious that he had a very big place in the family's hearts.

Now the big decision: what to wear! She had a lovely new dress for the party night, and another couple that she thought she would wear for other special nights out. She decided that tonight *was* a special night, so grabbed one of the dresses and pulled it on. It would be nice to see Marios' face when he saw her all dressed up and not just in her beach clothes.

As she headed down the stairs a short while later, she could hear voices out on the terrace. It sounded like Filippos and her dad, and they were quite loud, laughing away with each other.

'Here she comes! Now, young lady, what have you done with my son? He hasn't arrived yet.'

'Please excuse my husband,' said the beautiful woman sitting next to Filippos. 'He has had a few too many drinks and he and your dad have been riling each other up all afternoon. I'm Nadia, by the way, and it's really lovely to meet you. Paul's been telling us all about you. Can I get you a drink?'

'If you're off to get Jenny a drink, my love, can you fetch Paul and myself each another, please?'

'I'll bring you each a water. You two need to slow down a little.'

'Yeah, give us a chance to catch up!' Jenny joked.

'I'm afraid that won't be possible as these two seem determined to relive their youth. Evangelina has already told them to slow down but it fell on deaf ears. I think I hear my son's bike, so the mystery of where he is, is evidently about to be solved.' Nadia laughed as she headed inside to grab the next round of drinks.

Jenny's stomach fluttered with nerves. She was excited to see Marios again but they both knew they had to play it cool as there was no way they wanted their parents to know that they had spent the afternoon kissing.

Nadia returned and poured Jenny a glass of white wine, and then topped up Filippos and Paul's glass, even though she'd been on at them to switch to water. Marios stepped onto the terrace just then and he looked lovely. His hair was still damp from a shower and he had a nice, crisp, blue shirt and cream shorts on. He had scrubbed up well and she couldn't help thinking how sexy he was, but he also had that shy look on his face again. Was that because his parents were here? She wanted to stand up, go over to him, and give him a big kiss, but sadly that wasn't going to happen.

'Here he is! I was worried about you, son. I thought this young lady might have done something to you.'

Marios blushed and looked very uncomfortable, and though Jenny wanted to say something to take the attention off him, her mind was blank. Thankfully, Evangelina appeared and distracted everyone.

'Dinner will be another hour or so, so here's a tray of nibbles. Helena and myself have just got a few more things to sort and then we'll be out to join you. Marios, can you believe the state of your father? It's like the old days; when he and Paul got together and opened a bottle of wine there was no stopping them. I've never known which one was to blame, but one thing is for sure – he won't be making it to the boat tomorrow! Thank goodness the trips haven't started yet.'

'What did you kids get up to today?' asked Filippos.

'Marios showed me around the harbour. We're saving other places on the island for another day.'

'Another day. Does that mean you'll need more time off?' he asked his son.

Nadia interrupted before Marios could answer. 'Don't tease him, Filippos, of course he should take the time off. Part of why you've both worked so hard the last few months was so that you wouldn't have to work while all Evangelina's guests are here.'

'I know, though I don't think it will get better than tonight. To be honest, I can't believe Mum has even invited one or two of them. They were always such characters, and not in a good way.'

'I've invited them because they helped us run this hotel over the years and are part of what has made it the success it is,' Evangelina said sharply as she joined them. 'I know your favourite time was when Paul worked here, but you did get on well with the others. Ok, perhaps you didn't party with them, but they're good people.'

'Ok, ok,' said Filippos, raising his hands in a gesture of surrender. 'Let's run through who will be arriving tomorrow.'

'Stepanie and her daughter, Tonia. You remember Stepanie? You liked her when she worked those four or five seasons for us.'

'She was good with the customers but—'

'But she helped us make a lot of money. Once she got behind that bar the holiday makers happily parted with their cash, so though she might not have been as quick with her jobs as others, she was a valuable asset. Then there's Emma, who got on with the job very quietly, the complete opposite to Stepanie. Also, Sandra and her son, Craig, are coming. She was a mixture of the two; not loud and bubbly like Stepanie, but chattier than Emma.'

'Did you invite James?' Filippos asked. 'I always suspected he had a soft spot for you,' he whispered to Nadia, placing a protective arm around her shoulder.

Helena chimed in, 'He was coming but he's cancelled, and it wasn't just Nadia; he liked everyone, isn't that right, Mum?'

'Yes, he did. Now, are we ready to eat? Everyone head to the table and Helena and I will fetch the food. Marios, could you please top up everyone's drinks?'

Jenny was very conscious of Marios and didn't think it was a good idea to sit next to him because she knew if they were together the others would notice the connection between them. So, she put herself between her dad and Nadia, which left three seats opposite. Hopefully Helena would sit in the middle so Jenny wouldn't be looking directly at Marios; in a way that would be worse than being next to him! She watched as he went around the table pouring the wine and when he got to her, she could see he was shaking. Hopefully no one else had noticed. Helena brought out the biggest bowl of salad Jenny had ever seen, followed by Evangelina with a massive tray with a steaming hot moussaka. The smell was unbelievable.

'Please dive in! I just need to fetch the garlic bread.'

'You sit down, Mum, I'll get it,' said Helena.

Jenny was in luck. Evangelina sat opposite her and Marios next to her.

Helena returned with the garlic bread on two plates, putting one either end of the table, and then walked over to the empty seat next to Paul.

Jenny couldn't help but notice the look on her dad's face when Helena sat down, or the smile on Helena's as she looked at him. Oh my goodness, was it possible that Jenny wasn't the only one embarking on a Greek romance?

'...Jenny?'

'Sorry, Nadia, I was miles away, what did you say?'

'I asked if you'd like me to pass the bread.'

'Yes, please.'

As she put the bread on her side plate, she noticed something else – she hadn't been the only one to notice the interaction between Helena and her dad, so had Evangelina. She was now looking between them with a mysterious smile.

Filippos started to talk, which was a bit of a relief as it distracted Jenny from her racing thoughts.

'Mum, this is lovely and the perfect start to the week's celebrations. It feels just like old times around the table, but now it's even better as Marios and Jenny have joined us.'

'It makes me wonder what your father would think if he was here now. With everyone coming back to the island, I think he would be very happy.'

Nadia agreed. 'He would, Evangelina. But he

would also be having a go at Filippos for drinking too much.'

Everyone couldn't help but laugh at that, knowing how true it was.

'A very good point,' Evangelina agreed. 'Make sure to help yourselves to more moussaka and salad, everyone, there's lots to go around. And it's not like you to be slow with your food, Marios, dig in! You're a growing young man.'

Marios caught Jenny's eye and blushed, and she had to look down into her plate until she'd managed to control the grin that stretched across her face.

For the next two hours there was lots of chatting, Filippos telling stories of old. The only one not really joining in with the conversation was Helena, but Jenny got the impression this was normal, as her family didn't seem at all surprised she was quiet.

'Seeing as the ladies have done all the cooking and serving, it seems only fair we clear away,' Filippos announced. 'On your feet, Marios, you can give me a hand taking everything back to the kitchen.'

Paul got to his feet to help as well but Filippo immediately waved him back down, saying he was a guest, and he should relax. And then it was like a competition to see who could carry the most to the kitchen in one trip, Marios or his dad. Within minutes the table was cleared, and everyone was laughing and joking.

As he sat back down, Filippos asked, 'Mum, what time do the other guests arrive tomorrow?'

'Not until late afternoon. I'm not sure if they'll all be arriving at the same time so I'll be around to greet them as and when they get here.'

'Each person is going to message as they're leaving Corfu so we'll have a rough idea of arrival times,' added Helena.

Paul spoke up. 'Well, Jenny and I will keep out of your way. I'm planning on taking her around the island by bus.'

Jenny could see her disappointment reflected on Marios' face. They had been hoping to spend the day together.

But before she had a chance to speak, Nadia said, 'Marios can borrow my car and show you around. That way you won't be hanging around waiting for buses all day. What do you say, Marios?'

'Fine by me as I've nothing planned.'

Evangelina caught Jenny's eye and smiled. 'That will be nice for you all. Given that we're all organised for the other guests and there's really nothing else to do, why don't you go with them as well, Helena? I think a day off will do you the power of good and I'm sure the four of you will have fun and find lots to chat about. Now that's sorted, it's time for me to go to bed. Thank you all for coming and sitting and eating at my table tonight. It's been a very special evening. Good night.'

Jenny looked over at her dad and then at Helena to find they were looking at each other with huge smiles on their faces. It turned out that Jenny and Marios were just the start of Evangelina's matchmaking projects!

Chapter 17

Voula was awake early to check the last few things off her list, number one being breakfast. She needed to see what this hotel had to offer, and she wanted to try and make conversation with a couple of the other guests to see what they'd like, what they'd disliked, and whether the experience had lived up to their expectations. But all of that had to be done subtly, so as to not draw too much unwanted attention, or annoy her fellow guests by waylaying them for too long.

As she sat on the balcony, she thought back to last night. The food at dinner was excellent and there was nothing she could complain about because the service had been impeccable. The whole evening had been special and if there was one word that summed up her stay here, it had to be 'calm'. The word made her smile as 'calm' was something she'd rarely had in either her working or private lives.

Heading downstairs, she went over her plan to make notes on both the service and the presentation. If she was going to deliver an experience at the same high level, her sister-in-law Nadia would have to up her game. And with Helena already up in arms, Voula would have to approach Nadia extra carefully. She needed everyone in the family on her side and on board with this refurb and rebranding.

Walking through the reception she saw a young couple checking out and she slowed down and stopped to look at one of the paintings so she could listen in on their conversation with the receptionist.

'Thank you so much, the whole experience has been wonderful, everything from the room to the food. We've had a very special time here and it will be a week we will never forget.'

High praise indeed! After breakfast she'd try to make conversation with an older couple, whose expectations would likely be a lot higher, having a lot more travel under their belts and more comparisons against which to grade their experience at this hotel. She thought it would be a shame to be sat indoors on such a lovely morning, so she headed out to find a table on the terrace. She picked her spot and within seconds a young waitress was there to offer tea, coffee, and juice.

'Coffee would be lovely, thank you, and an orange juice, please.'

In no time at all the waitress was back with the drinks and pointed out where the buffet was. After last night's meal Voula wasn't overly hungry, but for research purposes she wanted to go up to the buffet at least twice. She drank her juice and then headed over to grab a little fruit and yogurt. She spotted it at the far end of the buffet but decided she would go the long way around to take everything in, and to pass by where a chef was stood making omelettes and pancakes. As she got closer, he said good morning and smiled. She returned the smile as she walked past a heated counter with bacon, sausages, and other cooked items. Once at the fruit she made up a small bowl of different sorts before putting yogurt and honey on top.

As she sat back down at her table, she breathed a sigh of relief knowing that Nadia would have no problem creating similar buffet options. Sitting with her coffee she felt relaxed and like she was on a real holiday. She had achieved everything she had come here to do, perhaps more so. After finishing the fruit, she went back up and fetched an omelette, which was beautifully light and fluffy, with just enough cheese.

To think, if she hadn't seen this hotel online, she

would never have had the fabulous idea of refurbishing the family business! Now, having seen it in person, all the practical things that needed to be done were becoming clear in her head, and she really believed she could achieve all of them, with one exception – she needed to find out about putting the infinity pool at the front of the hotel. It was going to be the most expensive part of the project, and she'd need a surveyor's report before she even started to look for a company to build it, but the result would absolutely be worth it.

Looking at the time she saw she had a while before she needed to check out of her room, so she made her way over to the outside bar area.

She had just taken out her phone to review her notes when the hotel manager – Athena's son – appeared at her elbow.

'Miss Aetos. Please allow me to introduce myself; my name is Dimitri, and I am the manager here. May I join you for a moment?'

'Of course. You have a fabulous hotel here; you must be so proud.'

'Thank you. As I believe you know, it's my mum's hotel – her dream.'

'Yes, and it must be nice for you to see her be so successful, and of course get to work here at this gorgeous hotel.'

'Yes, I'm pleased for her. She has worked very hard and for many years to get to this point. I, on the other hand, hate every moment. For a start, when I wake up every morning I know nothing I do or say will be right. I have lost count of how many times I've sat down with my mother and asked her to clarify what she requires of me but she just says, "you're the manager, so act as a manager". So I do, only to be told I'm doing it wrong. It's infuriating.'

Voula was a bit taken aback by the man's vehemence, but she had to empathise.

'I sort of understand. My family have a business, and I knew from an early age I didn't want to be a part of it because my parents' way was the only acceptable way, in their eyes, and if I even dared to suggest something it would immediately be deemed wrong and inappropriate.'

'That's it exactly. I can see why you'd want to escape and build your career on Rhodes. I'm sorry to have interrupted you this morning, but when my mum said you were here spying it was the first bit of excitement I've had in ages and I just had to meet you.'

Voula was surprised to learn he knew she was a hotel manager – though apparently his sources were not all that up to date as they didn't know she had resigned. 'I take it you or your mum looked into me?'

He nodded. 'She Google searched your name and photos of you came up with mentions of the hotel you manage.'

'The dreaded internet. Nothing is secret anymore, is it? It's been nice chatting but I need to go and check out so the room can be readied for the next guests. I wish you well, Dimitri, and really hope you can get to the point where you start to enjoy your time here. It really is a lovely business.'

'Thank you, but I don't think the hotel industry will ever be for me. Once my mum realises that, hopefully we can both move on. Have a nice journey back and good luck with recreating this back on the island of Rhodes.'

As she got back to her room and put the last few bits of clothes and toiletries in her hand luggage, she thought about what Dimitri had said. She felt sorry for him, but he was an adult, and so he should stand up for himself and tell his mum he didn't want to be part of her business. Before she made her way down to reception, Voula took one last look around the room. Apart from electrical work, which would be expensive no matter what, she was confident that she could recreate this look on a reasonable budget.

As she walked out of the lift and into reception, she spotted the one person she was hoping to avoid: Athena. She knew she wouldn't be able to get away without a conversation, but first she would check out and get the receptionist to order her a taxi. At least that way she had an escape plan in place.

'Good morning, Miss Aetos,' Athena called as Voula stepped away from the desk, her check out complete. 'I really hope your stay was nice and, of course, fruitful.' She winked.

'I've had a wonderful stay, thank you. You really do have the most beautiful hotel here. It's such a calming atmosphere.'

'Thank you, that's very kind. Now if only I could sort the issue of my son's lack of interest sooner rather than later. If not, I'll need to give someone else the chance to carry my dream forward.'

'I think that's my taxi that's just pulled up,' said Voula, eager to end the conversation. 'Thanks again. The next time I need a dose of calm I'll know just where to come.'

'Voula, you could have three hundred and sixty-five days of calm if you came here and ran the hotel for me.'

Voula's jaw dropped. What had Athena just said?

'Here, take my card. Once you've had a chance to think about it, that's my direct number,' said Athena, tapping the card. 'I'll look forward to hearing from you. For now, have a lovely flight home.'

Chapter 18
Saturday 14th April

Helena was in her bungalow with the first coffee of the day, looking over her to-do list. Most of the jobs had already been crossed off and the rest didn't need to be done until tomorrow, so she could actually relax and enjoy the day out today. Marios had suggested they drive to Thagistri, which was one of her favourite places on the island. It would be quiet as the season hadn't started properly yet, and the beach was sheltered from the breeze so would be the perfect place to spend a few hours.

As she looked through her wardrobe for something nice to wear, she laughed to herself. This was the second day in a row she was putting extra thought into her appearance, and it had been years since that had happened! She could barely believe she was – kind of – going out on a date. Sitting next to Paul at the table last night she had felt a connection that was so much more than just old friends reunited, and she could tell the feelings weren't one sided by the way he'd looked at her and the smile on his face. There had even been some parts of the evening when it felt as though it was just the two of them sat together alone.

After sorting out an outfit she headed across the courtyard to the hotel so she could start to prepare a picnic. She noticed the kitchen window was open, which meant her mum was already up, probably preparing breakfast.

'You beat me to it!' she greeted her mum warmly. 'I would have been happy to sort the breakfast out so you could have a slow start to the day after our late night.'

'You're fine, Helena. It's your day off and it's only for two people so it's taking no time at all. Tomorrow will be a different story as all the others will have arrived and there will be a lot more mouths to feed. Why don't you sort out what you want to take with you to eat at the beach? There's a lot to choose from as the fridges are full. As for last night, it was lovely to sit around the table all together, and your brother made me laugh so much. I expect he'll have a bad head today and that's before Nadia lays into him for drinking so much. Did you notice that Marios seemed more like himself than he has since the break-up? I think he is quite taken with Jenny, and it's good for him to realise there's life out there after Natalia.'

As Evangelina bid her farewell and headed out onto the terrace with her coffee, Helena had to laugh to herself, having noticed that her mum managed to mention everyone apart from Paul. She knew Evangelina would have noticed them with their heads bent together, catching up just the two of them, and she appreciated that she was letting her have a little space and not rushing to matchmake, the way she had with Jenny and Marios.

Thinking about the next couple of weeks and her mum's upcoming party, she realised she was feeling ok about moving on and leaving the hotel to Voula. What her future held, she hadn't a clue, but those thoughts could be put on hold until the visitors were gone and the celebrations were over.

She finished packing the cool box with savoury things then texted Marios to ask him to stop at the bakery and pick up some fresh sweet pastries. As she put her phone down, she could hear voices outside on the terrace. It sounded like Paul and Jenny were up and chatting to Evangelina so she would make a fresh pot of coffee to take out to them.

'I'll just nip in and get the breakfast things,' said

Evangelina after Helena joined them and everyone had said their hellos.

'No, you sit and chat, Mum. You'll have a busy afternoon when the others arrive so you need to rest up while you can.'

'That reminds me, I've had a text from Sandra to say she's not coming as she isn't very well, but her son Craig is still planning on joining us. It's a little odd as none of us know him, and I hope he doesn't feel out of place.'

'I expect Craig will feel like me,' Jenny suggested. 'His mum likely talked a lot about being here, just like Dad has, so he probably feels he knows everyone already.'

'You're probably right. I think he's the same sort of age as you and Marios so at least he'll have people his age to talk to,' said Evangelina.

After breakfast Paul and Jenny went back to their rooms to get ready to go, and once Helena had tidied around in the kitchen, she went back to her bungalow to change. As she looked at the dress she'd picked out and left hanging up on the wardrobe door, she worried it was a bit too dressy, but she wanted to look nice, so decided to be brave.

'Oh, you look lovely, Jenny!'

'Thank you, Helena, and so do you. I love that dress! Let's just hope the lads scrub up as well as we do.'

Paul pretended indignation. 'Excuse me? I don't know about Marios, but your father here has put a lot of effort into how he looks today.'

'Yes, you look very handsome, Dad. What do you think, Helena?'

Jenny realised immediately that she'd said the wrong thing and embarrassed Helena, but thankfully the awkward moment was broken by the sound of a car pulling up on the drive. Marios stepped out looking extremely sexy in his t-shirt and shorts.

'Morning! All ready to go? I've got the pastries, Helena, and I've filled my cool box with lots of bottles of water. I hope everyone has remembered their beach things. I doubt it will be warm enough to get in the sea just yet, as it's still a little early in the year, but it's worth a shot.'

'Can you just help me with the food, Marios? It's all packed up in the kitchen,' said Helena.

Once everything was in the boot of the car Paul got in the front passenger's seat and the two women got in the back. They headed out of the harbour town, nephew and aunt pointing things out and talking about the different coves and towns they were passing.

'A lot of this is coming back to me, which is shocking after so many years have passed. I notice quite a bit has changed, too. For instance, the roads seem a lot better maintained.'

'They are,' agreed Helena. 'The island authorities realised they had to increase investment in the island's infrastructure so that more visitors would come here on holiday. Before he died, my dad was on a community committee that kept pushing for better facilities, and he was very proud of what they achieved.'

'Oh yes, my grandad was a stubborn chap, and it was to his benefit! Once he dug his heels in there was no moving him. Now, here we are. I expect you won't recognise this car park, Paul, as it's not been here very long.'

'You're right, I don't recognise the lot, but I do recognise the place as this is where I used to come with your mum, dad, and aunt. They were good days, weren't they, Helena? We had lots of happy times on this beach.'

Jenny noticed tears gathering in Helena's eyes but couldn't figure out if they were because she was happy or sad. Marios parked the car in the shade of a tree and they all got out and got their things together. It was early for the lunch Helena had packed so they left the picnic in the trunk and just took the cool box full of bottled water with them.

'If I'm right, I think we used to walk along a track and then cut through a gap in the trees to get to the sand.'

'You are right,' said Helena. 'You have a good memory.'

'I can't wait to put my feet in the beautiful clear blue sea,' said Jenny as they headed off.

Marios laughed and said, 'It might be clear and blue but this time of year it's cold as well because there hasn't been enough sun to warm it up yet.'

'I don't mind. I haven't come all this way to Greece to not have a paddle.'

'Ok, but you've been warned. You're my witness, Paul; if your daughter gets frostbite, I'm not responsible.'

This had them all laughing as they walked along the track and then Paul stopped and pointed.

'Here we are! Oh my goodness, it feels like just yesterday I was here.'

They all walked through the gap in the trees Paul had remembered and stepped onto the sand. Apart from a few people in the distance, they had the place to themselves.

'It's paradise!' exclaimed Jenny. 'And to think you gave all this up to go back to a cold, wet England.'

'Yes, darling, but I had my reasons to go home,' said Paul, sounding a bit cryptic. Jenny glanced at her dad and caught him looking a bit wistfully at Helena, who was studiously avoiding meeting Paul's gaze.

They walked over to an area of the sand where there were rocks for them to lean on.

'I'm not wasting time sitting down,' said Jenny as Paul and Helena lowered themselves onto the beach towels they'd brought. 'You three can stay here but I'm going down to the water as I have some serious paddling to do.'

'I'll come with you. If we turn left at the water's edge, we can follow the beach to the bend there in the distance. It has a great view of one of the busier towns.'

'Come on, Marios, race you to the sea!' called Jenny, taking off towards the water.

'Paul, your daughter is bonkers!' said Marios, laughing. 'It's like coming to the beach with a five-year-old. Will you be ok here if we go for a walk?'

'Of course! On your way back, why don't you stop at the car and get the food?'

'Sounds good. See you both in a little while.'

And off Marios went, chasing Jenny down the beach.

'She's a real credit to you,' said Helena, watching the two young people laughing and splashing one another.

'I don't know what I would have done without her after my wife left. She sort of ... took control and organised me, pointing me in the right direction. She got me back on my feet and what she has done with my new apartment is fabulous. I really wouldn't have known where to start with interiors and all those types of things.'

'It sounds like you two are very close.'

'We are. It seems as though you have that same connection with Marios.'

'I do. I would have liked to have children of my own, but it wasn't to be, so I'm very lucky to have Marios in my life, and that Filippos and Nadia have included me in their family dynamic from day one.'

'And they're lucky to have you,' said Paul, kindness clear in his tone.

They sat in a comfortable silence for a while before Helena turned to Paul, wanting to ask about something that had been bugging her.

'Earlier, when Jenny asked how you could leave beautiful Greece and go back to England, you said you *had* to go. What did you mean by that?'

Paul looked serious, and she worried she shouldn't have asked the question.

'I'm sorry, you don't need to answer,' she offered, giving him an out if he wanted one.

'No, it's ok, and I don't mind telling you. It was simple: I wanted to be with you, and I couldn't because you were with Sotirios. From where I stood you seemed happy together, and I certainly wasn't going to do or say anything to spoil that, so I had to leave.'

Helena turned away from Paul and looked across to the other side of the beach. She wanted to say something but the words wouldn't come out of her mouth. Knowing for certain that Paul had had feelings for her back then made her realise just how different her life could have been if she had made different choices. A sadness enveloped her and her heart felt heavy. If only she could turn back time.

Chapter 19

'Go on then, put your feet in and let me time you to see how long you can stand the cold.'

Jenny did as he said, and though the water was freezing she wasn't going to let him see it on her face, so she fixed a smile on and said it was lovely.

'I think I'd best walk on the sand for a bit as my feet are sinking here in the water,' she said once she was sure she couldn't take the cold for a second longer.

'Liar. It's cold and you want to get out,' said Marios. She could see he was laughing away to himself at her expense, but she didn't mind as it was all a bit of fun.

'Ok,' Jenny admitted a bit sheepishly, 'you were right. It isn't as warm as I was hoping it would be. Now, lead the way. I need to get moving to warm myself back up!'

'Last night was fun,' said Marios as they meandered along the shore line.

'It was. Did you notice how well my dad and your aunt were getting on? I think your grandmother clocked it.'

He nodded. 'My mum did as well. She mentioned it on the way home, saying that if Helena hadn't been with Sotirios all those years ago she was sure my aunt and your dad would have got together, and he would have probably stayed here on Vekianos and not gone back to England.'

'They certainly seem to be enjoying each other's company now...' Jenny trailed off, looking thoughtful. She shook her head and focused on Marios. 'Enough about my dad. I want to hear everything about *you*, Marios, because I don't know anything apart from who you're related to, and the fact you work on a boat.'

'You also know something else.'

'I do?'

'I can't believe you've forgotten already. And here I thought it was memorable. Oh dear, I guess I'm just going to have to remind you.'

With that he pulled Jenny close and kissed her.

'I never expected you'd forget what a good kisser I am,' he said when he finally pulled away, pretending to pout.

She smiled and apologised before leaning close to whisper, 'Perhaps you'll have to keep reminding me, so I don't forget again.'

He didn't need telling twice, and in no time at all they were both lost in another kiss. Afterward, they held hands as they walked along in silence, until eventually Jenny realised he hadn't actually answered her question.

'Let's sit for a bit so you can talk to me about yourself. I want to know more about this chap that keeps kissing me,' she said, playfully.

'To be honest with you, I'm pretty boring and there's nothing really to tell. You already know that I've lived my whole life here on Vekianos. I worked in the family hotel until I was old enough to work on my dad's boat, and I've been there ever since. That's about it, really.'

'So tell me more about the boat. Do you like your job?'

'Yeah, I enjoy it. My dad steers and I do all the physical stuff with the ropes and the sails. On a normal day, my dad will be chatting to the holidaymakers on board while music plays, and when we get close to the beach in Antipaxos we stop so people can have a swim off the boat, which everyone always appreciates, especially on the hot days. From there, we sail to the caves and again the visitors can have a swim. We then head to Paxos and moor up for five or six hours while the tourists go sightseeing, and then we make the journey back, which is always a great atmosphere as Dad puts the party music on, which you can imagine goes down a treat. And that's my day.'

'It sounds like so much fun and something I'd like to experience for myself. Is it a similar itinerary on the days you go to Parga?'

'No, it's actually completely different as we just sail there and back, a bit like a taxi service. We drop people off and bring others back to spend the day here on Vekianos. I'm not complaining though. It's good to have different types of day.'

'What do you do when you're waiting for the visitors to come back onboard in Paxos?'

'All sorts of things; it just depends on what needs fixing or cleaning that day as there's always something that needs to be done. Did you want to walk a little further or turn back here?'

'I think it's time to put my feet back in the sea. No, I'm only joking,' she rushed to add. 'That won't be happening today! I think I'll have to come back in the summer for that. Let's go a bit further and then turn back.'

As they continued on, Jenny wondered if she should ask Marios about his ex, or if that would come across as being too nosey. She decided it probably was and because she didn't want to ruin the day, she kept the questions to herself.

'This is lovely and so peaceful,' she said. 'I expect as the weeks go on it will be a lot busier here on the beach, and on the island in general.'

'Yes, but it doesn't ever get overcrowded like a few of the other islands. It's more off the beaten path.'

'I really like the fact that it feels like we have the place to ourselves.'

'Can you see over there?' Marios pointed. 'That's Keriaphos, a busy but small town with lots of restaurants and tourist shops. In the height of the summer it gets very busy and at night there's a lovely atmosphere. Perhaps we could go over one evening and have something to eat?'

'I'd like that very much.' Jenny smiled. 'We should probably turn around now and fetch the picnic.'

'Sounds good, but maybe there's time for another kiss first?'

'Plenty of time, I think.'

Coming up for air several minutes later, they joined hands and turned back the way they'd come.

'All this kissing has made me hungry!' joked Jenny.

Marios laughed but then turned serious for a moment. 'Jenny, I think there's something I need to tell you.'

'Oh?' she asked, feeling a bit worried.

'It's about my ex...' he began.

'You don't have to tell me if you don't want to,' she said, kindly. 'It's really none of my business.'

'I know, but I think it will answer a few of the questions I suspect you've been avoiding asking.' He came to a stop and looked down into Jenny's eyes. 'Her name was Natalia and we met three or four years ago when she came here from Athens to work for the season. That first summer was magical but once the season was over, she went back to Athens for the winter months. I missed her, and she said she missed me, too. Just after Christmas I went to visit her but something was off between us from the moment I landed. I didn't like the big, busy city and things between us felt different than they did here on the island.'

'That's a shame. Did you ever go and visit her again after that, or was that the only time?'

'No, I just went the once, and I think she held it against me. No matter how much time I devoted to her, or how many gifts I lavished on her, it never seemed to make her happy.'

'I'm sorry to hear that.'

'You don't need to be sorry. I really thought I loved Natalia, so it was hard to have my friends and my mum and dad saying she took me for granted. I told them they didn't understand her and they couldn't see what I saw. I think the more people that said they didn't like her, the more I felt I had to defend her.'

'What other people think shouldn't count. It's you that was in a relationship with her so only you could know the truth. You had to live your life the way you wanted to, regardless of what others said and thought.'

'I know, but I realise now that they were right and I was wrong. They saw the real Natalia when I couldn't.'

'But you know now, and you have moved on, which is a good thing.'

'I need to be honest with you and admit that I only came to that conclusion these last few days. Your arrival has changed my perspective on things, Jenny.'

Before she had time to digest what he'd said, he bent and kissed her. Unlike their previous kisses, this was completely different, full of passion and like nothing she had ever experienced before in her life. She had hastily dismissed the idea of a Greek island romance when her dad suggested it might happen, but perhaps she might want one after all...

Chapter 20

As the car turned onto the hotel drive and the day came to a close, Helena found herself wanting to stay back on that beach laughing and chatting to Paul instead of going into the hotel where the other guests would be waiting. She just wasn't really in the mood for them after having had such a lovely day away from all the stress and strain of daily life.

'Thank you so much, Marios,' said Paul as the car pulled to a stop. 'It's been a great day.'

They shared smiles and all thanked Helena again for preparing such a delicious picnic feast, and then they said their goodbyes to Marios, and he drove off. Helena, Paul, and Jenny decided to go back to their rooms to shower and change clothes, and agreed they would meet on the terrace in a bit to join the newly arrived guests.

Showered and dressed a short while later, Helena sat on the edge of her bed, memories from decades ago when Paul was working at the hotel flooding through her mind. But knowing now that Paul had carried a torch for her back then, the familiar memories seemed somehow different. Why had he never said anything about his feelings at the time? He'd said he didn't want to get in the way of her relationship, but she wished he'd told her how he felt. She knew she needed to go and meet the new arrivals, so she put her thoughts on hold for the time being and finished getting ready.

As Jenny walked out onto the terrace, she realised how odd it was that all of these people had something big in common – having all done the same jobs at the same place – but had never met.

She wondered if they would compare notes, chatting about what they liked and disliked about working here. She got to the door leading out to the terrace and could see Evangelina chatting to two women so she headed over to join them.

'Jenny! Let me introduce you to Emma and Stepanie. Why don't you all get to know one another while I get you a drink. Red or white?'

'White, please. It's nice to meet you both,' she said to the new arrivals. 'I was just thinking as I was coming down the stairs how odd it must be for you, coming back here and meeting people you've only heard of.'

Stepanie spoke first. 'It is, isn't it? Do you work here now?'

'Oh, no, I've never worked here. I've come with my dad, Paul, who worked here many years ago... And talk of the devil, here he is. Dad, this is Emma and Stepanie.'

As Paul introduced himself Jenny couldn't help but notice the two women were like chalk and cheese in so many ways. Emma was incredibly quiet and quite plain, whereas Stepanie was glamorous and forthright.

'I can't believe I'm finally meeting the famous Paul!' Stepanie said. 'Of course, you must know that you were the one we've all had to live up to. Your work here set the benchmark for everyone that followed after you!' She paused as Evangelina walked across the terrace to rejoin the group.

'Oh dear, I feel bad now,' said Paul.

'Don't feel bad,' said Jenny, supportively. 'You were a trailblazer! I'm certainly finding out a lot more about you on this trip.' She laughed. 'Helena mentioned your daughter was coming with you, Stepanie. Is she going to be joining us tonight?'

'Yes, in a bit. She dropped her luggage and then went off to discover what the town has to offer. I think she's of the opinion that we will all be too old to socialise with. Helena, you haven't changed a bit!' she said, greeting her with an appraising look. 'Still wearing those floaty skirts and sporting the same hairstyle I see. How ... brave.' Before Helena could respond, Stepanie had turned back to Jenny. 'When I was here working, Helena and I were the perfect team – me chatting and entertaining the guests and Helena pottering in the background.'

'By which you mean, Helena did all the work while you chatted and did nothing,' said Emma, an eyebrow arched.

Jenny silently cheered Emma on. Even from their short acquaintance she could tell Stepanie wasn't the nicest of people. It would do her good to eat some humble pie.

Helena broke the awkward silence, saying kindly, 'You're right, we were a good team, Stepanie. To be honest, everyone I've worked with here over the years has been good. Once a routine is set for the season everything tends to flow nicely, which I'm always grateful for. Now, if you will excuse me, I need to go and give Nadia a hand with tonight's buffet. Please help yourself to nibbles and more wine in the meantime. I think we're just waiting on one more to arrive – Sandra's son, Craig. And, of course, Filippos and his son Marios will be joining us as well.'

'What are you laughing at?' Nadia asked Helena as she walked back into the kitchen.

'Stepanie hasn't changed a bit over all these years. She's still making out like she owns the hotel. But like Dad used to say, she kept the holiday makers happy and they spent money so who were we to complain? I was shocked to see Emma take a swipe at her though. I think that's a first as I've never known her to speak up like that before. Perhaps the years have toughened her up, although she does still look a bit sad and miserable.'

'Not words that could be used to describe you today. You are positively glowing!'

'I don't know what you mean,' said Helena, going a bit red in the face with embarrassment. 'I might have had a little sun on the beach but—'

'It has nothing to do with the beach. No, I suspect it's all to do with a certain someone coming back to the island, someone who is also glowing this evening.'

'You've got it all wrong. Paul and I have just been chatting and talking about old times.'

'If you say so...' Nadia laughed as they turned their attention to finalising the buffet.

Out on the terrace Evangelina was holding court and telling lots of stories from the past. But then the nice atmosphere was interrupted by a shout.

'It's time to get this party started! My mum, Sandra, couldn't come but you won't be disappointed as I will be twice as much fun,' Craig greeted the group, before turning and raking an appreciative gaze over Jenny. 'And what's your name? I didn't realise there would be young, gorgeous females here. I think we're going to have a *great* time.' He leered, causing Jenny to lean away.

Thankfully Evangelia stepped forward to greet him and Jenny was able to slip away while Craig's attention was otherwise occupied.

First Stepanie being rude to Helena and now Craig acting like he should be the centre of attention? It was clear to Jenny that the rest of the trip would be nothing like last night around the table, or on the beach today. What a shame.

'I'm sorry to bother you, Helena, as I can see you're busy with the food, but someone else has just arrived: Craig.'

'Thank you, Jenny, I will go and show him to his

room.'

'You don't happen to have a room on the other side of the island, or come to that on a different island, do you?'

'Oh dear. That bad, is he?'

As Helena rushed out of the kitchen, Jenny turned to Nadia. 'Can I help with anything while Helena sorts out Mr "I Love Myself"?'

'There always has to be one, doesn't there? Or I should say two, counting Tonia.'

'Tonia?' asked Jenny.

'Oh, you've not met her yet, have you? She's Stepanie's daughter. It sounds like she and Craig will be two peas in a pod. The week is certainly turning up a few unwelcome surprises, but there have been highlights, too – my son, for instance, is happier than I've seen him for a very long time, and that makes *me* happy.' She winked. 'And yes, it would be great if you could help. There are a few bowls of salad over there, would you be able to grab them and follow me?'

Jenny helped Nadia carry the food out and put it on a table just outside the doors to the terrace. They each made half a dozen trips and every time they came out all they could hear was Craig's voice.

'Hey, doll, I'll have another drink. Beer this time,' Craig called over when they were nearly finished getting everything ready for dinner.

Jenny and Nadia looked at each other and then ignored him. As they returned to the kitchen Nadia laughed and said, 'I wonder which one of us is the doll?'

Helena walked in just as they were picking up the last of the platters. She was shaking her head and when Nadia asked what was wrong, Helena sighed. 'It was all too good to be true. We had a lovely day and then this Craig chap arrives and I can already see that the evening is going to be disastrous.'

'Oh, Helena, it can always get worse. You and Jenny have yet to meet Tonia!' Nadia laughed but Helena's grimace worsened. 'Who knows, perhaps she and Craig might get on well and they can entertain each other,' Nadia offered. 'That would solve the problem nicely, and then we'll just have Stepanie to deal with, which will be easy as the more she drinks the quieter she gets. Right, which one of us wants to be the "doll" and take Craig his beer?'

Evangelina walked in just as Nadia asked the question and said, 'I think I will. It's time to nip this problem in the bud.'

Jenny smiled and took the last platter outside. She really didn't want to miss this! But just then Filippos and Marios appeared, and all Jenny's attention was taken up with admiring how handsome Marios was looking in his crisp white shirt and tailored navy trousers. She walked over to greet father and son.

'You two have scrubbed up well! You're just in time to meet the new arrival, Craig. It's all turning a little interesting.'

'What is that noise?' Filippos asked. 'I thought I heard a car pull up and now it sounds like people are arguing. I'll go and have a look.'

Jenny and Marios followed Filippos at a distance and found him talking calmly to a woman who was shouting at him. The young woman appeared to have had one drink too many and Jenny wondered if this was the infamous Tonia, Stepanie's daughter. The woman brushed past Filippos and stormed through the hotel and out onto the terrace. Before anyone could say anything about her abrupt arrival, she picked up a bottle of red wine and then fell against the table of food, which sent the beautifully prepared platters everywhere. Marios moved to try and help Tonia but she fell towards him, the red wine covering him from head to toe.

Chapter 21

Sat on her little balcony eating a bowl of pasta after a busy day of cleaning her apartment and readying it to go on the market, Voula's phone rang with a call from her brother.

'Filippos! Everything ok? It's not like you to call out of the blue.'

'Nothing major, but I did feel I needed to call you. Mum's guests have arrived, and, well...'

As Filippos explained what had happened with Craig and Tonia, and how everything was spoiled and Evangelina went to her room upset, Voula was disappointed for her mum and siblings. She knew they'd all been looking forward to tonight.

'I feel bad now that we talked her into having a party. On paper it should have been lovely, all the people Mum and Dad enjoyed working with coming back together, but it's already falling apart – and most of them are here for at least a week or more! Mum is insisting that the party be cancelled but we can't let her retire on this horrible note.'

'I really don't know what to say. I'd love to help the situation but what can I do when I'm here on Rhodes?'

'That's the main reason I'm calling – I'm asking you to come back. We need to give Mum a lovely time so that her lasting memories are her family and closest friends around her, and without you here on Vekianos things won't feel right. Even if you can only make it for a couple of days, please say yes.'

'Ok, I'll do it,' Voula agreed.

Once off the phone Voula's first thought was that she knew she had to go back to the island, but she also didn't feel ready yet. What if Helena changed her mind and told their mum about Voula's plans? Or what if it was harder than usual to maintain her 'in control Voula' face? Ultimately, she had no choice. Her family needed her, so she would go.

Pouring another glass of wine, she opened her laptop. She had one more job to do before heading to bed, and that was to send an email to Athena. She would thank her for the very generous job offer, and explain that she had to turn her down because she had her own hotel project to undertake. If anyone could understand the need to chase and achieve a dream, it was Athena.

As she climbed into bed, she thought about how alike she and Athena were. They probably would have gotten on very well together if circumstances had been different and Voula had been in a position to take the job. Perhaps if it wasn't for the excitement of all the impending changes on Vekianos, her life could have been on Mykonos. As she pondered the possibilities, she fell into a deep sleep.

Chapter 22
Sunday 15th April

Helena had barely slept. It had taken three hours to clear up the horrible mess Tonia had caused and to see Evangelina so upset had been heartbreaking. This was not what these last few weeks were meant to be about, and as much as Nadia had tried to reassure Helena that everything would be ok, she wasn't convinced. The only thing she knew for sure was that sitting here exhausted in her little bungalow wasn't going to help the situation. She needed to get over to the hotel and help her sister-in-law with getting the breakfast sorted for the guests, not that some of them even deserved it.

She couldn't help thinking that it was all her fault. After all, she was the one who had insisted on inviting these people to the hotel.

'You look like you've had a rough night,' said Nadia, coming over to give her a supportive hug as soon as she stepped into the kitchen a few minutes later. 'Filippos didn't even go to bed. He was in the chair in the sitting room when I got up this morning, and he looked about as exhausted as you do. Look, I'll say to you what I said to him: it's a new day and anything is possible. We know who we're dealing with now we've met the visitors – we know their characters and how they behave – so we can be one step ahead, and foresee any potential problems. Plus, we know that as well as the family we also have Jenny and Paul on our side to help control any situations that arise.'

'Thank you for that. I should say it more often, but you are by far the best thing that ever happened to our family. And it's not just me that thinks so, my dad used to say it all the time.'

Nadia nodded, a sad smile on her face. 'He used to tell me all the time.' Nadia reached out and hugged Helena tightly before stepping away and rubbing her eyes. 'Now, enough of all this sentimental business! We have to get this show on the road and hopefully make it a slightly different show to yesterday.'

'What do you mean?'

'Well yesterday's show was all love and romance, with Jenny and Marios, and you and Paul...'

Helena made to interrupt but Nadia continued.

'...Whereas today's show will be more of a crime thriller because if Tonia takes one step out of line or further upsets Evangelina in *any* way, I will be there to annihilate her. She won't know what hit her!'

'Please tell me you won't *actually* hit her.'

'Of course not! But there is more than one way to sort that young lady out,' said Nadia, sounding and looking very ominous.

They laughed and hugged again before Helena went to set up the terrace for breakfast and Nadia prepared the food. Helena marvelled to herself at what a good team they were, and then thought sadly about the fact that it would soon come to an end. With all the changes Voula had planned for the hotel, would Nadia stay or would she move on as well?

Walking onto the terrace Helena was surprised to see that the tables and chairs were all in place, so all she had to do was lay the tables. Nadia hadn't mentioned she had done that so who—

Helena stopped abruptly as she noticed Paul carrying a chair from around the corner.

'I wondered who had put all the tables in place. You really shouldn't be doing that as you're a guest, but thank you. I would have done it last night but as you're well aware, the floor was very wet after—'

'After nothing,' interrupted Paul. 'What

happened last night doesn't need to be mentioned again. It's all over with and in the past, and today is another day. To tell the truth, I've enjoyed setting everything up. It's brought back so many happy memories from all those years ago, and that's largely what this holiday is all about for me: reliving the memories, and also making new ones. For instance, our time on the beach yesterday, which was very special to me.'

'It really was a lovely day, Paul, which was completely spoiled by a few individuals last night.'

'I don't think what happened here needs to have anything to do with yesterday on the beach. Oh, look, here comes Jenny.'

'Morning, Dad, hi, Helena. I just caught what you said, and I was thinking while I was in the shower this morning that there will come a time when we'll all laugh about this. Hopefully sooner rather than later.'

'I wish I had your faith, Jenny, but I can't see my mum laughing about any of it,' said Helena, a bit sadly.

'Is there anything I can do to help?' asked Jenny.

'Actually there is something you could do that would take the pressure away from everything here at the hotel and hopefully bring a smile back on Evangelina's face ... but I suspect it's not something you're going to enjoy,' said Paul.

'I don't mind, I just want everything to go back to how it was when we first arrived.'

She could put up with anything to restore a little calm to the hotel.

'I think you'd best sit down before I tell you, and remember, it's all to make Evangelina feel better. I think you should suggest taking Craig out for the day, perhaps to the beach or to a bar. We just need to get him out of the way. I would say take Tonia as well, but something tells me that with the amount she drank yesterday it could be a couple of days before she surfaces. As for Stepanie, well, I think she will be very subdued and keep out of the way.'

He was right, she wasn't going to like this one little bit! The thought of being with Craig all day made her shudder but how could she say no? Perhaps she could lose him in a bar down in the harbour, but thinking that, perhaps that wasn't the best idea. The last thing they needed was him coming back like Tonia had. No, it would have to be a beach day away from alcohol.

Helena jumped in before Jenny had time to answer. 'You can't ask Jenny to do that, it's not fair to her.'

'It's fine, and like you say, it will ensure things are calm and quiet here. There is one thing though... Would anyone mind if I just happen to put him on a boat that's not returning to Vekianos for a week or so?'

That had them all laughing and as they turned around there was Nadia with a big flask of coffee. 'I see that normality has returned to the hotel,' she said. 'Thank goodness!'

Emma appeared then with that same wary look she'd had since arriving, and they all greeted her warmly, hoping to make her feel even more welcome.

'Do we know how Evangelina is after everything that happened last night?' asked Emma.

'Mum will be fine, I promise. Now, help yourself to some coffee while I head back into the kitchen to help Nadia finish off the food.'

'So, Emma, am I right in thinking you were the one who worked here the season after my dad and before Stepanie?' asked Jenny as they found their seats.

'Yes, that's right.'

She lapsed into silence again and Jenny took a deep breath. It would be a long week if it was this hard to draw Emma into conversation!

They were saved from the awkward silence by the sound of Emma's phone ringing and as she answered she stood and walked off the terrace into the garden.

'I'm not really in the mood to be out with Craig today but I'm starting to think it's a far better option than being here with Emma,' Jenny whispered to her dad. 'Talk about pulling teeth! Why has she bothered to come if she's going to be silent and miserable the whole time?'

'I don't know, darling, but then I suppose Stepanie will fill that silence when she comes down for breakfast. Maybe it's better only one of them likes the sound of her own voice?'

'Don't say that! Oh, she's coming back... Is everything ok?' asked Jenny, politely.

'Yes, everything is lovely, thank you. Ooh! Here comes Helena with a big basket of pastries. It's such a treat to sit out here in the morning sun with the beautiful view in front of us. How lucky are we?'

Paul and Jenny stared at each other as Helena placed the pastries in the middle of the table. Jenny couldn't figure out what had just happened. Who was this different Emma? How could one person change so much with just one phone call?

'Dive in while they're still warm,' encouraged Helena. 'There are cereals, ham, and cheese on the table inside, and I will fetch more coffee. I won't be a minute.'

'Have you two got any plans for today?' asked the new and much chattier version of Emma that had now joined them.

'I'm mostly staying here, though I might have a little walk later, and Jenny is going to take Craig out and show him around the harbour.'

'That will be nice. I was thinking only this morning how nice the two of you young people looked together.'

'You might think that, but I have to confess that the only reason I'm taking him out is so that he doesn't annoy Evangelina and get on everyone else's nerves, which he's sure to do if he stays around the hotel all day.'

'Oh? It won't be a problem for me as I'm off out for the day. I'm meeting an old friend. That's actually who just called. I let him know I would be here and he insisted on showing me around. He mentioned he's recently single so it looks like my visit here to Vekianos is going to be more interesting than I'd thought. I'm not too hungry so I think I'd best head off and find a suitable outfit for the day. See you later!'

'What just happened?' asked Jenny, bemused.

'I'm not sure, but could you pass me the coffee pot, please?'

'It's empty. Helena said she would grab more so I'll go see if I can chivvy her along.'

As Jenny walked through the lounge, she could see Helena stood at the front door looking very confused.

'Are you ok, Helena? Is something wrong?'

'Yes and no. Stepanie and Tonia have just left in a taxi.'

'Because of yesterday?' asked Jenny.

'Yes, Stepanie said she feels she can't stay and face everyone because she's too embarrassed. It's sad as it wasn't her fault but her daughter's. Oh, this week is turning into a complete disaster!'

Chapter 23

Voula was at her desk facing the obstacle to her plans for the family hotel: the swimming pool. Everything was hinging on this pool because with no pool, there was no way forward with the project.

A text came through, disrupting her concentration, but she wasn't mad as it was from her nephew Marios. He explained that the party was off and thanked her for her help but said he wouldn't be contacting her with any more queries. She started to reply but realised it would be better if she called instead.

'I'm sorry to have bothered you,' said Marios, after they'd exchanged hellos. 'I so appreciate all the weeks of advice but Grandma isn't having a party now.'

'No, it's going ahead. I will make sure of that.'

'But how?'

'I'm coming back and between us we'll make it happen. Mum deserves the best send-off party Vekianos has ever seen. Now, I need to get on with my work, but I'll get back to you with a plan of action ASAP. In the meantime, please reassure your dad and aunt that the party will still go ahead.'

'Ok, but I think you need to tell Grandma yourself because she won't listen to any of the family here.'

'Not a problem. I'll do it tonight.'

As she came off the phone, she laughed at her word choice. The truth was it was going to be a nightmare trying to persuade her mum. But before all of that, she needed to resolve her swimming pool issue.

Five hours later she had researched pool installation companies and created a shortlist based on their packages and reviews, and made enquiries about having a survey done to make sure the ground was suitable and the set-up safe enough to install a pool. Her eyes hurt from being on the laptop for so long, so it was definitely time to switch it off and take a break.

Seeing it as a good opportunity to call her sister, she rang Helena.

'I've heard the news about Mum's party,' she said, 'so I'm just calling to tell you I'm coming back for it and between Marios and myself we're determined to make it happen, so there's no need for you to worry about anything.'

'Ok, but I don't think I'm the one you should be telling that to.'

'I know. I need to talk to Mum, which I intend to, but I wanted to tell you first.'

'Thank you. By the way, two guests have already left this morning. Stepanie and her daughter are still on the island but they've found somewhere else to stay.'

'I take it she's still planning to come to the party? Knowing her from all those years ago she'll undoubtedly want to be the centre of attention. Apart from that, is everything else ok? Are you geared up for the start of the season?'

There was silence and Voula wasn't sure what to say or ask next.

Finally, Helena spoke. 'The tour operators have been enquiring about next year and we have to decide which company, or companies, to go with.'

'I thought that might happen. If you could stall them until I come back, we can talk about it then.'

'To be honest, there's nothing to talk about. All I need to know is when you intend to take over and—'

'I'm not "taking over",' interrupted Voula. 'We'll

be doing this together, Helena. It's always going to be a family-run hotel, but now it will be more of a modern high-end retreat that caters to a wealthier clientele.'

'No, Voula, it's your thing and I don't want to be a part of it. I remember the last time you tried to change things and I really can't go through all that upset again. Now, if that's everything, I need to go and see to the guests. Goodbye.'

Helena hung up before Voula could respond.

Oh dear, that hadn't gone as well as Voula had hoped. Still, one thing at a time. The priority now was to make sure the party went ahead and that their mum left the island happy and ready to enjoy her retirement.

Chapter 24

By the time Jenny and Craig had left the hotel, it was nearly lunchtime. He hadn't stumbled out of his room until quite late, but as breakfast was over and there was no food for him it didn't take much persuasion to convince him to get ready quickly and join her for a day out. In fact, he was very keen. *Too* keen for her liking, if Jenny was honest.

'Shall we grab some food first and then do a bit of a sightseeing tour?' she asked.

'Yes, food, and a beer, and a sit in the sunshine sounds like the perfect day for me, doll.'

'Can I ask you a favour? Please call me Jenny. I'm not a doll.'

'Normally my girls like to be called doll.'

'They might do, but I'm most definitely *not* your girl.'

'Not yet. We're on holiday! It's all about having a laugh and I can tell you're excited about being with me. Now, where is the food? I'm starving.'

Jenny had been annoyed that Craig was still asleep at midday, but now she was beginning to wish he'd slept the whole day so that she could have avoided him entirely.

'When I go on holiday I can usually find lots of places that serve English food – you know, a big, all-day breakfast – but I'm not seeing any here. It's all foreign.'

Jenny was nonplussed. 'You're annoyed that the restaurants are serving Greek food ... in Greece?'

'You get it,' said Craig, nodding to himself as though she'd agreed with him.

Jenny took a deep breath. How many more hours of this would she have to endure?

'There's a place over there that looks fine, and I'm sure you could get steak and chips.'

'Lead the way, doll – sorry, *Jenny*. Steak and chips accompanied by a beer will be the perfect start to the day.'

Jenny laughed to herself. Start of the day? It was nearly afternoon as they sat down! She ordered a coffee and of course Craig had a beer, and as they waited for their food, she wondered what on earth they could talk about. She had nothing whatsoever in common with him apart from the fact that they were staying in the same hotel.

'This is better, don't you think, Jenny? See, I got it right the first time,' he said, smugly.

'What is better?'

'Being here rather than back at that old people's home. You have to admit it's not much fun. If it wasn't a free holiday I think I would complain.'

Jenny didn't know what to say and then she laughed a little too loud as she wondered if the reason his mum hadn't come was because she knew what he would be like, and was too embarrassed to be around him.

'What are you laughing about?' asked Craig, looking annoyed.

'What were you expecting of this holiday? Like, what did your mum tell you the holiday was all about?'

'She just said she was invited to a party at the island hotel where she once worked.'

'So, she said nothing about a retirement party?'

'She might have, but I just heard "party" and "Greek island", and I instantly thought Ibiza... Why are you laughing?'

'Ibiza is in Spain and is a total party island. This is a very small – very quiet – Greek island.'

'Yes, but both are islands with sunshine. How could they be all that different...? Don't move!

There's an insect on your hair and it's big. Stay very still while I remove it.'

He stretched over and touched the side of her face, and she wasn't sure if it was the insect or him touching her that was more upsetting. It felt it was taking forever to remove it, and she breathed a sigh of relief when he finally sat back.

'Good job I was here to rescue you. Here comes the food, and just in time as I need another beer.'

As he got stuck into his steak and chips, she wondered if she could just eat and then leave him. But then what would happen if he wandered back to the hotel? No, she'd best stay out with him until at least the early evening.

'Was that good? You seemed to enjoy it,' she said as he finished his meal.

'Yes, one more beer and then I'll be ready to have a sleep on the beach. It's very quiet here, isn't it?' he said, looking around them. 'I think there was more life up at the hotel!'

'That's because the season hasn't started yet. The holiday makers will only start coming in a few weeks, when the weather gets better.'

'Oh, so why are we here now and not in a few weeks?'

She couldn't be bothered to explain to him – again – that this was a free holiday before the season started and he should count his blessings that he'd been invited. He wouldn't understand.

Once they'd finished they headed to the beach. Jenny had her fingers crossed that he would fall asleep and she could read a book on her phone, but almost immediately it became clear that wasn't going to happen.

'Lead me to a sun lounger! It's time to get a tan. I have to make the lads at home jealous when they see how brown I am. Talking of the lads, let's have a selfie so I can show them I've scored.'

That was *it*. Jenny was up and out of her seat, absolutely fuming. There would be no photo and he absolutely had *not* scored. Not today, or at any other time on this holiday. As she stood up, she caught her foot in the strap of her bag and as she went to walk away, she fell. Craig stopped her falling flat on her face by catching her, and though the last thing she needed was to be in his arms staring right into his eyes, she was thankful not to have hit the ground.

Then he spoke and ruined whatever goodwill he might have earned by helping her. 'If not for me, you might have hurt yourself! Or was it intentional? C'mon, doll, admit you just wanted to be in my arms.'

She nearly slapped him.

'It was an *accident*,' she hissed, scrambling away from him.

'If you say so. But give it a few hours and see if you don't want it to happen again.' He smiled smugly. 'Right, doll, wake me up when the excitement starts, though somehow I don't think that's going to happen, not on this island.'

He took his t-shirt off and reclined on the lounger, and was asleep in no time, a happy relief for Jenny. After covering herself in sun cream she looked at her phone. There was a text from her dad to say they had been invited to eat with Filippos and Nadia at their place that evening, along with Evangelina and Helena, but they didn't need to be there until eight o'clock.

Texting back a thumbs up, she was warmed by the prospect of another evening with Marios – this time preferably without him covered in red wine.

She texted Marios.

Looking forward to seeing you at your mum and dad's tonight, Jenny xx

Her day was – finally – turning out better than she'd thought after all.

*

It was over two hours before Craig woke up, and as he was stirring, she thought perhaps she should pretend to be asleep so that he might just lie there in silence and leave her in peace. It was worth a go.

She heard him grumbling to himself but then a silence followed. Just as she thought she'd managed to fool him, she felt his lips on hers. Gasping, she pushed him away as forcefully as she could.

'What on earth are you doing?!'

'I was waking you up just like Sleeping Beauty in the film. I know how you girls like all that sloppy stuff.'

'I can tell you that *this* girl *doesn't*. Don't even think about doing that again. *Ever.*'

'Playing hard to get then? Let's see what happens once you have a few drinks inside you. No doubt I'll be chasing you off.'

That was it, she'd had enough. Her task of keeping him occupied was officially over because she was not spending one more minute in his company. He could cause whatever trouble he liked at the hotel; he wasn't her problem anymore.

As she gathered her things her phone beeped with a text from Marios.

Won't be there tonight

Well, that was a shock. Why wouldn't he be there? And if that was the case, perhaps she wouldn't bother to go. She'd had a hellish day and it was probably best to stay at the hotel and just let her dad and the family chat about the old days.

'Why the sad face? You're out with Craig! I've noticed a lot of younger people work here on the island so they must party somewhere, and I'm an expert at sniffing out a good time. Come on, get your bag. It's time to find out where the action is. And by the way, yes, you can.'

'Yes I can what?' she asked, warily.

'Trip on your bag again so I can catch you.'

She ignored him as she packed her things. She didn't enjoy Craig's company but perhaps one or two drinks would be just what she needed to get over her disappointment about not seeing Marios tonight.

She sighed and then let him lead the way, quickly texting her dad to say she'd had a change of mind and wouldn't be going to dinner after all.

'Keep up, doll! I'm on a mission to give you a good time, but before that we need a few drinks.'

Perhaps this was a terrible idea and she should just walk off and head back to the hotel. But then, that would mean seeing her dad before he left and no doubt he'd try to persuade her into going with him tonight. She wasn't in the mood for that either so that only left following Craig as an option.

Eventually they reached the streets behind the harbour, and it wasn't looking as touristy as some of the other places she'd been on the island. And to give him credit, she could see a bar with younger people sat outside up ahead.

'Take a seat. I suppose you want a fancy cocktail thing with one of those umbrellas in.'

'No, I'm having a beer.'

'A girl that likes to drink beer? That's fine by me; I like a cheap date.'

She didn't answer, just laughed. He really didn't have a clue what came out his mouth.

Determined to salvage the day, she asked him about himself once the beers had arrived. 'What do you do for a living and how do you spend your spare time? Do you have any hobbies?'

'Football. It's all about the match.'

'So, you're a footballer? Are you in the premier league?'

'No, I don't play it, I watch it with my mates,' he said, sounding exasperated. 'I work in a factory.'

'What sort of factory?'

'A big one.'

She wasn't getting anywhere with this conversation so she excused herself and went off to the bathroom. How had she got herself into this situation? It was so bad, it was almost – *almost* – funny. As she walked back outside, she could see a woman in her seat. She must have been in her fifties and her hands were all over Craig. He looked like he was enjoying it, so perhaps this could be Jenny's get out of jail free card?

'Doll, you're back! This is another doll, and she said I looked lonely and needed a good feed, so if you don't mind, I'm going back to her place with her. See you later.' He stood to leave and then turned back and whispered, 'Actually, I don't think I'll be back today. Something tells me this doll has other plans once she's fed me. This island is starting to get exciting after all.'

Half an hour later Jenny was still laughing as she sat on the harbour wall. It had been the perfect outcome and she hoped the other 'doll' would entertain Craig for the rest of his holiday so Jenny could spend her time with Marios instead. Thinking about the gorgeous Greek, she got out her phone and texted him.

I've missed you today. Are you free tomorrow to have a day out? Jenny xx

There was no reply from him so she headed back up to the hotel. As she got to the main door she bumped into Emma, who was towing a big suitcase and a carry-on bag.

'Are you off somewhere?' asked Jenny.

'Yes. Do you know where Evangelina or Helena are?'

'They've gone out for the evening. Are you leaving for good?'

'Only the hotel, not the island. You know my

friend that I caught up with today? He's suggested I stay with him for the rest of my trip.'

'Oh, that will be nice for you.'

'Yes, but could you do me a favour? When you see Helena will you explain to her that I've gone? And, of course, please reassure her I'll still be at the party. Here's my taxi. Bye!'

With that, she was gone, and it hit Jenny that everything was back to normal, and it was just her and her dad staying at the hotel. She smiled to herself just as her phone beeped with a text from Marios.

From what I've seen today it didn't look like you were missing me at all. I'm busy tomorrow.

What the heck was that about?

Chapter 25

As Jenny sat on her balcony with her first cup of coffee of the day, she was feeling sorry for herself. She knew she had no right to be feeling like this, as she had everything going for her, but after Marios' abrupt rejection the night before she couldn't help but feel low. Still, if he was silly enough to think she had any interest in Craig, and that their spending the day out together was anything more than a favour to her dad and Helena, it was his loss. No, she wasn't going to let him spoil her day.

As she made her way down the stairs and out onto the terrace a while later, she could see she was the first one up. But that wasn't saying much as there were no longer any other guests beyond her and her dad.

'Morning, Jenny, sleep well?' asked Nadia.

'Yes, thanks. I needed it after the day out I had with Craig.' She shuddered. 'Hopefully it did the trick and will keep him away from here for the day.'

'It definitely helped. Evangelina was in good spirits and has agreed the party can go ahead so we are – sort of – all back to normal. I say "sort of" because my son is in a wicked mood today. I hope you don't mind me asking, but have you and Marios fallen out?'

'I think he has with me. It's a long story, but I get the impression he saw Craig and I out together yesterday and he's put two and two together and made five. He obviously doesn't know I was asked by my dad and Helena to keep Craig out of Evangelina's way.'

Nadia laughed sadly. 'Sorry, Jenny, that's typical of my son. He's just like his father; they never think things through. Leave it to me and I will put him straight. Is that why neither of you came for dinner last night?'

'Yes, and I'm sorry to have let you down. Did the five of you have a nice time?'

'We did, thank you, but there were only four of us as Evangelina decided to stay here. It was a very cosy evening, especially for two people,' she said, in a tone that hinted there was a lot more to the story. 'If you want to take a seat I'll fetch you some coffee. By the way, I hear Emma has left us as well?'

Jenny nodded. 'Can you believe it?'

Nadia shook her head and walked inside.

As it was just her and dad for breakfast, Jenny thought that perhaps she should see how he was feeling. This holiday was certainly not turning out the way they had both planned, and the party hadn't even happened yet!

'I have just called my son and told him what an idiot he has been so I expect before long you might get a call,' Nadia announced as she poured Jenny a fruit juice.

'You really didn't need to do that but thank you. I think I can hear Dad and Helena chatting,' she said, turning towards the terrace door.

'Nadia tells me the party is going ahead after all. That's great news,' Jenny said to Helena.

'Yes, we're all back on track and Filippos has persuaded my sister Voula to come over from Rhodes for it. I think that's what swung it for my mum. I need to sort a few things out, so I'd better head off. Enjoy your breakfast.'

With that Helena and Nadia headed back inside and Jenny could see how her dad's eyes followed them. It made her smile. He deserved every bit of happiness. She didn't want to do anything to spook him or spoil it, so she'd have to do her best to not question him about Helena unless he broached the subject first.

'Thank you for yesterday, darling, I imagine it wasn't a nice day for you, but it really helped the situation here with Evangelina.'

'Actually, it was so bad that it was almost funny. If I had a penny for every time he called me "doll" I think I would be very rich. But fingers crossed he's out of the way for a while. I suspect that if that woman he met has any say in it, Craig won't see the light of day until he has to catch the plane home.'

They were still laughing when Evangelina joined them a few minutes later.

Jenny smiled as her dad got up to pull back the chair for her. He fitted in so well with this lovely family.

'I hear I owe you a thank you,' Evangelina said to Jenny

'It was fine, and it's over with now.'

'Still, I appreciate it. Any plans for today? You're welcome to stay here and enjoy the hotel. Don't feel you need to be on the go at all times – you're meant to be relaxing! I'm off out with Nadia after breakfast to find a fabulous party dress – Nadia's words, not mine – as she says it's important I look my best.'

'I'm sure a little shopping therapy will be perfect,' said Jenny.

'I doubt there will be anything therapeutic about it for me, but I'll go along with it to keep the family happy. That sounds like Marios' bike out front. I wonder what brings him here so early in the morning,' she said, wandering off to greet her grandson.

'What's so urgent you needed to talk to me right away, Marios?' asked Helena.

'I've been so stupid,' he said, looking despondent.

'Look, go through to the bar and I'll fetch us a

drink and then we'll sort out whatever your problem is. Just give me a minute.'

'Helena, is that my son I can hear?' asked Nadia as Helena stepped into the kitchen. 'Has he told you what he's done? He spotted Jenny out with that Craig chap and looked at the situation in all the wrong ways. He's evidently come to apologise for being rude to her and I have to give him points for coming here rather than phoning or texting.'

'Oh, dear. But who does he remind you of?' Helena tried to stifle a laugh.

'Yes, Filippos used to pull the exact same kinds of stunts.' Nadia rolled her eyes. 'Men! Why are they all so alike?'

'Actually, I'd argue there are some who are very different,' said Helena, glancing in the direction of the terrace.

'What do you mean...? Ah, I see. I should have known.' Nadia winked. 'All joking aside though, I'm happy you and Paul are having a nice time together. You deserve it so much.'

'Thank you for that. I'm enjoying being with him and...' She hesitated, then took a deep breath and continued. 'You're the only one I can say this to, but ... I've been thinking about how things in my life could have been so different if Paul hadn't left the island and Sotirios hadn't been around. Sometimes you can't see the woods for the trees, can you? What I mean is that I should have stood back and took a breather. Should have considered everything in a different way. Sadly, it's now too late.'

'Too late? What rubbish! This is a second chance at a whole new future for you. Go and grab it with both hands, Helena, and enjoy every minute of it.'

Helena didn't know what to say so she just hugged her sister-in-law. Finally she pulled away.

'Now, you have a nephew to sort out.'

'Oh yes, I almost forgot! Let me just get him that

drink.'

'Sorry, Marios, your mum and I got distracted. Here's your coffee. Now, tell me what the problem is.'

He explained how he'd seen Craig and Jenny together and completely misunderstood what he was witnessing.

'And so you thought the worst,' said Helena, nodding. 'I honestly don't think you've been all that silly. You've only known Jenny for a few days and who is to say she isn't the type of girl who keeps things casual and likes having more than one boyfriend on the go at one time?'

'Thank you for trying to make me feel better but we both know Jenny isn't that kind of girl.'

'Well, if that's the case, drink your coffee and go and apologise. Jenny and Paul should have finished their breakfast by now, and you don't want to waste another day, do you?'

'Thank you, Aunt Helena. I promise I won't.'

Helena smiled as she watched him head off out onto the terrace. How was he so grown up already? It didn't seem five minutes since he was first trying to crawl... But he wasn't a boy anymore, he was a man, and she was very proud of him.

'We'll miss these breakfasts when we go home,' said Paul, already sounding wistful even though their holiday was nowhere near over.

'I don't think the breakfast is the only thing you'll miss,' Jenny half-whispered to herself.

'Is it that obvious?' asked Paul, looking sheepish.

Jenny blushed, embarrassed that he'd heard her. 'Your face lights up every time Helena appears and she's just the same. It's really sweet and I can't ever remember you being like this. I mean, of course you've always been happy when it was just the two of us together, but when you're with Helena it's different. You look so relaxed and content.'

'I think you could be right.'

'So, what shall we do today, Dad?'

'I think that question has been answered for you. Here comes Marios. I'll leave you two to chat. I think I might go for a little walk down into the harbour.'

With that Paul stood up and gave Jenny a kiss before going back inside.

'Good morning, Marios. Come and pull up a chair. It's nice to see you,' said Jenny, a bit shyly.

'Do you mean that? I'm not sure if I would feel the same if you'd treated me the horrible way I treated you. It's just ... I was so stupid. I saw Craig stroking your hair and face and...' He trailed off as Jenny began to laugh.

'I had a bug of some sort in my hair that he was trying to get out for me.'

'Like I said, I was stupid.'

'It's all forgotten. It's in the past and it's time to move on.'

'That's very understanding of you, but I would still like to make it up to you. Do you have any plans for today?'

'Yes, I do. I'm off out for the day with a very handsome man who works on one of the tourist boats. He's going to show me this gorgeous island and hopefully, if I'm really lucky, he might kiss me like he did the day before yesterday.'

Marios' face lit up and he leaned forward and gave her just what she wanted.

'I think I'd best go up to my room and get changed,' she said as they pulled apart a while later. 'I don't think either of us wants to miss a minute of the day ahead.'

Chapter 26

Helena caught sight of her reflection in the mirror as she was walking back through the hotel lounge towards the kitchen and she burst out laughing. The whole thing was madness! Why had they talked Evangelina into having a party? But more than that, what else could go wrong? Well, she actually knew the answer to that last one. There was no doubt that Voula's return would herald some kind of disaster. She heard the front door opening and turned to see Paul coming in.

'Did you have a nice walk? I'm off to make some lunch so if there's anything you're craving just let me know.'

'I'll have the same as you if you're sure it's not too much trouble.'

'Not at all. Two Greek salads with lots of feta will soon be on their way. Why don't you meet me on the terrace in fifteen minutes?'

'Sounds great. Would you like a hand with anything?'

'No, it's ok, I have it all under control.'

After preparing the food she went and fetched a cold bottle of wine from the bar and two glasses. Taking them out to the terrace she could see Paul stood looking out to sea. It was a sight she remembered from years ago. Her mum and dad had always used to say that Paul was one of the only members of staff they employed who really appreciated the view and made time in his day to stop and take it all in.

'Here we go. If you could open the bottle and pour it, I'll go and fetch the food. I've warmed some bread to go with it.'

As Paul turned around she could see he looked just as happy as she felt, and she felt the magic of the moment keenly. When her phone beeped she jumped, looking down at it to find a text from Nadia.

Disastrous shopping trip but bought some fabric and we are now off to see Renata the dressmaker to see what she can come up with. Won't be back for a few hours. Wish me luck!!

Helena texted back:

Rather you than me.

She put the salads, bread and condiments on a tray and headed back out to Paul.

'Sounds like Nadia is having a bad shopping trip with Mum, but if anyone can control the situation it's my sister-in-law.'

Paul laughed and picked up his glass to toast the chef. The two of them said '*yamas*' and then there was an awkward silence as they both slowly started to eat. Helena didn't know what to talk about. Ten minutes ago she had felt excited to be spending time with him, so why had things changed?

'You've gone quiet,' said Paul gently. 'Is something wrong?'

'I'm fine, I just get these moments when I'm a little overwhelmed with everything – Mum retiring, the party, Voula coming back... Everything just fills my head at once.'

'That's completely understandable. Perhaps it would help if you broke everything down into different compartments so that it all feels more manageable? It was how I learned to deal with things when my wife left,' he added quietly.

'What do you mean by "break things down"?' she asked, curious.

'There's so much to take care of when a marriage comes to an end. The house had to be sold and I had to find somewhere new to live, we had to divide our belongings, we had to figure out all the financials...

And then there was the emotional toll: processing the end of a relationship while dealing with the well-intentioned pity of my friends and extended family, which hindered more than helped. So, I learned to deal with one thing at a time by putting everything into imaginary boxes in my head. It sounds a bit silly saying it out loud.'

'It's not silly at all if it worked for you. That's all that matters, don't you think?'

'I suppose so. It did stop me feeling too overwhelmed and panicking, and one by one those boxes were emptied as things were sorted. As I see it, some of the boxes you might be carrying are already sorted given that Emma and Stepanie have moved elsewhere, and Craig's attention is tied up away from the hotel. Now the next one is probably the party, am I right?'

Helena nodded.

'From what I understand Marios and Voula are organising that, but it's only natural that you might be worrying as you want everything to be perfect for your mum. But if you interfered Marios might have a crisis of confidence. Better for you to mark that box as 'taken care of' in your mind and leave it in his more than capable hands. I know he's going to make you proud and get everything sorted.'

'You're right, there's less to worry about than I thought. That just leaves the biggest box – Voula coming back to Vekianos for good.'

'Can I ask what Voula's specific plans are? You said she wants to turn the hotel into a five-star luxury destination, but surely that will take a lot of money? And then there's the fact it might not succeed. Vekianos is a small island and from what I've seen in the past the people who stay in those types of hotels expect there to be posh shops and jewellers, as well as glitzy bars and restaurants, close by. There's nothing like that here on this island, and thank goodness for that! People don't come here for infinity pools, they want the gorgeous beaches with the clear blue seas and the quaint, authentic hotels, shops, and restaurants.'

'Yes, but there are more and more luxury villas with pools popping up around the island.'

'Maybe, but I'd argue that most visitors still want easy access to the little harbour and the beaches, which means staying in the more centrally located hotels.'

'I know what you're saying but Voula is right about one thing, this hotel is very old and dated. All the pine furniture is from the seventies and the heavy, dark, patterned curtains are so far from chic. Visitors these days want nice big showers with waterfall shower heads, not baths with a shower curtain. It all needs updating.'

'So that's Voula's plan? Update everything to the point where it's barely recognisable?'

Helena shrugged. 'I suspect so.'

'But what about your plans? Have you thought that perhaps you could work together?'

'To be completely honest, it just wouldn't work. We're too different and our visions for the hotel are sure to clash. No, I'm just going to focus on this upcoming season – my last at the hotel – and I'll figure out my future when our last guest leaves in October. I have lots of contacts here on the island so I'm sure to find a job somewhere next year.'

'And what will Evangelia think when she finds out about Voula's plans? And more importantly, about you leaving her beloved hotel?'

'I think she'll understand why I can't work here. She is our mother after all.' Helena laughed, but it was a bit hollow. 'It won't be a surprise to her that our working together isn't a great idea. As for Voula's plans ... I think Mum will be happy the hotel is moving forward and staying in the family. I think one of her fears over the years has been that we'll sell the hotel after she passes, so it will be a relief for her to see how invested Voula is in making it a success.'

'But you haven't said what she'll think of all the changes Voula will be making.'

'She knows things need to be modernised and as she'll be in Parga and won't see any of the work happening, I think she'll be fine with it. Now how about a dessert? I have a lovely fresh gateau with mango and cream.'

'Ok then, if you insist,' joked Paul. 'I'm sure I can manage it, but only if it's a small piece.'

'You sure?' Helena arched an eyebrow.

'Absolutely not. Give me the biggest piece you have, please.' Paul grinned.

'I'll be going home the size of a house at this rate with all the lovely food I've enjoyed,' said Paul, putting down his spoon a while later. 'Do you mind if we go back to what we were talking about before dessert? You said Evangelina knows things need to be modernised, but couldn't *you* organise that?'

'I could,' she hedged, 'but it's too late to do it for this season and Voula will be here when we close for the winter. There's also the matter of the money involved with refurbishing everything. It won't be cheap.'

'I don't think it would be that expensive to make some minor updates. For a start, a shower cubicle could easily be fitted where the bath is so no drains or water pipes would need to be moved. Can I show you something on my phone? Just give me a second.'

Helena wasn't sure what Paul was getting at and she worried that if he showed her something she liked it would just make it worse that she was being forced to leave the business.

'Here now, look at these photos. This is the biggest budget hotel company in the UK. They have thousands of hotels that are what you'd call "cheap and cheerful" and they're excellent value for money. The great thing about them is that it doesn't matter which city or town you're in, you're guaranteed that every room is the same.'

'I don't understand what you're getting at.'

'Each room is furnished to a modern standard, but basic. There's a bed and a headboard with a shelf either side, a wardrobe and a tea and coffee station. It's everything the guest needs for a comfortable stay with none of the frills that typically drive up the price.'

'Unlike our rooms, which have so much clutter in them.'

'My point is, you don't have to spend a lot of money to give your guests exactly what they need and if you redid one room at a time you could do it at a pace that wouldn't bankrupt you. Also, if it's the same as when I worked here, then once the guests have finished breakfast they're off out to the beach and don't come back until it's time to get ready to go out to eat in the evening, so the work could be done throughout the season, the builders moving on to the next each time a room is completed. Doing a bigger overhaul now to make the rooms more timeless would mean they just need a fresh coat of paint every couple of years going forward, which means you'll save money in the long run.'

'I could pick a single fabric for the curtains and go with that throughout, which would allow me to bulk buy the fabric and save some money,' said Helena, building on Paul's vision.

'Exactly!' Paul smiled.

'For some reason I've always thought it would be a major task that would have to be done during the winter when the hotel is closed, but your idea of going room by room and concentrating the work during the hours the guests are out could work really well.' She thought for a moment and then shook her head. 'But why would I bother to do it when after a few months Voula will come in and rip it all out, putting her own plans into action?'

'You do it because it will stop her. Your mum will see what a fabulous job you've done and won't let her change it, and then in the winter you can concentrate on the outside of the building.'

'Yeah, a fresh coat of paint is more than overdue. That's a priority.'

'I hope I've given you something to think about. Maybe you can put it into one of those imaginary boxes and from time to time open it up and give it some further thought? And perhaps you might chat to Filippos and Nadia and see what they have to say? And, of course, you'll need to find someone who could do the actual work.'

'That's the easy bit as I know the perfect person for the job: you. You started your working life here on Vekianos, so why not come full circle, and finish it out by coming back here to the hotel?'

Chapter 27

Jenny was ready for her day out. She had a sensible outfit suitable for being on the back of a bike and she was excited to be spending the day with Marios.

Marios had a huge smile on his face when she emerged from the hotel, and put out his hand to take Jenny's bag off her. He was a real gentleman and she liked it.

'Where are we off to?'

'I thought we could go over to Keriaphos. I think you'll really like it.'

'Sounds perfect.'

Marios took out a crash helmet for her and put her bag in the box on the back of the bike. As she put on the helmet he balanced the bike and then helped her get settled behind him. This was the bit she had been most looking forward to: holding on tight to Marios while he drove. She was fairly confident that he would enjoy it as much as she would.

The journey didn't take long and as they reached the top of a hill Marios turned his head slightly and shouted back to her, 'Hold on tight! This is a little steep but it's better than having to walk down and back.'

As he slowly drove down Jenny glimpsed the sea in between the buildings, and once down on the flat the road narrowed and they entered a lovely little town. Marios parked the bike and balanced it while she got off, then took the beach bag out and locked up the two crash helmets.

'I thought we'd grab coffee and cake first, if that's ok with you? A friend of mine works in a café just down from here.'

'Sounds great to me, lead the way.'

As they got to the door of the café a lad welcomed them and chatted away to Marios in Greek. Jenny didn't have a clue what they were saying apart from one word: 'Natalia'. They grabbed a spot at a table outside and she could imagine the little town busy on a summer night, the atmosphere buzzing.

'Have you two known one another a long time?' she asked, motioning to his friend.

'We went to school together and he also went into the family business. This is his dad's café. It gets very busy during the season so it's nice to be able to pop in when it's calm.'

'Tell me more about the season and the boat. I expect you see lots of different types of people, all ages and nationalities. Which bit of the job do you enjoy the most?'

'All of it, really. My dad and I work well together and if we have a good crowd on board, it's great. Sometimes there's a mix of serious visitors and happy out-to-have-fun ones, so it can be a little awkward, but to see the way their faces change when they spot a dolphin, everyone onboard sharing in the moment, it's unifying and so special.'

'What a magical job to have. You sound really content with your life.'

'Are you not content with yours?'

'I mean, I'm happy. I enjoyed the job I was doing and I know I did it well as I progressed up the ladder in the company and achieved a lot while I was there.'

'If you loved it so much, why didn't you go with them when they relocated? I know you've said you didn't want to move away from your dad but surely you could have visited one another?'

'Strangely, since I've been here on holiday I've started to wonder if not wanting to move away from my dad was just an excuse not to relocate.'

'Paul just wants you to be happy so I'm sure he'd

support you if you changed your mind. And who knows, maybe he has a move of his own in the cards.'

'My dad and your Aunt Helena do seem to be getting closer by the day, don't they? I'm very happy to see him smiling and enjoying himself, but I am getting a bit worried about what will happen when the holiday is over. I might suggest he make the holiday a bit longer. It's not as though he has anything to rush back to in the UK.'

'Would it be a problem for you if he stayed?'

'No, not at all.'

'It would free you up to move with your company.'

'I don't think so. I've made up my mind that I want a new challenge, something different, though I don't know what that might be.'

'Well, if you fancy a *magical* job, my dad still has one going on his boat.'

'Now that is a *very* tempting offer. Six months in beautiful Greece? How lovely that would be! Sadly, I need to get back and start looking for a new job. Shall we take a look around this gorgeous little town?' she asked as she drank the last of her coffee. 'I just need to pop to the bathroom and then I'm ready.'

As she walked inside, she took a deep breath. She hadn't been lying when she'd said it would be lovely to spend a whole summer on this island, enjoying the sunshine and the food, but best of all being with Marios. But sadly, that was the type of thing that happened in fairy stories, not real life.

When she headed back to the table, she could see Marios looking towards her and smiling. It had been a very long time since anyone had looked at her that way and it made her feel nice. Special.

'I'm ready. Where first?'

'I thought we could have a few hours on the beach. It's just down the road a little and there's a little cove I think you might enjoy seeing.'

'Great! Lead the way.'

'I just need to pay and say goodbye to my friend. Be right back.'

Watching the exchange, Jenny saw Marios' friend refuse to take any money for the coffee and cake, and she heard Natalia's name used again, noting how Marios scowled. He really didn't look that happy.

As they walked down the road, she could tell Marios was in deep thought, and wondered if it had something to do with the ex-girlfriend. Perhaps he wasn't as over her as he'd thought?

'Here we are, it's just down this little boardwalk.'

'Oh, this is so sweet! I bet you can't get a spot in the height of summer.'

'Thankfully, today we have our pick.'

They found a spot and both got their towels out to sit on. She commented as she sat down, 'Are there many little towns and beaches around the island like this?'

'Yes and no. There are quite a few towns but a lot of them are twenty minutes or so from a beach. This is one of the most popular as it has everything so close together.'

'I see the appeal. Your friend was really nice and he seemed happy to see you.'

'It's always nice to see him. I wouldn't have the patience to do what he does day in and day out, chatting to every holiday maker.'

'But you must talk to the visitors on the boat trips. I can't imagine you ignoring them.'

'Yes, but that's different as we're sailing. They're taking in all the views and only occasionally asking about the islands in the distance, whereas he's dealing with constant questions about the menu and having to give directions to this or that. Did you want to walk down to the edge of the sea and put your feet in?'

'No, I learned my lesson the other day.' She laughed. 'Perhaps if we had come here on holiday in a few months' time it would be different, but saying that, if we'd come when the season had already started, you and I wouldn't have had days out like this as you would be busy working.'

'Yes, very true. Another few weeks and we'll start to climb the hill.'

She looked at him, a bit confused, and he explained, 'The way I look at it, once we get into May we're at the bottom of the hill, and week by week we climb it until we get to the top in August, and then we start to head back down, and around the second week in October we reach the bottom again and shut the boat up for the winter. People have asked me over the years if I get bored with it, doing the same thing year after year, and though perhaps I should be, I just never am. Ok, there are days in the summer where I think to myself that I don't want to work, but once the boat is full of happy people and we're heading to another island I find a kind of peace and wouldn't want to be anywhere else in the world. I'm very lucky.'

'Do you think it will be different this year as you haven't got Natalia to share the summer with?' she asked, dreading the answer.

There was silence, and Jenny quickly changed the subject.

'But the big change this summer will be with the hotel and the family. Your grandmother won't be here on the island, which is going to be odd for all of you. I also get the impression from my dad that your aunts aren't really seeing eye to eye on things when it comes to the hotel.'

'You know about that? Yeah, Voula has big plans to put in an infinity pool in a bid to attract rich, chic guests. I'm keeping out of it, but I know my mum and dad will be there for Helena one hundred percent.'

Marios reached for Jenny's hand and she felt a tingle race through her whole body. Looking at him she moved closer. She couldn't wait any longer, she just had to kiss him, and she knew she wouldn't be pulling away for some time.

For the next few hours there was no talk of families, jobs, the future, or the past, just kissing and discussing the beautiful island they were on and the places Marios wanted to show her over the next week.

But their peaceful interlude was interrupted by the beep of Marios' phone. As he reached for it his smile dropped and his whole body went tense, only relaxing after he checked the screen.

'Is everything ok?'

'Yes, it's my Aunt Voula. She wants to chat about the party later today.'

Jenny nodded but couldn't help wondering why Marios had been so nervous to see who was messaging him. Was he expecting it to be Natalia?

'Do you fancy something to eat? We could grab a pizza or pasta,' Marios suggested.

'Yes, that would be nice.'

'The main "nice restaurant" here in Keriaphos isn't open yet for the season, so we'll have to go back to the harbour, but we could have a walk around before we go and perhaps have a drink?'

Jenny nodded and they collected their things. Once back across the boardwalk and onto the road Marios led the way to a nearby café, saying he was surprised at how busy it was.

'I'm getting a little taste of the buzz this town has and it's lovely,' said Jenny, smiling as multiple people called out greetings to Marios. 'I could easily sit here and people watch all day, but I'm starting to get really hungry. Do you mind if we drink up and head off?'

'Of course! We missed out on lunch, didn't we, and it's been quite a few hours now since those cakes.'

They walked back to the bike and before Marios handed Jenny the crash helmet there was time for one more kiss. It felt like the perfect day and as Jenny got on the back of the bike she held Marios even closer around the waist as they roared out of the town.

It wasn't long until they were back in the harbour and Marios parked the bike in a side street. They walked down towards the sea wall, the pair of them laughing like two teenagers.

'Which way to food, left or right?'

'It's just along here on the left. It's the one with all the tables outside. Can you see it?'

Jenny nodded and just as they approached the restaurant they heard someone call out to Marios. He stopped dead in his tracks and turned around.

'Natalia? What are you doing here?'

'I hear there's a party happening soon, and as I was sort of family for a few years I thought I should be here. Aren't you pleased to see me?' she asked, casting a look over Jenny.

And just like that, the perfect day came to a screeching halt.

Chapter 28

As Jenny walked away she knew she had done the right thing by letting Marios and Natalia chat, even though she could tell by his face that Natalia was the last person he wanted to be left alone with. It appeared that this wasn't going to be a short stay for Natalia as she had three suitcases and a bag with her, suggesting she was back for good. But why? Especially when she'd said she was going to be working somewhere else this year. Though Jenny was disappointed she wouldn't be spending the evening with Marios, it wasn't as if they had a future together. It was just a holiday romance after all.

Jenny wondered what to do now and as she was absolutely starving – all that talk of pizza and pasta hadn't helped – she decided she would head along the quayside until she saw somewhere suitable open. Peering down a side street that looked promising, she was surprised to find her dad coming towards her. She waved like mad but he didn't see her until the last second, looking right through her as though he was miles away.

Paul was in a world of his own. His head was all over the place, and he hadn't felt this out of sorts since his wife had said she was leaving. What had he done today? Why had he gone on and on at Helena about what she could do to the hotel? He had seriously overstepped the mark by making her think everything would be so easy and straightforward. On a practical level, the hotel was an old building so no one could know what problems might crop up once the plumbing and electrical work started.

And for her to have asked him to stay and do the work himself? It was madness! He'd panicked and rushed off, but now he wondered why he hadn't answered her. There was no need for him to rush back to England as he had nothing to go back for, and he could easily do the needed work, so why couldn't he stay? The simple truth was that he wasn't sure he was ready for a relationship with Helena, and moving here felt tantamount to making an unbreakable vow. Because he would never do anything that might hurt Helena. She'd been through too much already.

'Oh, hello, darling,' he said, startled to find Jenny waving her hand in his face. 'I didn't see you there.'

'I know. I've been shouting and waving for half a block. Are you ok?'

'Yes, I've just come out for a walk with a view to getting something to eat. Where is Marios?' he asked, realising his daughter was alone.

'It's a bit of a long story. I'm famished so let's find somewhere to eat so I can tell you all about it.'

'Good idea.'

They were nearly at the end of the sea wall when they spotted an open restaurant. Jenny was so hungry she was past the point of caring what they served; she just wanted food of any type.

'This looks perfect. Did you want to sit inside or out?'

'It's warm enough to sit outside, if that's ok with you?' asked Paul.

A waiter greeted them and showed them to a table. Before he walked away to prepare their drinks, Jenny asked if they could have a tzatziki with lots of bread while they looked at the menu.

'All I've had since breakfast is some cake,' she explained to her dad when he looked at her quizzically.

The wine arrived and Jenny started to relax and put the day behind her as she recapped it for her dad.

'Oh dear. And you say it looks like she's here to stay?'

'I think so, and she will probably be at the party as she reckons she's part of the family.'

Paul chuckled. 'I doubt Nadia would agree, and Evangelina either, come to that. So, apart from the sudden end to your day out, did you have a nice time?'

'I did. We went to a sweet little town with a beach. I can't remember the name but it definitely started with a K.'

'That must be Keriaphos. I know it well.'

'Oh, here comes the tzatziki. Let's order while the waiter is here.'

'We'll both have the moussaka, please,' Paul said to the waiter.

'This bread is delicious. Now, how has your day been?'

'A little awkward I'm afraid. Helena and I were chatting about the hotel and how tired it looked, and she was saying it was such a big job and very expensive to refurbish it. I told her about a hotel concept I've seen in the UK that might work here and not be too expensive.'

'And what did she say to that?'

Paul smiled. 'She said why don't I stay and do the work for her. Of course, that's not going to happen. I have my new apartment and commitments back in the UK. I can't just come here and work.'

Jenny didn't really know what to say. She knew her dad would do a brilliant job of it, and that it would make him happy, but he seemed so hesitant. Why?

And then she remembered what Marios had said earlier.

'Well, you aren't the only one who has been offered a job on the island. Marios suggested I stay and work on his dad's boat for the summer, but that's not going to happen. How could I give up everything in England to do that?'

'But what would you have to give up? I actually think a break here and working in the sunshine would do you a world of good.'

She didn't have an answer to that but thankfully the waiter arrived at just that point with the moussaka and the conversation stopped. Part of her knew her dad was right, and there was nothing stopping her working on the boat.

Well, perhaps there was one thing – the return of Natalia.

They got stuck into their meal and the conversation was food focused for the next little while, both trying to talk about anything and everything other than their futures. Eventually they got onto the topic of the party.

'Do you think the party will be ok? I know Voula's return isn't what Helena wants, but Marios seems very relieved she will be back to take control of the planning.'

'I get that impression too. Reading between the lines though, I think Evangelina just wants to have her three children here all together, so if she gets that she'll be happy. It's what happens when she leaves that I worry about, but I suppose what will be, will be. I'm a bit surprised Filippos hasn't said anything, and I'm beginning to wonder if he's completely in the dark about Voula's plans.'

'If he did know he would have told Nadia, and she definitely would have something to say about it.'

'I like Nadia. I think she's the glue holding everything together. And you're right, I'm sure she wouldn't mince her words with Voula. She doesn't with Filippos!' Paul laughed.

Jenny was glad to see her dad laughing. He wasn't himself tonight, and she suspected it had something to do with his growing feelings for Helena. It hadn't been that long since her mum had nearly destroyed him. Was he ready and willing to give his heart to someone else? They'd always been open and honest with one another, especially since her mum had left, so she knew the time had come when she needed to say something.

'Dad, can I ask you something?'

'Always!'

'Are you regretting coming back here after all these years?'

'No, I don't think so, though the trip is turning out differently than I'd anticipated, and I never expected to be offered a chance to return and become a hotel employee again.'

'Does that mean you're considering it?'

'I don't know. I guess I wouldn't object to getting a paint brush out and helping Helena here and there. In fact, I think I would rather enjoy it.'

'Is it just the painting you would enjoy? Or is there something else? Like ... spending time with Helena?'

'I don't know, and that's the problem. Listen, would you mind if I went for a little walk? I feel dreadful leaving you to go back up to the hotel by yourself, but I really need to clear a lot of stuff out of this old mind.'

'Of course not. I'm quite tired and an early night will do me good.'

'Thank you. For everything. I really don't know where I would be or how I ever would have got through the last year without you.'

'I know.' She hugged him tightly. 'Now, go for your walk. I'm going to have a tea and then head up the hill.'

Paul stood up and squeezed Jenny's arm before saying good night and heading off. Once he was gone Jenny decided not to have that tea after all. She asked for the bill and headed back to the hotel.

She thought the job renovating the hotel could be just what her dad needed, and if he decided to stay she could come and visit him once she'd gotten her own life back on track.

When she reached the hotel she headed towards the bar to grab a bottle of water, but as she passed the door to the terrace she spotted Helena sat taking in the view.

'Hi, Helena.'

'Hello, Jenny. I'm sorry about how your day ended with Marios.'

'So, you know Natalia is back?'

'Yes, Marios called me. He wanted me to make sure you were ok.'

'I'm fine. I had dinner with my dad down in the harbour, which was really nice.'

'Has Paul gone to his room?'

'No, he decided to take a walk to clear his head before coming back up.'

'Oh dear, I expect that has something to do with me.'

'Only he could say,' Jenny offered, knowing it wasn't her place to say anything. Her dad would talk to Helena when he was ready.

'Would you like to sit and have a drink with me?'

'That would be nice. No nibbles though as I'm full to the brim with bread and moussaka.'

Helena smiled. 'It's my experience that nothing pairs better than wine and a chat.'

As Jenny settled into her seat Helena poured her a glass.

'Here you go. My nephew was so worried he had upset you.'

'We had a lovely day, and it would have been nice to finish it off with a meal, but I understand that he and Natalia have things to sort out.'

'My mum and Nadia are not happy she's back.'

'But you don't feel the same?'

'I don't really know. I just want him to be happy, and if that's with her, I'll be pleased for him. But that doesn't mean I like the way she treated him, or the way he acted when they were together, always at her beck and call.'

'From what I can see she's back to stay ... and also looking forward to the party.'

'Yes, now that could be a problem, but thankfully not one of mine.'

'Dad was telling me he's been trying to persuade you to refurbish the rooms. He said you asked him to help.'

'I did, but I scared him off, I think.'

'I wouldn't be so sure. You said I've brought the fun back into Marios' life, and I believe you've done the same for my dad.'

'I really loved his ideas and I know it would work brilliantly, but there's still the obstacle of my sister.'

'I haven't met her yet but somehow I don't think she stands a chance against you. Both Evangelina and Filippos will be very excited about you refurbishing everything and putting your stamp on the hotel, and Nadia is a force to be reckoned with. Helena, can I ask you something a bit personal?'

'You can, but I can't guarantee I'll answer.' Helena laughed lightly.

'Is it the refurbishment you really want? Or is it the prospect of my dad coming back here for good?'

'I think you already know the answer to that. If Paul was here by my side, I would be the happiest person on Vekianos.'

Chapter 29
Monday 16th April

Jenny hadn't seen her dad when he came back the night before, so was eager to get down to breakfast to check how he was feeling.

'Even after my walk last night I was still full when I got back to the room!' said Paul once they were both settled at the breakfast table on the terrace.

'I felt the same. I need to avoid letting myself get that hungry again!' Jenny laughed.

'What can I get you, Jenny?' asked Nadia, holding a tray of drinks. 'Please don't disappoint me and say you want nothing cooked as you're still full from last night like your dad.'

'Sorry, but I'd best stick to just pastries this morning.'

'Are you sure? What with Helena having left for Corfu early today I'm feeling at a loose end, just rattling around the kitchen with nothing to do, and you'll need fuel today as Voula returns tonight.' Nadia gave an exaggerated shudder. 'Prepare yourselves for the atmosphere to change. Helena will go very quiet, and Evangelina will be picking and choosing her words, but in a shock to no one, I will be myself, and if there's something I don't agree with I won't be afraid to speak up. I'll leave you both to get on with your breakfast for now but if you change your mind about something cooked just shout.'

'We will,' said Paul. 'By the way, do we know what time the visitor is arriving?'

'No, but there will be no mistaking when she gets here.'

With that Nadia headed back to the kitchen and

Jenny reached for the plate of pastries while her dad poured the coffee.

'I have to admit I'm a bit excited to finally be meeting Voula. I feel I already know her from all the things people have been saying. How are you feeling about seeing her again after the way she treated you?'

'Oh, I'll be just fine. I'm looking forward to seeing what you make of her though. You're very good with quickly sussing people out. Speaking of, did you see Helena when you got back last night? How did she seem?'

'Yes, we sat and had a drink and a chat. She seemed ok. I'm surprised she didn't say anything about going to Corfu today. Perhaps it was a spur of the moment thing? Or something to do with the party?'

'Maybe. I don't really know now what I should do today as I was hoping to spend it with Helena.'

'As my daughter's away, why not spend it with me and help take my mind off of this party?' said Evangelina, startling them both as they hadn't heard her emerge onto the terrace.

'Good morning!' said Paul, warmly. 'Take a seat and join us. I would love nothing more than to spend my day with you so thank you for the offer.'

'I'm warning you in advance that I *will* be grumpy.'

'No, you won't, because there's no reason to be. The party will be fun!'

'If you say so, Paul, but before that I need to sort my grandson out and tell him again how this Natalia girl is taking him for a fool.'

This was a subject Jenny didn't want to get involved in so she quickly drank her coffee and made an excuse to leave. 'I hope you both don't mind me heading out, but I thought I would take a walk or maybe catch a bus somewhere.'

'What you should be doing is going and knocking some sense into that grandson of mine.'

'I don't think he needs me interfering in his life. Who knows, perhaps this is the best thing that could happen, Natalia coming back. You never know, she might be a different person than the one that left. I'll see you both tonight and I'm looking forward to meeting Voula.'

Jenny waved goodbye then went up to her room to pick up her bag. She was excited at the prospect of a day out by herself, and not having to chat to anyone. True, everyone she'd met here had been so friendly, but today she needed some head space to think about her dad and Helena, and also to think through what it might be like living in her dad's apartment without him there. One thing was for sure, she would be able to thoroughly throw herself into a new career without having to worry about her dad.

As she wandered down the little streets, she noticed there seemed to be more people around than the day before, and businesses that had still been closed for the winter months when they first arrived were starting to open, ready for the impending summer season.

As she approached the sea wall she thought briefly about walking in the direction of Filippos' boat, but the last thing she needed was to bump into Marios, particularly if he was with Natalia. No, she would go in the other direction, and head away from the harbour. Her dad had said the coastal path was nice and there were places to stop, sit, and enjoy the view.

She popped into a nearby shop to get a big bottle of water and as she was exiting and cramming the bottle in her bag, she heard someone say her name. She looked behind her and spotted Filippos.

'Oh, hello, Filippos! How are you doing?'

'Fine, thank you. I'm just on my way to the boat. I expect you're avoiding being at the villa with Voula's impending return?'

'No, not at all. I'm actually looking forward to meeting her.'

'You won't be saying that this time tomorrow!' He laughed. 'I heard you ran into our other new arrival yesterday. I'm sure that was a treat for you.'

Jenny shrugged, trying to appear unbothered. 'Natalia seemed nice.'

'Don't let Nadia hear you say that. As far as I'm concerned, Marios has to be allowed to make his own mistakes. He'll pick himself up and move on when the time comes. In the meantime, he doesn't need his mum or my mum interfering in his romances. But talking of Marios, he told me he's trying to persuade you to stay on Vekianos so you can come and work on the boat with us.'

'Yes, but I'm sure he was only joking. I would be useless! I know nothing about boats.'

'You wouldn't need to. I sail the boat, Marios deals with ropes and sails and everything else, and you would have the glamorous job of handing out sick bags. Only joking. I'm sure you would be great at interacting with the customers.'

'Perhaps now Natalia is back she might be looking for a job.'

'Oh no, that's definitely not happening. I might not be willing to interfere in my son's love life, but that young lady isn't coming anywhere near my boat.'

'Why do you say that?'

'Because she's not reliable. I've lost count of how many jobs she's lost here on the island for poor time keeping. It's bad enough being late when you're working in a shop or a restaurant, but when you're working on a boat it's even worse. You have to be on time to catch the tides.'

'So swimming to catch up with the boat isn't an option? Gotcha. Sorry, I couldn't resist,' she teased.

'See? This is why you would be such a great fit. You have a wonderful sense of humour. I guess my son and I have this next week before you and your dad leave to persuade you to stay. Talking of your dad, he seems to really be enjoying his visit.'

'Yes, apparently it's just like the old days.'

'I don't know about that. I've gotten the impression it's different for him this time.'

'What do you mean?'

'Why not come to the boat with me and I'll explain over a coffee?'

Jenny agreed, and they arrived at the boat in no time at all.

Filippos jumped across from the jetty to the deck of the boat and then took Jenny's hand to help her balance as she made the leap. It was nice to be back on the gorgeous old boat. It had so much character and felt a lot bigger than the last time she'd visited, though she couldn't say why.

'You have a very special place to work every day,' she said as she looked around.

'I'm incredibly blessed.'

'And content, which few people truly are, which makes it extra special.'

Filippos' phone ringing interrupted them, and he looked at the screen and shouted, 'Yes! We're safe for another night.'

Jenny was confused and was relieved when Filippos explained what he meant.

'That was Nadia saying she's just had a call from Voula to say she's catching the last boat from Corfu. She'll be arriving quite late, so my mum isn't having the big family meal tonight.'

'You are wicked. I really can't imagine she's that bad, but you're starting to make me nervous about meeting her.'

'Sorry, I don't mean to. I'm sure you'll get on fine with her,' he said, reassuringly. 'Would you like a look around my kingdom?' She nodded. 'Great! Follow me.'

For the next twenty minutes Filippos gave Jenny a guided tour of the whole boat, even opening cupboards and pointing out where everything was kept. It almost felt like an induction to a new job, which made her smile.

'Time for a ship's coffee. You go pick a spot and I'll get it sorted.'

'Where do you normally sit?'

'Right at the back looking out to sea.'

'Ok then, that's where I'll be waiting for my coffee.'

As she walked the length of the boat, she thought about what it might feel like working here. It was a gorgeous, old-fashioned boat, and she knew working alongside Filippos would be a lovely experience. Every day would be different and probably rather exciting.

'Here we are,' said Filippos, handing her a mug. 'I never get bored looking out over the sea, though you'd think I would after all these years.'

'I get that. My dad has spent most of the time we've been here staring out in silence, and he says the same – that it's just magical. What did you mean earlier, when you said things were different now for my dad?'

'I need to start back at the beginning, when my dad first employed him. Anyone that Mum and Dad took on to work for them was treated as family, though it's no secret your dad was one of my mum's favourites. It wasn't just because he was a hard worker, or that he fit into the family seamlessly, it was because she – well, everyone, really – could see there was a special connection between him and Helena.'

'But she was with her boyfriend then.'

'Yes, and that was the problem. Nadia reckoned that if he wasn't careful he would lose Helena to your dad, and told Sotirios so, so for a while he started to treat her a lot better, which I think clouded the waters and made it hard for my sister to see or even acknowledge her bond with Paul. Sotirios was clever but he was ultimately a waste of space who used poor Helena, something that continued for years after your dad had left the island.'

'That's so sad. From what I can see she hasn't moved on from him as there isn't another man in her life.'

'That's what I would have said up until a week or so ago, but now your dad is back they're like two teenagers again, their connection just as strong as it always was, which is lovely to see. The big question is what happens next. He's talked a lot to me about how he has retired and doesn't know what he'll do next with his life, so I'm really hoping he'll consider staying here.'

'I would be happy for him to come and help Helena refurbish the hotel. It would be nice for them to have the time to explore whatever is developing between them and it would mean Helena wouldn't be pushed out by Voula... Oops, the look on your face says you don't know about that. I've really put my two big feet in it, haven't I? Well, now that I've mentioned that bit, I suppose I should tell you what I know. But please promise me you won't say anything until after the party.'

'You have completely lost me, Jenny. Of course, I guessed Helena would make changes when Mum goes over to Parga, as it's no secret that the bedrooms and bathrooms desperately need updating, but where does Voula come into all of this? I promise not to say anything, just please tell me what's going on.'

As Jenny explained Filippos stared at her in shock and dismay.

'How has all of this been going on without me knowing? And not just me but also Nadia? She doesn't usually miss a trick.'

'My dad and Helena only talked about a potential refurbishment a day or two ago, and I get the impression Voula was caught measuring for the swimming pool when she was last here. I'm so sorry to have spilled the beans like this.'

'Don't be sorry. I promise I won't say anything until after the party, I'm just grateful for your dad stepping in and persuading Helena to stay, especially if it means he might stay too. No one deserves happiness more than those two. But that does leave us with one big problem. Though saying that, I think there might be an easy solution.'

'What do you mean?'

'I'm talking about you.'

'How am I a problem?'

'Well, if your dad's working here in Greece while you head back to England, you'll soon be missing each other and that won't be good for either of you.'

'Yes, but I can visit.'

'That's definitely one option, but there's a better one – you come and work on the boat with Marios and me. That way, you and your dad can be in each other's lives every day of the week. Problem solved!'

Jenny laughed. Filippos certainly was persuasive!

Chapter 30

Helena couldn't really believe what she was doing. It wasn't like her to do anything in the spur of the moment, and even more than that, to do something without telling her mum. But she knew she had to. Since chatting to Paul her mind couldn't switch off, thoughts and possibilities swirling through her thoughts. She was excited about what she might be able to do with the hotel and she felt confident for the first time in years, which made her smile with happiness. She could almost hear her dad saying, 'Come on, Helena, you decide. There will be a time when your mum and I won't be around, and you'll have to decide on things for the hotel. You need to be confident enough to do it.' It looked as though today was going to be the day.

She stopped at a restaurant in the harbour in Corfu and made a plan to ensure this little trip was ruled by her head and not her heart. But maybe there was no avoiding her heart being involved. After all, she still wasn't entirely sure if she was doing this so that Paul would stay on Vekianos, or if she was doing it for the good of the hotel.

An hour later she had a bullet point list and was feeling calm and ready to do business. After a short taxi ride, she arrived at the offices of the biggest builder's merchants on the island. She took a deep breath as she stood outside the doors, and reminded herself what she was here to discuss: toilets, shower cubicles and wash hand basins. She could only hope that she found a salesperson that wouldn't treat her like a pushover and try to upsell her.

Walking in the huge doors she could see at once she had picked the right place as it wasn't one of those glamorous showrooms, where you're afraid to touch anything. Hopefully that was reflected in the prices. She made her way to the bathroom section and was almost immediately overwhelmed by choice. After getting her notebook and pen out she felt a lot calmer, and she reminded herself that her guiding principles today were practicality and price.

'Good morning, can I help you?'

Helena was relieved to find that the salesperson was a woman.

'Yes, please. What I'm looking for is... You see, I've come over from Vekianos and my plans... I'm so sorry, I'm getting myself a little muddled and tongue tied.'

'Why don't we take a seat, and you can talk me through what you're looking for? My name is Claudia, and this is my father's business. I know from experience it's a little daunting to be faced with so many choices. Whoever would have thought that there could be so many toilets to choose from?' Claudia laughed.

Already feeling more relaxed, Helena followed her over to a little table and they sat. Helena explained that this was a research trip, and she was only looking to price things up on this visit so that she could come up with a budget. She mentioned she would need ten of everything for the family hotel and Claudia told her there would be a considerable discount because of the quantity she was buying, which was welcome news.

'So, you're looking for items that are sleek, modern, and affordable, both easy to install and maintain,' summarised Claudia. 'I think we can definitely help you. We can also give you a good price on other things that go into a refurbishment, such as electricals and lighting.'

It was such a relief for Helena to know that so much could be organised through one company, and

Claudia's enthusiasm for the project added to Helena's excitement.

Before she knew it, the hours had flown by and they'd outlined and priced out a whole plan for the refurbishment.

'I really couldn't have achieved any of this without your help. It's so kind of you to take the time,' said Helena.

'I've enjoyed it thoroughly! And if you decide to go this way with your plans it will be a very good thing for my dad's company, so we'll both come out as winners.' Claudia smiled warmly. 'Now, are you sure we've covered everything?'

'I think so, but I have your phone number and email address if I have any more questions. Again, thank you so much.'

Looking at the time as she left the shop, Helena realised she wouldn't have enough time to get to the harbour for the next boat back to Vekianos, so she decided she would go and look around the shops. Perhaps she might even treat herself to a new dress to celebrate the successful day she'd had. Stood waiting for the taxi to arrive to take her into Corfu town, it hit her what had just happened. She had found her confidence and coming out of her meeting with Claudia she now really wanted this refurbishment to go ahead, so she could take the hotel forward, just like her dad had done all those years ago.

Chapter 31

Voula was one of the first off the plane, and as she only had hand luggage, she was able to head straight out of the airport. Checking the schedule online she saw she had the choice of three boats over to Vekianos, which would give her plenty of time to sort through her list before she arrived and was swept up in the whirlwind of her family.

As she waited in the taxi rank, her phone rang. She didn't recognise the number but something made her answer the call.

'Voula speaking.'

'Voula, it's Athena. Are you free to chat?'

Voula walked away from the taxi rank, finding a seat away from the crowd.

'Hi, Athena, yes, of course.'

'I know you're a busy woman so I will cut to the chase: my situation here is not improving. Dimitri and I are at an impasse and I need to replace him. Before I advertise for a new manager, I wanted to ask you one more time if you would consider taking the job. Do I hear a plane in the background? Oh no, have I caught you just as you're about to board a flight?'

'No, the opposite. I've just arrived in Corfu. I'm heading to see my family on Vekianos as my mum is retiring from the family business.'

Voula instantly regretted her admission. Why had she said that? Now Athena would start to put one and two together.

'Oh, I didn't realise you were from there. How lovely for you. Look, I will let you go but please do think about the offer; I just know we could work so well together. Goodbye for now and enjoy your time with your family.'

As Voula entered the building merchant's a while later, she was still thinking about the call. If it wasn't for her mum's retirement she might have taken Athena up on her offer, but the timing just wasn't right.

She headed to the enquiry desk where she was greeted warmly.

'Can I help you?' asked the receptionist.

'Yes, I need a salesperson who specialises in bathroom fittings.'

Within minutes a smart looking woman was heading towards Voula.

'Hi, I'm Claudia, how can I help you?'

'Do you know bathroom fittings?'

'I should do, my family owns this business.'

The look on Claudia's face told Voula she had come with the wrong attitude and started off on the wrong foot with this woman.

'Shall we head over to the bathroom section and then we can take it from there?' offered Claudia.

Voula nodded and smiled, trying to get things back to an even keel.

Once they were settled at a table, Voula explained what she was looking for.

'I will need ten of everything and the vision is high end luxury, so it has to make a statement and have the wow factor. It's for a hotel and my goal is for the guests to have their breath taken away when they walk into the bathroom.'

'Sounds very exciting! When it comes to the top of the range stock we usually need to order from the catalogues as so much of it is custom, but we might have a few samples in stock to give you an idea of what we could achieve. I could also show you some photos I have here on the iPad of other bathroom fittings we've supplied to businesses here on Corfu.

Is yours a new build or a refurbishment?'

'A refurbishment, but over on Vekianos.'

The woman suddenly seemed to go all strange.

'Is everything ok? You seem shocked I mentioned Vekianos but as you're the nearest supplier for the island surely you've had other business owners come visit you?'

'No, I'm not shocked, just a bit surprised by your request as it was only a couple of hours ago that I had someone else here from Vekianos doing the exact same thing – refurbishing a ten-room hotel on the island.'

'Did you get the name of the hotel? I'd like to know what my competition looks like.'

'Sorry but I'm not able to disclose those details. As a businesswoman yourself, I'm sure you can understand how important confidentiality is.'

'Yes, of course, but you were the one who started this by telling me about the other business,' said Voula, feeling a bit defensive.

'I'm very sorry. That was my mistake. Let's turn back to your requirements...'

The next two hours were spent going through all the company had to offer, Voula making a note of the prices and dimensions of everything. She also gave each bathroom suite example Claudia presented her with a score out of ten, which would help when making her final choice.

'Thank you, it's been a very interesting and informative afternoon and you've been a huge help. Although I'm not placing an order today, I can assure you that you will have my business when I'm ready to begin.'

'Wonderful! While you're here, can I also show you our vast selection of wall and floor tiles?'

'That's kind of you but all the tiles for my project have already been sourced and ordered from a merchant in Italy.'

'How lovely. I'm sure this project is going to look stunning when it's all finished.'

'I hope so. I'd best get going. Thank you again, goodbye.'

It was eight-thirty in the evening when Voula got off the boat in Vekianos harbour. Wheeling her case through the little streets she saw a man coming towards her and for a moment thought she recognised him from years ago. As he stood to one side to let her pass their eyes met and he stared at her strangely.

'Voula? It's you, isn't it? Everyone has been waiting for you to arrive.'

Voula could only stare at the man, confused by his familiarity.

'It's Paul,' he replied. 'I worked for your parents many years ago...'

Having seen so many temporary workers come and go from the hotel over the years she couldn't immediately place him.

'Perhaps this will help you to remember – I was the lad that you took out on a date to make an old boyfriend jealous...?'

She grimaced, the memories coming back to her all at once.

'Right! Paul! You were the one my mum and dad liked the most out of all the employees they had over the years. Welcome back! If it's not too late, I'd like to apologise for my dreadful, childish behaviour way back when.'

'Apology accepted. To be honest with you, I got over it many years ago. Now, let me help you with your case and get you up to the hotel.'

'But you were going in the opposite direction. Are you off somewhere? I don't want to hold you up.'

'It's not important. I was only going for a drink down in the harbour.'

'That's just what I need. If you don't mind me joining you, that is? I think a big drink will set me up to face the family.'

'You make it sound as if you don't want to.'

'No, sorry, of course I do. It's just always such a big deal when I come back, and I never quite know the reception I'll get.'

'I think you've got that all wrong. I know how much Evangelina is looking forward to you being here, and of course Marcos will be very grateful for your help with the party.'

'Yes, and my sister and brother will stop being their normal happy selves and go all quiet as the wicked sister has returned. But saying that, my sister-in-law will make up for it. She's never been one to mince her words.'

'Families!' Paul laughed. 'They're all the same in the end, the ups and downs keeping everyone on their toes. Now, how about that drink?'

'Excellent, but I'm buying as a thank you for forgiving me for my rudeness all those years ago.'

With that Paul's phone rang. 'Excuse me, Voula, it's Helena,' Paul said before answering. 'Hi, everything ok?'

'Yes, I was just wondering if you fancy a drink on the terrace? I have something to tell you about my trip to Corfu today.'

'That would be nice. I'm in the harbour at the moment having a drink with Voula, but I would think we'll both be back up at the hotel within the hour.'

'Actually, you know what? I hadn't realised the time,' Helena said in a rush, sounding off all of a sudden. 'Perhaps we should leave it until tomorrow. Yes, I think I'll have an early night instead. Enjoy your drink with Voula. Good night.'

Paul sighed. Helena was upset. Again. Why couldn't he get things right with her?

Chapter 32
Tuesday 17th April

Jenny was a little nervous as she was getting ready to go down to breakfast. Today was the day she would be meeting Voula, the woman that she had heard so much about over the last few days. She was also still thinking about the job offer from Filippos. It was so tempting to spend a summer sailing around these beautiful waters and enjoying life here on this island without a care in the world, but what about Natalia? For a start, how would she react to Jenny working with Marios? And thinking of Marios, would she be able to work with him given how close they'd gotten before Natalia returned? There was so much to consider, but it would have to wait as it was time to head downstairs for breakfast.

As she walked out onto the terrace she found the breakfast table was laid but she was the first one to arrive. As she sat down Nadia appeared with a coffee pot in her hand.

'Good morning, Jenny, how are you today? Filippos said you stopped by the boat yesterday and I probably need to apologise for what he said.'

'I'm not sure what you mean.'

'The conversation you had.'

Oh no, had Filippos mentioned Voula's plans to come back and run the hotel?

'Please don't worry about turning down the job on the boat. I told him it was a lot to expect you to give up an exciting life in England to sail around the islands here, handing out bottles of water to holiday visitors.'

'To be honest, Nadia, I don't have an exciting life back at home and handing out bottles of water is actually very tempting given how gorgeous the working environment would be. But I don't think Natalia would be impressed with me working with Marios.'

'The girl is the bane of my life. I want to just jump in and tell her what I think of her, but of course I won't as that would upset Marios. I just wish he could see through her the way I can. All I can do is hope that one day he wakes up to the fact she uses him. Enough of all that though. Can I make you anything this morning?'

'Could we wait until my dad comes down?'

'Of course!'

'Thanks. By the way, no Helena today?'

'No, she messaged me last night to say she would be off out early today.' Nadia moved closer to Jenny and whispered, 'I think it's probably because Voula is back. Now, I need to get back to the kitchen as I have things in the oven.'

Jenny picked up her mug of coffee and walked down to the edge of the garden and looked out to sea. There were one or two boats on the horizon and the sun was shining on them. This really was paradise. And it could be her home for the summer if she accepted the job offer from Filippos. She turned back and looked up at the hotel. The view from here was so different from looking up from the harbour. The paint was flaky and the building really wasn't looking at its best.

As she walked back to the breakfast table, she spotted Evangelina walking out of the hotel onto the terrace.

'Good morning, Evangelina, it's another gorgeous day here in paradise!'

'Summer is creeping up on us and it's bringing the most beautiful weather. I saw you were taking a look at the old building. It's in desperate need of a coat of paint, isn't it, and the bedrooms need updating as well.'

'Perhaps Helena will get it sorted when she takes over. It will give her the chance to stamp her own identity onto the hotel.'

'Yes, or Voula.'

'With all Voula's knowledge on hotels she could certainly help her sister. Wouldn't that be lovely, the two of them working together?'

'Somehow I doubt that's going to happen. Helena will likely leave if Voula takes control.'

'You think Voula's coming back for good?' asked Jenny, surprised – but also not surprised – at how in tune Evangelina was with this hotel and her family.

'She hasn't said as much to me but I'm capable of putting two and two together. The minute I decided to move over to Parga I knew Voula would jump at the chance of running this place. Strangely, no one else seems to have realised... But you're being oddly quiet. Can I assume you know something?'

'I don't know that it's any of my business to say anything.'

'But it might be your business if my daughter and your father get together and he ends up staying here and helping her run the hotel. Would you have a problem with that?'

Jenny shook her head. 'I just want my dad to be happy, and if that's here with Helena then I'll be very happy for them both.'

'And so will I. Helena needs something more in her life than this business and it would make me very happy to see them together.'

'But what happens if...'

'If Voula takes over the hotel instead? Between you and I, that's not going to happen, though I do worry that a lot of harsh words will be spoken and a lot of upset caused before we get to that point, which is unfortunate. But I can't worry about that right now because we have the party to focus on.'

'At least that's guaranteed to be fun.'

'Fun isn't the word I would choose to use, but I will go along with it. Oh, here come Voula now.'

'Good morning, Mum. Ah, you must be Jenny! It's nice to meet you. Your dad has told me so much about you already. How are you liking our lovely island?'

'It's amazing. I can see why my dad loves it so much.'

Nadia and Paul appeared just then, bringing a certain tension into the air.

'How are we all today?' asked Paul.

Evangelina was the first to answer. 'For the time being, we are all well, I think.'

'Now that everyone is here, what can I cook for you?' asked Nadia.

'It has to be an omelette for me,' replied Paul.

'Yes, the same for me,' said Jenny.

'And you, Voula?' asked Nadia, her tone noticeably colder.

'My usual, please.'

'Three omelettes it is then. I won't be long.'

'No Helena this morning, Mum?' asked Voula.

'She was up and out early today, just like yesterday when she went over to Corfu. I think she's visiting her friends over in Keriaphos today.'

Jenny noticed an odd look crossed Voula's face, as if she was thinking something through, but before she could question it, Evangelina spoke.

'So, what plans do you all have for today?'

'I thought Dad and I could have a day out somewhere.'

'That would be lovely, darling.'

'I'm having a party meeting with Marios,' added Voula.

'By the way, Voula, Marios' ... *friend* is back on the island, so you will need to add Natalia to the guest list.'

'I thought they were over,' said Voula, her confusion evident.

'So did we, but as per usual that young lady clicks her fingers and Marios jumps to attention. We will see how long she stays though. She'll need to find a job and as we all know that not many businesses want to employ her.'

Nadia returned a little later with the food and as she put it down Voula said, 'Mum tells me Natalia is back.'

'Yes, and I'm not saying a word about it. I've said enough about her over the years. Can I get anyone more coffee?' asked Nadia, changing the subject entirely.

'I have things to be getting on with for now but shall we catch up over lunch later, Voula?'

'Sorry, Mum, but I need to pop over and see someone in Keriaphos.'

'What is it with that town today? Both my daughters visiting it... Perhaps you will bump into each other and have lunch together. That would be nice for both of you.'

Voula didn't answer, only smiled, and Jenny realised that if Marios was coming to the hotel for a planning meeting with his aunt, he might bring Natalia with him. If so, she wanted to be out of the way. Quickly eating her food, she planned to make an excuse to go to her room, but it was too late. As she finished the last few bites, she heard Marios pull up outside on his bike.

'Have a lovely day, all of you, and remember that we're having a family dinner here tonight,' Evangelina called over her shoulder as she headed inside.

Before too long Nadia was back with Marios in tow and Jenny could tell he was nervous. Was that because he was having a meeting with Voula? Or was it because he didn't know what sort of welcome he would get from Jenny? She decided to be the one to break the ice because at the end of the day she was only here on holiday and theirs had been an innocent hook-up, just some kisses and cuddles, whereas what he'd had with Natalia was obviously special even though his mum or grandmother didn't necessarily think so.

She excused herself to get ready to head out and quietly asked Marios to meet her out front of the hotel in a few minutes.

'How are the party plans coming?' she asked when he joined her.

'They're ok. We were meant to chat about them today but Voula is in a hurry to go somewhere so we're meeting up tomorrow instead.'

Jenny nodded, not sure how to broach the topic of Natalia.

'My dad told me he offered you the job on the boat. Is it something you might consider now that your dad and Helena are getting closer?'

'It's very tempting to spend a summer sailing around this beautiful island, and working alongside you and your dad would be fun, but...'

'But?'

'Don't you think Natalia would mind us working together?'

Marios barked a laugh. 'Oh, she wouldn't be happy about it *at all.*'

'So that's my answer then. I won't be working here on Vekianos this summer. My dad's going to be ready any minute, so I'd better go.'

And she turned and walked back into the hotel, leaving Marios a bit stunned and wondering what had just happened.

Chapter 33

Helena was feeling very happy with herself. Her meeting with her friend, Dimos, who was a plumber, had gone well, and she decided to celebrate with a late lunch here in Keriaphos before heading back to the hotel. It would give her time to look at her notes while they were fresh in her mind.

She found a restaurant and ordered a club sandwich and a glass of wine. She was feeling so much more positive than she had earlier this morning, and she couldn't believe her luck that Dimos had availability this summer and could focus on modernising the hotel's bathrooms.

Turning over the pages in her notebook she kept coming back to the one she had headed 'Mum and Dad's Apartment'. She already knew she wasn't going to move into it as she would likely miss her little bungalow too much, so it made sense to divide it up into more hotel rooms. There were a few problems, of course – none of the windows had a sea view, plus it would cost a lot of money to divide it up into bedrooms and add all the necessary plumbing – but it would be such a waste leaving it empty when it could be earning her more income.

The waiter brought the club sandwich and the wine, and she put the notebook back in her bag. As she looked up, she was surprised to see Voula walking down the road. What was she doing here?

And then the penny dropped. Helena had thought Dimos was acting a little strange when she first mentioned her plans, and he'd asked more than once if the bathroom refurbishment project had been talked about as a family. Apparently, she hadn't been the only sister to get in touch with him. Needing to know what was going on she waved her sister over.

'Join me?' asked Helena.

'Gladly. It looks like I'm one step behind you again, just like yesterday,' said Voula, sounding a bit sarcastic.

'I'm not sure what you mean.'

'I take it you've already been to see Dimos? I know you were at the builder's showroom in Corfu yesterday as well. It looks like we have a problem, don't you think?'

'No, no problem that I can see. I'm refurbishing the hotel and putting my own stamp on it.'

'But we've already talked about my plans to make it a luxury retreat,' said Voula, annoyed.

'*You* talked about it. I didn't agree to anything.'

'This is silly. There's no point in us falling out over something we can work on together. C'mon, it can be our joint project. Can't you just picture it? The hotel will look stunning and we can charge a lot more money for the rooms, and you wouldn't have to work all those long hours as there would be two of us to share the burden.'

'I'm sorry, Voula, but I've decided to continue on just as our parents have for all these years. The hotel will still offer the same warm and welcoming experience, but with new, modern touches in the rooms.'

'How are you going to fund a renovation?'

'I'm not, the business will be paying for it.'

Voula was just about to say something but Helena could see she was having second thoughts, and in the end, she stood and walked away in silence. Helena carried on eating but knew that even though she might have won this battle with her sister, it didn't mean the war was over. No, Voula would only come back stronger.

Back at the hotel Helena ran into Paul.

'Have you a minute to spare?' asked Paul.

Helena nodded, but was unsure what he might say ... or how she'd feel about it.

'I won't keep you long, it's just that ... I'm not sure if I might have upset you... What I'm trying to say is that yesterday, on the phone, you didn't sound very happy...'

'The truth is that I wasn't. You were obviously in the middle of something with Voula, so I thought it best if I got out of the way. Now, if you will excuse me.'

As she pushed past him and walked away, she felt horrible. She shouldn't be talking to Paul like that, but it was the truth. She *had* been upset.

Evangelina was in her happy place – her kitchen – and doing what she loved best – cooking for her family. Nothing in life was better than that.

'What can I do to help,' asked Filippos. 'I know you won't let me near the food but there must be something I can contribute.'

'You're right, why don't you handle the drinks? And Nadia can sort the table settings as she does it far better than anyone else.' Evangelina smiled across the kitchen at her beloved daughter-in-law.

'Thank you, Evangelina. Filippos, remember that when your mum says "drinks", she means for everyone, not just yourself.'

'Ok, I did know *that*,' said Filippos, pulling his wife in close and tickling her.

Evangelina laughed. 'Nothing gets past you, Nadia, and oh how you do make me laugh. My poor son doesn't stand a chance against the two of us, does he?'

With that Filippos took the hump and left the kitchen and they both had a giggle.

'Are you looking forward to the family dinner tonight?' asked Nadia. 'It will be different with Voula being here, and I suspect you won't get two words out of Helena.'

'I know, and it doesn't help that she's in a strange mood already. I was stood in the back courtyard earlier and I saw her have a confrontation with Paul. I couldn't hear what they were saying but that happy, flirty vibe they've had was gone, and it almost looked like they had fallen out.'

'Oh dear. Hopefully Filippos and Paul will entertain us. They can usually be counted on because the more they drink the funnier they get. I'm going to get started on laying the table. There's eight of us, right? A nice even number.'

'Actually, it's nine. Marios has asked me if he can bring Natalia with him, but I did get the impression he would have liked it if I said no.'

'Looks like we're in for a fun night!' said Nadia, sarcastically. 'Perhaps instead of getting Filippos and Paul drunk we should just get drunk ourselves! At least then we won't know half of what's happening.'

Filippos came back in just then, asking, 'What's so funny? I can hear you both laughing from outside.'

'Help me carry everything out to the table,' said Nadia. 'There's something I need to ask you.'

Filippos grabbed the plates and cutlery while Nadia handled the glasses.

'So, what do you need from me?' he asked once they were alone.

'Do you know something that I should have known about?'

'I don't know what you mean,' he said, nervously.

'Do you or do you not have a secret you're keeping from me?' She paused and stared at him shrewdly. 'Yes, you have, I can tell by your face.'

'Ok, I do, but I was sworn to secrecy until after the big party. I promise I was going to tell you then.'

'Now you are the one talking in riddles. I meant Marios bringing Natalia tonight, but forget that for now. Spill the beans, mister. What were you going to wait until after the party to tell me?'

'Oh, this is a mess.' Filippos ran a hand over his face, looking pained. 'If I tell you, you have to promise me you won't say anything until after Mum's moved over to Parga.'

'No promises. Now, I'm waiting.'

'Voula wants to come back to Vekianos and run the hotel.' He said it on a single breath, then braced for the impact of his words.

Before Nadia could respond though, Helena appeared on the terrace and asked, 'Is there anything I can do to help?'

'No, we're ok, thanks. But perhaps your mum could do with a hand in the kitchen.'

'Ok, the table looks really nice tonight.' Helena smiled and waved goodbye, heading towards the kitchen.

'Now, husband of mine, explain *everything* to me. Have you talked to Voula about this?'

'No, but from what I can gather she wants to modernise the hotel, and you have to agree it desperately needs it.'

'But where does that leave Helena? And me as well? Voula is the last person I want to take orders from. Perhaps I should come and work on the boat with you and Marios. Don't look so worried, Filippos,' she added, 'I'm not serious. Could you even imagine?' She laughed.

'Nadia, please promise me you won't say anything until after the party. I know you wouldn't want Mum upset.'

'I promise. Now let's get everything sorted for tonight.'

As Helena walked into the kitchen, her only thought

was that she just wanted the evening to be over with already.

'Hi, Mum, can I help with anything?'

'Yes, you can. I need the salad put into a bowl ... no, I think two bowls, one for each end of the table.'

'No problem.'

As Helena set to work her mum asked bluntly, 'Have you and Paul had a falling out?'

'No, of course not! What makes you think that?' she asked, flustered.

'Nothing really, I just get the impression that something has changed between you two. Does it have something to do with your sister coming back? I know she had a drink with Paul in the town last night, but surely that hasn't upset you. After all, you more than anyone know how keen he is on you, and always has been.'

Helena realised she had been a bit stupid to get so upset with Paul. She needed to make it right, but how?

Out on the terrace Jenny and Paul were chatting to Filippos as he was pouring them a drink.

'You look lovely, Jenny,' said Nadia as she hurried past carrying a tray of food. 'That's such a gorgeous dress and with your tan you are really glowing.'

'Thank you, I really like this dress. I was going to save it for the party, but I just felt tonight was the time to wear it. Is Marios going to join us?'

'Yes, and unfortunately he won't be alone. He asked if he could bring Natalia.' Nadia rolled her eyes.

'I'm sure it will be fine.'

'Fine is not the word I would use, but I will – with great difficulty – keep my mouth shut.' She paused and turned towards the door before turning back to Jenny. 'I can hear another voice coming that

I'll need to avoid giving a piece of my mind to.'

Jenny looked up and saw Voula walking out onto the terrace with Evangelina. She looked lovely in a casual summer dress.

'I hope my son is looking after you with drinks,' said Evangelina. 'The food is almost ready so we'll just wait for Marios and Natalia to arrive and then we can sit at the table.'

'Are you ok, Dad?' whispered Jenny.

'Yes, thank you, darling. Are *you* ok? I didn't realise Marios was bringing his friend.'

'I think you mean "girlfriend", and yes, I promise I'm completely ok with it. There's nothing for you to worry about. My and Marios' friendship was just a bit of holiday fun.'

Marios and Natalia arrived just then, and she headed right over to Evangelina. Jenny could hear her say how lovely it was to be back on the island and express her excitement about the party, and though Evangelina was very polite, she quickly made an excuse to go to the kitchen. Within minutes she was back with Helena, both carrying the food, and Nadia organised everyone to sit down, making sure Natalia was sat between Marios and Filippos. Helena was next to Paul and Jenny heard her whisper, 'I'm sorry for how I acted earlier today. I was out of order. I think it's all the business with the hotel that has me on edge.'

Everyone was soon settled and for a few minutes there was a contented silence as they all started to eat. Jenny kept her eyes on Evangelina as she knew she would be in control of the evening. She also noticed how her dad and Helena kept turning towards each other and smiling. Marios had his head down and was eating without making eye contact with anyone.

The first to speak was Nadia. 'Voula, I haven't asked how everything on Rhodes is going. Have you got a new job yet?'

Jenny immediately suspected what Nadia was getting at and it was clear by her answer that Voula did as well.

'Thank you for your interest, Nadia, but no, nothing yet, as I'm still considering quite a few options. Now, talking of jobs, I had heard you weren't coming back to the island this year, Natalia, as you got a job elsewhere, so are you just visiting?'

'I had a few opportunities on another island but ultimately they weren't really for me, and of course Marios has been begging me to come back here.'

'So you have a job lined up here on Vekianos?' asked Nadia, sounding sceptical.

'Yes, I'm going to help someone run their business, making it a lot slicker and more productive. It's a bit drab and it needs someone like me, with fresh eyes and great style, to move it forward. I'm excited and I'm sure once I tell them my vision, they will be over the moon. Perhaps, as the business owner is here at the table, now is the time to share the big news.'

'I hope you don't mean the hotel, Natalia. I could possibly offer you a few days cleaning, but that's all,' said Helena.

'Oh, no, it's not the hotel, and I certainly won't be cleaning anything any time soon. No, I'm going to help make the boat more successful! Filippos has a job going and I'm the perfect person to sail the business into the future.' She smiled smugly.

Jenny could see by the look on everyone's faces that they were too shocked to respond. What a madam! Who did she think she was?

Before she could stop herself, Jenny found herself saying, 'I'm sorry to disappoint you, Natalia, but there aren't any open jobs on Filippos' *very successful* boat as I'm working the season with Marios and his dad. And you know what? Something tells me the three of us will get on just fine without any improvements whatsoever. Now, this is such a tasty meal you've prepared, Evangelina, could I possibly have another serving?' She held out her plate and smiled brightly at her host, whose own smile was growing by the second.

Natalia was immediately on her feet and walking inside, Marios following her like a puppy. The looks on everyone else's faces were a picture, and Jenny wondered what she'd just done.

The simple answer was that she had got herself a job here on Vekianos for the summer. A job she'd had no intention of taking twelve hours earlier.

Chapter 34

It was three hours later, and what she had said was still just sinking in. Jenny couldn't believe the words had come out of her mouth, and for her to have said it without giving it any thought...! And as for the aftermath, Natalia storming out with Marios chasing after and then Filippos pouring more wine to celebrate his new employee as well as trying to calm Nadia, the latter blustering about Natalia's reaction with lots of muttering of 'who does that girl think she is'. The best reaction had come from Jenny's dad, his face lighting up at the prospect of her staying here with him on the island. Of course, not everything was cut and dried. There was still the not-so-little matter of Voula and her grand plans to sort.

As Filippos topped up the glasses one last time, Jenny picked hers up and walked across the grass to the fence. Looking down into the harbour it sank in that it would be her new workplace. Had she done the right thing accepting the job? She really wasn't sure, but how could a summer working here on Vekianos not be enjoyable? As she walked to the little bench at the end of the garden, she could sense someone following behind her.

'Are you ok, Jenny? Not regretting your decision, I hope,' said Evangelina.

'Oh, no, I'm excited. Who wouldn't want to spend a summer of their life on a beautiful boat in the glorious Greek sunshine, and with two fabulous chaps as co-workers?'

'You know, my late husband was so disappointed that Filippos didn't want to get involved with the hotel, and it was several years before he accepted that his son had done the right thing striking out on his own. In the end, it brought him so much joy to see his son not just successful and happy, but also so content going out in that boat seven days a week from April to October. It's not like a job to him, he truly loves it. And now, to see Marios enjoying it as well... Well, it's very rewarding and makes me happy.'

'I'm so sorry again for causing a scene at dinner. I didn't plan to say it, it just sort of came out.'

'I have to admit I found it very funny, and I think you've done us all a huge favour because if you hadn't stepped in, Nadia would have ... well, I'm not sure what she would have done, so it's probably best we didn't find out! She's so happy you've taken the job, though not as happy as someone else. Your dad's whole face lit up just at the idea of it. I hope that means he'll be staying as well.'

'I do, too. He and Helena seem so well matched.'

'I know what you mean, and I can see them working well together and having a fun time.'

'But then there's the problem of Voula and her plans. Do you think it's what she really wants, or it's just the best option as she doesn't currently have a job?'

'I suspect it's a combination of things, but ultimately she has as much right to be running the hotel as Helena. I love them equally so I'm not getting involved. They need to sort it between themselves. Now, my dear, it's time for this old woman to go off to her bed, and between you and me, I would love to wake up to find that the party is already over.'

'You don't mean that really.'

'We'll see. Good night, and thank you for being a part of this family.'

'The business family, you mean?'

'We'll see,' said Evangelina, a mysterious glint in her eyes.

As she walked away Jenny turned back to the view. What an evening it had been. Everyone had thought it was the party that was going to be dramatic, only to have this quiet family dinner erupt in drama!

'I think I'll say good night,' said Nadia, walking over to join Jenny. 'I need to take Filippos home before he opens another bottle or two of wine. Thank you again for taking up his offer. I know you're in for a lovely summer.'

'I'm looking forward to it. Nadia?' Jenny added just as the woman turned to walk away. 'Do you think Natalia will leave the island?'

'I think she'll go wherever she can find someone to support her. If it's my son, she'll stay, but if a better offer comes along, she will be gone. I'll see you tomorrow.'

Jenny spotted her dad helping Helena take everything back to the kitchen and though she felt the urge to offer her help, she also didn't want to interrupt. They looked so sweet together, giggling away.

Voula had just come back from her room with a shawl around her shoulders and after pouring herself a glass of wine she walked towards Jenny.

'Would you like some company?'

'Yes, please, take a seat. This view never gets boring.'

'I know what you mean. I can appreciate it now but when I was a teenager living here I definitely didn't. I felt so trapped. The island being as small as it is, everyone knew everything about each other, which I hated. I could also never understand how everyone else seemed fine with it, the friends I grew up with were so happy to stay here, never feeling the same ambition to leave that I did. But do you know what? Now I'm in my fifties I envy them. Look at my brother, for instance. He's so content. He wants nothing more out of life than what he's got. How great is that?'

'Is that why you want to come back and take over the hotel? Are you seeking a sense of calm, Voula?'

'No, I just feel it's time for the business to move forward, and with my mum leaving it's the perfect opportunity. I still need to persuade my sister it's the right thing to do, but I really believe we can work well as a team. She now has your dad back in her life, and if we do it my way, she would have more time to spend with him.'

'People don't like change, do they? I say that from experience because if it wasn't for the company I worked for moving locations, I would never have left. Ultimately, it might have been the best thing that happened to me. I was so set in my ways, working more hours each week than what I was being paid to do, which impacted my quality of life. I'm looking forward to a relaxed summer on the boat and having the time to reset. How about you? Have the recent changes in your job been the kick start you needed?'

'They have. It's very daunting starting again at my time of life, but I do believe everything happens for a reason.'

'I completely agree. Timing is so important as well, isn't it? If this holiday offer had come two years ago, my dad and I would never have been able to come because my mum wouldn't have let my dad accept it and I never would have been able to bring myself to take the time off work. There's something I want to ask you, Voula, but I don't know if it's my place so please don't feel you need to answer, but ... what will happen if you don't get your way with the hotel?'

'I don't mind sharing that I think it will all come down to money. I know my mum says she won't get involved, but she's counting on her share of the hotel's profits to cover her expenses and ultimately my idea will bring in a lot more income than Helena's. When everything is on paper in black and white the evidence in my favour will be clear, but before it comes to that, I'm hoping to convince my sister to come onboard with my vision so that we can work together, rather than against one another.'

Chapter 35
Wednesday 18th April

Helena was the first one up the next morning and was focused on preparing breakfast when her mum walked into the kitchen.

'Any word from that grandson of mine?' asked Evangelina.

'Yes, he texted me last night to say he was sorry for Natalia's behaviour.'

'It shouldn't be him apologising, it should be her!' Evangelina shook her head as she poured herself a glass of water and added a slice of lemon. 'What are you up to today? I'll be doing my best to keep out of the way as Voula and Marios will be making the final arrangement for tomorrow's party.'

'I was thinking the same so Paul and I are going out for the day. Just think, Mum, in two days' time it will all be over.'

'Hooray! Only joking,' she rushed to add. 'I know you've all gone to a lot of trouble on my behalf, and I appreciate it.' Evangelina pulled Helena into a quick hug and then patted her cheek.

'I've been putting off asking but ... have you decided on your moving date yet?'

'Yes, I think I'll go the week before the hotel reopens for the season. You know as well as I do that if I'm here when the first guest arrives, I'll just end up staying.'

'And that wouldn't be a problem at all. This isn't just your business, it's your home and the island you love. If you want to stay, but need space from the hotel, we could find you a house here. We have savings that will cover it, Mum.'

'No, that money is there to refurbish the hotel

and bring it up to date, just like your father did in the seventies after he took over from his father.'

'Please tell me that's not the reason you're moving? Mum, that money is *yours*, not mine.'

'No, it's for you. Now, I don't want to talk about this again. I'm moving to Parga and that's it.'

As Evangelina picked up the coffee pot and went through to the terrace, Helena's head felt as though it was about to explode. Something had to be done. There was no way she was going to let her mum move away and be unhappy because of some misguided notion that she needed to give her savings away.

'Everything ok?' asked Voula, taking in the faraway expression on Helena's face as she stepped into the kitchen.

'Yes, everything is fine,' she said, brusquely.

Taking the pastries out onto the terrace she found Paul chatting to Evangelina.

'Would it be possible if we postpone heading out for a couple of hours?' Helena asked Paul. 'Marios has asked if I'm free for a chat down in the harbour.'

'Of course! We have all day so please don't rush on my account.'

Once back in her bungalow she called Nadia. 'We have a problem. Are you both at home?'

'Yes, your brother has a bad head so I can't see him going anywhere today.'

'Good, I'm on the way.'

Helena quickly changed her clothes, picked up her phone and bag, and she was off down the hill in no time.

The front door of Filippos and Nadia's house was unlocked, and Helena walked right in, finding her brother looking a bit worse for wear, a familiar sight from when he was younger.

She wasted no time at all, blurting, 'Mum doesn't actually want to move to Parga and she's only doing it because she thinks her life savings need to be spent refurbishing the hotel.'

Nadia spoke first. 'Take a breath, Helena, and let's talk it through. Do you want to take a seat?'

As Helena nodded and sank onto the sofa, Filippos asked, 'What makes you think that?'

'I don't just think it, she told me! What are we going to do? How can we persuade her to stay? Nadia, you don't usually miss anything. Had you not realised she had ulterior motives?'

'I knew something was off, but I thought it was just nerves about going somewhere new. To be honest, I thought she would go, experience it, and then come to the realisation on her own that she should come back. I didn't think she would stay there forever.'

'We need a solution because I will do anything to keep her here on the island with us.'

'There *is* a solution that would benefit Evangelina, but it wouldn't make any of us happy,' said Nadia, hesitantly. 'We could let Voula do what she wants to the hotel.' When Filippos and Helena looked at her in stunned silence, she rushed to continue. 'Look, we all know that Voula's best placed to fund the project independently, and that way the business' savings would be free to buy Evangelina her new home.'

There was silence as they all thought through the implications of this plan. Helena's first reaction was disappointment, because letting Voula take over the hotel would mean that all her own dreams and plans would be shattered, but ultimately this wasn't about Helena, this was about her mum's happiness in her retirement. And that was so much more important.

'You're right, Nadia,' agreed Helena. 'It's not what any of us want but I appreciate you playing devil's advocate and encouraging us to look at this from all directions.'

As Helena got up out of the chair Nadia reached out to place a hand on her arm. 'But if you aren't going to be modernising the hotel, where does that leave your and Paul's relationship?'

'I don't know,' said Helena, sadly. 'I expect he'll go back to England.'

'There's also Jenny to consider. She agreed to work on Filippos' boat largely because her dad would be here. Perhaps she'll go as well.'

'I think I'm the one who needs to leave Vekianos. Everyone seems to be having a new start, so perhaps it's my turn to make one as well,' said Helena.

Chapter 36

'How's your head feeling?' Jenny whispered to her dad as he joined her on the terrace for breakfast.

'Sore.' Paul grimaced. 'I'm hoping a good breakfast will help me shake it as Helena and I are going out for the day, and I want to be able to enjoy every minute.'

Paul smiled and his grin grew as his phone rang. Jenny assumed it must be a call from Helena.

As he hung up a moment later, however, the grin was gone.

'Is everything ok?' asked Jenny.

'No. That was Helena cancelling our date.'

'Did she say why?'

'Just that there was some kind of "family situation". But Evangelina and Voula don't seem affected by it,' Paul whispered to his daughter, looking across the terrace to the two women who were talking quietly.

'I'm sorry you won't have the day you expected, but what if we hung out instead? We could catch the bus to Keriaphos and enjoy the shops and beach.'

'That sounds really nice,' said Paul, trying to smile for Jenny as they tucked into the pastries.

As Voula said goodbye to everyone as they headed out for the day, she poured herself a coffee and took it down to the edge of the garden to look out to sea. She had been surprised to hear that Helena had called off her date with Paul, and wondered if it had something to do with Marios and Natalia. Perhaps when Marios arrived to go over the party details he might enlighten her.

As she walked back inside and set up in the

kitchen for the party planning meeting, she heard Marios' bike pull up outside. He came in like a whirlwind, asking after his grandmother and Helena.

'Your aunt had to pop out and see someone. I thought it might have been you.'

'No, not me,' he said, shaking his head.

Now Voula knew something was definitely off. There wasn't anything she could do about it now, however, so she and Marios headed out onto the terrace for their meeting.

As they settled at one of the tables Voula had to smile at the obvious reminder of how different generations worked. Her nephew hadn't brought anything other than his phone, whereas she had a whole file of paperwork.

She was pleasantly surprised, however, to find that he was much more organised than she'd initially given him credit for. The caterers were booked, he'd arranged to borrow tables and chairs from the local hall that was used for council meetings, and he'd even found a band to provide music and entertainment. The only things left on the to-do list were cleaning and tidying.

'I'm impressed, Marios. You've done a phenomenal job with the planning.'

'Thanks, but to be honest I've only done what you asked. It's not like I had to spend much time thinking about what needed to be done.'

'But all the same, you got it sorted, and your grandmother will be very pleased and proud of you. I have to ask – will Natalia be coming to the party after what happened last night? No one at that table was impressed with what she had to say about your dad's business, and if it wasn't for Jenny stepping in I suspect your mum and grandmother might have gone full throttle.'

'I know, but ... well ... she's just like that.' He shrugged, looking a bit embarrassed.

'How did you two leave things last night?'

'She's demanding that my dad fire Jenny before she's even started.'

'And what's your view on the subject? Do you want Jenny working on the boat? Or would you perhaps prefer Natalia?'

'To be honest, I think Jenny's a much better fit for the role, but... Oh, Voula, it's a complete mess. I tried everything to persuade Natalia to come back but now she has I'm in a pickle. How can I refuse her request after she's done exactly what I asked her to do?'

'I'm sorry it's all become so complicated.'

'It's ok, it's no one's fault but my own. But I shouldn't be letting my personal drama distract us. The party should be the focus. I just hope Gran will enjoy it.'

'She will because she knows how much care and effort you've put into it.'

'Thank you again for helping me with all of this. I couldn't have done it without you.'

'Of course you could have.' She gave him a hug and waved him off from the front door of the hotel.

Once Marios had gone, Voula was able to switch off from the party and focus on the hotel. Her plans for the outside, the bedrooms, and the bathrooms were all set, so she turned her attention to the restaurant and bar. The kitchen was fine and would need just a few tweaks, but given she didn't have the square footage of the Mykonos hotel, she thought it might be prudent to combine the restaurant and bar, rather than keeping them as the two separate areas they currently were.

She spent time taking photos and sketching a potential floor plan before making a sandwich and pouring a glass of wine. As she settled for lunch at a table on the terrace, she heard someone coming in through the reception area. Putting her notes under a magazine she called out, 'Mum, I'm out here!' But turning around it wasn't Evangelina she saw, as she'd expected, but Helena. And she looked serious.

'I think we need to have a chat before Mum gets back,' said Helena.

'Fine by me. Grab a seat.'

Helena felt ready to scream and shout but what was the point? Ultimately, this wasn't about her and Voula, it was about their mum's happiness, and so they needed to come together and approach this as a united team. But she'd have to ease into things. Taking a deep breath she sat next to her sister.

'Have you and Marios finalised everything for tomorrow? I know he's really appreciated all the help you've given him. I've never seen him so nervous about anything.'

'He's done a great job and I swear all I did was point him in the right direction. He sorted everything from there on. I'm looking forward to meeting Mum's guests. I'd expected them all to be here when I arrived, but as fate would have it, for one reason or another they've all gone to stay elsewhere on the island.'

'Thankfully lots of Mum's friends will be here, so if the likes of Craig and Tonia kick off, they will soon be lost in the crowd.'

'Hopefully it doesn't come to that. So, what did we need to talk about before Mum gets back?'

'Voula, Mum doesn't want to move to Parga. She's only doing it because she thinks it's the right thing to do.'

'I don't understand.'

'She knows the hotel needs to be updated as it hasn't had any serious renovations since the seventies when all the pine furniture arrived.'

'I remember that day very clearly. Dad was so proud that he was in a financial position to update everything, and there's no denying that he invested well. The furniture has lasted really well, even if it is looking a bit dated now.'

'Yes. Now, Mum is insisting that her savings be used to update the hotel, but that means there's nothing left for her to live on, and that's the reason she's moving away. It's not because she needs distance from the hotel, as she's been claiming.'

'That makes so much sense now you say it. I was shocked when she said she was leaving Vekianos, but I genuinely believed her claim that she wanted to move in with Aunt Dora and leave the hotel behind her.'

'We all did. Well, apart from Nadia. Apparently, she assumed it would be a temporary move, perhaps just for one season. She really does know us better than we know ourselves. Anyway, I digress. I really can't believe I never realised Mum didn't genuinely want to go, and I feel terrible that she's convinced herself that the money she's saved isn't hers to spend as she sees fit. That's why I've come up with a solution.'

'You've figured out a way to persuade her to stay?'

'Yes, we're going to convince her to buy a little house here on Vekianos.'

'But that wouldn't leave any money for you to renovate the hotel.'

'You're right, and that's where you come in. I will run the hotel for this season and then, come October, you can put your plans into action. In short, the hotel is yours to do with as you please. I won't be challenging you. Mum's future happiness has to come first. It's more important than any ideas I might have had about moving the hotel forward.'

Chapter 37
Thursday 19th April

After yesterday's chat with Voula, Helena had just gone through the motions. Nothing was mentioned to Evangelina when she returned, and after a quiet dinner the three of them had all gone off to their rooms for an early night. This morning was already a busy one, a van having arrived with the tables and chairs for the party, and final preparations well underway.

Filippos was going to take their mum out for the day to stop her getting stressed about the party, and Nadia was going to get stuck into the cleaning with Helena, not that there was that much to do as the hotel was always kept spotless. As Helena looked out into the garden, she could see Marios and Voula sorting out where the tables and chairs should be placed.

'Are you sure you don't want me to stay and help? I don't need to go out with Filippos,' asked Evangelina from the doorway.

'No, Mum, you go and switch off from all of this. And take comfort from the fact that come this time tomorrow it will all be over, and we will be back to normal.' Helena laughed.

'I'm not sure I know what normal is. Life here at the hotel has always been anything but normal – guests constantly coming and going, no two weeks alike – but I'm not complaining as I've never felt a desire to do "normal". Now, it's time that son of mine took me out and treated me to a nice lunch somewhere.'

'Have fun and please try to relax. I really think you'll enjoy the evening.'

With that Evangelina went to find Filippos and Helena went to look for Nadia.

As the two women got stuck into the cleaning, Nadia asked how Helena was feeling about the day before.

'I'm ok, thanks. I think perhaps, once the party is over, I might feel a bit sorry for myself, but I have a season to organise so I will soon snap out of it. I've talked to Voula now and told her she's free to do what she likes with the hotel come October because I won't be standing in her way.'

'And what did she say to that?'

'She thanked me and went on for ages about how she wanted me to be part of her plan.'

'And what did *you* say to that?'

'I said I'd give it some thought over the summer. She told me a bit about the spa treatment rooms she's envisioning installing in Mum and Dad's former apartment, and the infinity swimming pool, which she's clearly very nervous about as it requires lots of planning permissions. She even let her guard down enough to tell me that if the swimming pool didn't happen, it could put a stop to her plans completely.'

Nadia raised an eyebrow and Helena nodded.

'It all sounds as though it will be very grand and chic, with fancy food and a top chef in the kitchen, but I'm not sure this island is ready for that type of place. Still, she really does seem to know what she's talking about, and every detail has been thought out.'

'She might have convinced you, Helena, but not me. And did you say there would be a "fancy chef"? I take it that means I might not be needed for breakfast and lunch shifts? I guess I'll have to wait and see as she hasn't brought herself to let me in on her plans just yet.' Nadia huffed. 'Anyway, I'm not convinced yet it will actually happen, and we have something more important to focus on in the meantime – trying to convince Evangelina to stay on the island.'

Helena nodded. 'After I left you and before coming back up here yesterday, I looked at what houses are for sale here on Vekianos, and there are quite a few to choose from. Not that many down in the harbour though, and the ones that *are* available need a lot of work or are too small.'

'Remember that she won't need a lot of space; a bedroom, bathroom, small kitchen, and a living room would be perfect. It doesn't need to be a big, family home as any family get-togethers will still be here in the hotel.'

'That's a good point. I just want her to be happy and I feel bad that it's all turned into a bit of a mess. What do you think my dad would say if he was still here?'

'I know exactly what he would say – he'd say you shouldn't let Voula go through with her plans. Yes, he might take a little convincing to get rid of his beloved pine as he was so proud of it, but he was a smart businessman and would recognise the benefits to making some updates around here. What he wouldn't want – and what it seems like Voula is planning – is massive renovations that make the hotel unrecognisable.'

'You're right, but what can I do? I don't have the money to make the changes, and Voula does.' Helena sighed and returned her attention to dusting. 'Is anyone actually looking forward to this party?' she mused, almost to herself. 'I know I'm not.'

'But if there was no party there would be no Paul. Maybe you could look at it that way?' said Nadia, kindly.

'Right, Paul.' Helena sighed again. 'I asked him to stay and help refurbish the hotel, and now it's not happening he has no reason to be here.'

'Oh yes, he does! Helena, he's *crazy* about you,

and you guys would be so good together. That's what you should be focusing on: being with him in the present. Don't worry about the future; it will work itself out in time.'

It was nearly time for the first guests to arrive and Voula was busy doing final checks; making sure the caterers had everything they needed in the hotel kitchen, that the little stage area for the band and singers was ready, that all the tables were looking lovely, and seeing where Marios had moved some of the big plant pots around to different areas to make more of an impact. All that Voula needed to do now was to have a quick shower and put her party frock on.

'Have you got five minutes for a chat before Filippo brings Evangelina back?' asked Nadia, stopping Voula on her way back to her room.

This was a conversation Voula hadn't been looking forward to. She and her sister-in-law were so different and had butted heads many times over the years. She always dreaded confrontations with Nadia, and she knew that the revelation of her plans for the hotel was likely to bring out the worst in her sister-in-law.

'Of course. Shall we start the party off a little early with a glass of wine?' asked Voula.

'Go on, then. Why not?'

Voula went into the bar and came back with a bottle and two glasses, ready to be told a few home truths, whether she wanted to hear them or not.

'I think you have to agree that Helena is as happy as any of us have ever seen her since Paul arrived.'

Voula nodded, unsure of where Nadia was going with this.

'And we all want that happiness to continue for her, correct?' asked Nadia, a hint of menace in her tone.

Voula nodded again, more hesitantly this time.

'And we want Paul to be happy as well, don't we? He's not had it easy these last few years, and I think a summer here at the hotel is just what he needs.'

Voula felt a little uncomfortable. Where was the shouting she'd expected about 'you can't do this' and 'you can't do that' and 'changing this hotel would break your father's heart'?

'Right?' Nadia pressed.

'Right,' said Voula, dragging the word out. 'What are you getting at here, Nadia?'

'I promise I'm coming to my point. Voula, what's your plan once you've finished renovating the hotel and making it look unrecognisable? Will you really want to stay here on Vekianos for the rest of your life? I think – and, of course, it's only my opinion – that you're using the opportunity to take over here at the hotel as a means to escape the life you're currently living. I can understand you wanting to get away from Rhodes and have a fresh start, but you know as well as I do that you won't enjoy the choice you've made in the long run. Oh, I know you'll thrive in the face of the challenges that come up, and love every minute of creating your dream exclusive boutique hotel, but have you actually taken the time to consider the big picture? When it's all done and day-to-day – and then year-to-year – life kicks in, then what? To me, that life doesn't have "Voula" written on it. Does it to you?'

Nadia leaned back, cocking her head towards the road outside the hotel. 'I think I can hear a car, and it's probably Filippos back with Evangelina. I'd best be going as we need to head home to get ready for the party, but I really hope you're going to think about what I've said here today.'

With that Nadia walked away. Voula sat silently with a heavy heart because she knew everything her sister-in-law had just said was right. Yet, what choice did she have but to carry on with the project? Vekianos was her only option for a new life.

But actually ... it wasn't, was it? Because she had the offer of a job on Mykonos.

Mykonos would certainly be the easier option, but she still felt a sense of responsibility, and a driving need to make the project here on Vekianos work, not just for herself, but for the rest of the family as well. She also needed to prove to them she wasn't just the cold, disconnected sister and daughter that came back now and again to visit. They had to see she was the one who could do what no one else could, the one who would take the family business to the next stage of its life.

Chapter 38

Dressed in her party dress, Jenny knocked on her dad's door. She had a bottle of wine in her hand, thinking they could sit on the balcony and have a glass or two before going down to the party as she didn't want to be the first to arrive. She also wanted to make sure her dad was ok. Although they'd had a lovely day out over in Keriaphos, he had been quieter than usual, and it bothered her to think that he was grappling with something on his own.

'What's all this?' asked Paul.

'I thought we could watch from your balcony as everyone is arriving and then we could go down fashionably late.'

'That's a good idea and will avoid us walking into the unexpected. A few locals have already arrived and there looks to be several generations of one family, the children running around on the lawn.'

'You get the glasses,' said Jenny as she uncorked the wine. 'I expect Filippos and Nadia will be here soon so they can greet everyone with Helena and Voula.'

'Do you think Natalia will be accompanying Marios, or do you think she'll be too embarrassed to turn up after that scene she made?'

'I suspect she'll be here. Oh, look, I can see Voula.' Jenny pointed down to where Voula was greeting the guests who had been milling around outside. 'She looks lovely. With her experience I know she'll be the perfect hostess, making sure everyone is having a good time. And here comes Evangelina. She looks so elegant. I know she's said repeatedly that she isn't looking forward to tonight, but I suspect she'll enjoy every minute.'

Paul nodded. 'Once she starts mingling with her guests she'll have a ball. It will be nice to see her celebrated. Few deserve it more.' He smiled warmly then laughed. 'Looks like you were right,' he said, pointing to Natalia, who had just arrived on Marios' arm.

'Ready to party? The music has just started so it looks like the perfect time to make our entrance,' said Jenny.

As they got to the bottom of the stairs, they ran into Nadia and Filippos.

Jenny spoke first. 'You look gorgeous, Nadia, and you look very handsome and dapper, Filippos.'

'Thank you, Jenny. You both look smashing as well,' said Nadia. 'I was just reminding my husband that this isn't an evening for him to relax and enjoy himself; this is work, and he needs to make sure things run smoothly, not leave everything to his sisters and Marios.'

'Orders received loud and clear, but promise you'll tell me when my duties are over, and I can sign off?' begged Filippos.

'Oh, that's easy to answer. You're off the clock only once we've walked through our front door later tonight.'

Everyone knew Nadia wasn't joking, and they all laughed heartily while Filippos pouted.

'Seeing as I'm "on duty", can I show you through to the bar? Or would you prefer I introduce you to some of the other guests first?' he asked Paul and Jenny.

'A drink, first,' said Jenny, her attention caught by the latest arrivals. 'Looks like Stepanie and Emma are here, but there's no sign of Tonia just yet.'

Nadia answered, 'Apparently, Tonia can't make it. Such a shame... No, that's not the word. What is it I mean?' She pretended to ponder for a moment. 'Oh, yes, what I meant was ... what a relief!' She laughed. 'I think we also might have forgotten to remind Craig that the party was tonight so that only leaves one problem guest, and I can easily handle her...' She broke off, looking around at Filippos, Paul and Jenny's confused expressions. 'Why are you all looking at me as if you don't know who I'm talking about?'

Jenny started, realising she knew the answer. 'Oh! You mean Natalia, don't you?' Nadia scowled and nodded. 'Perhaps I should go and break the ice? Talk about how excited I am to be working on the boat this season?' she teased.

Filippos shook his head. 'I think you've been spending too much time with my wife! Should I be scared?'

'Oh, you've not seen anything yet, Filippos!'

'Paul, I'm beginning to think I've made a mistake employing your daughter.'

They all laughed again before Paul and Jenny walked over to get a drink. It was getting busier on the hotel terrace and Jenny took in the local faces, many of whom she recognised from walking around down in the harbour.

'You're sure you don't mind about Natalia being here?' Paul whispered.

'Of course not. At the end of the day, Marios wants to be with her, and if he's happy, I'm happy.'

'Something tells me by the look on his face he isn't all that happy.'

'Then that's his problem, not mine. By the way, you know who we haven't seen yet? Helena. I thought she'd be out greeting the guests.'

'Me, too. Do you think we should go and talk to Emma and Stepanie? They look a little lost over there by themselves.'

'Yes, come on. I'm intrigued to hear what they've both been up to since moving out of the hotel.'

'You two have scrubbed up well,' said Emma

once they'd all said their hellos.

'You, too. What have you two been up to since we last saw you? Have you and Tonia had some good times together, Stepanie? And Emma, has the mystery man been wining, dining, and spoiling you?'

Emma answered first. 'Yes, there's been quite a lot of wining and dining, and we went over to Corfu for a couple of days as well. It's been wonderful.'

'Sadly, no one has been taking me out for meals, and I've not seen much of Tonia as she parties all night and sleeps through the day, but I've enjoyed spending time on the beach and Tonia and I have had some nice dinners before she headed out for the evening, so it's been ok overall,' said Stepanie. 'What about you two? What have you been up to?'

Before Jenny or Paul could answer Emma jumped in. 'I expect it's been so boring here, and no doubt you can't wait to get the party over with so you can head back to the UK for a bit of excitement.'

Jenny and Paul looked at each other, neither knowing how to answer that when Emma couldn't be further from the truth. Thankfully, Voula appeared just then and saved them.

'Voula! Do you remember Stepanie and Emma? We'll just leave you three to catch up,' said Jenny, starting to pull Paul away.

Having safely escaped over to the corner of the garden, both father and daughter took a deep breath.

'I wonder what's keeping Helena,' said Jenny, trying to see through the crowd. 'Do you think it's because she doesn't want to be here? There's no denying she's sad about her mum leaving, but perhaps it's hit her hard today that she'll soon be taking over everything.'

'I'm not sure. It's out of character for her to be late though. I think I'll walk over to her bungalow and check on her.'

'No, Dad, why don't you stay and catch up with

some of the locals you know? I'll go and see what's keeping her. I'm sure there's a simple explanation.'

Jenny walked around the back of the hotel until she got to Helena's bungalow, smiling to herself at how sweet and welcoming it looked, even tucked out of the way as it was. She knocked on the door, calling, 'Helena? It's only Jenny. I was just wondering ... is everything ok?'

'Just a minute,' called Helena.

When the older woman opened the door a moment later, she was dressed and ready for the party, but her face told a different story.

'I fell asleep and time has flown by me,' she said, looking and sounding frazzled. 'I just need to get my phone.'

'There's no rush,' said Jenny, gently. 'Why don't we sit and have a chat before going over? And you could check yourself in the mirror?' she suggested.

'Oh, dear.' Helena frowned. 'Do I look that bad?'

'Of course not, I just meant that the party will be going on for a long while yet so there's no hurry. I promise it's all very relaxed over there. I think all the talk and build up to it has been a lot worse than the actual event itself. I'm sure you'll enjoy it.'

'I'm confused... Sorry, I think you have the wrong end of the stick, Jenny. It's not the party I'm avoiding ... it's your dad.'

'My dad? You've completely lost me. I thought you two were getting on really well.'

'We are, but there's been a ... development. You see, I'm not going to be refurbishing the hotel. Voula will be taking over the hotel come October, so all the things I'd planned to do – the work I asked your dad to take on – is no longer happening.'

'Why though? What's happened to change your mind?'

Helena quickly filled Jenny in.

'I'm sure there must be another solution to all

this, but it can wait for tomorrow. For now, let's just go over and enjoy the party.'

Not giving Helena time to answer, Jenny stood up and opened the bungalow's front door. 'You look lovely, Helena, and it's time to show off your party dress.'

As they walked over to the hotel Jenny was busy mentally analysing everything she'd just heard. With the change of plan her dad could be back in England while she was here working on the boat – a job she'd only agreed to as it meant staying close to her dad. What a mess! But just as she had told Helena, all of that needed to be put to one side because tonight was all about making sure Evangelina had a lovely time.

Within seconds of their walking onto the terrace old friends were coming up and chatting to Helena, and Jenny could see her visibly relax and regain control. It was as if the last half an hour had never taken place.

As Jenny went to get Helena a glass of wine, she kept an eye out for her dad, knowing that he was likely to have questions, but also that it was important she brush them off as it wasn't her place to explain the hotel's situation. On her way back from the bar she spotted him talking to Stepanie and Emma and knew he probably needed rescuing, so quickly handed off the wine to Helena and crossed the lawn towards him.

Filippos stopped her halfway and beckoned her in close, whispering conspiratorially, 'Nadia is watching my every move but what she doesn't know is that every time I go to the bar to get other people their drinks, I'm having a quick one myself. I think I'll use this tactic going forward. I can see it now – me offering to take things back and forth from the kitchen, enjoying a tipple from my wine glass at the table and another from the bottle I've hidden in the kitchen!' He laughed uproariously and Jenny couldn't help but laugh right along with him as she continued on her way.

She suspected that Nadia knew exactly what her husband was up to and the only reason he was getting away with it was because his wife was letting him.

'You think you are so clever, but I can see *exactly* what you're up to,' said a cold voice, stopping Jenny in her tracks.

She turned to find Natalia closing in on her.

'I'm sorry, did you say something?' asked Jenny, trying to remain calm.

'I know your game. Fetching drinks for the family and pretending you're interested in everything they say. You think you're so clever, but I can see right through you.'

'What's your point, Natalia?' There was an edge of steel in Jenny's tone now. This girl was too much!

'My point is that you are buttering them up and being so lovely so that you can get to Marios and push me out of the way.'

'That's what you think?' Jenny laughed. 'You want Marios? He's yours. I'm not interested.'

'I don't believe that. For a start, I see the way you look at each other; the little smiles and the blushing...' Natalia mimed being sick. 'It sticks out a mile that you want him.'

'Look, I'm not going to stand here arguing with you all night. Yes, Marios and I got on well together before you came back, but when you did, he chose you. I respect that. What you two have is obviously very special.'

'It is and as long as you know that—'

'I have to say though, Natalia, there is one thing I've missed since you've come back.'

'And that is?'

'Kissing Marios.' Jenny smiled sweetly.

'You what? You *kissed* Marios?'

'Yes, but you weren't here so what's the problem?'

'The problem is that since I've returned to Vekianos he hasn't kissed me once, and now we know why that is, don't we?' With that, Natalie turned on her heel and stormed off into the crowd.

Chapter 39
Friday 20th April

'You're up early, Evangelina. I would have thought you'd take it easy and get a slow start today after all of last night's excitement,' said Paul.

Evangelina waved a hand. 'Ach, I'm fine. The van will be here soon to collect all the tables and chairs, and as Marios and his dad moved them all to the gate before leaving last night I volunteered to let the driver in to pick it all up. Did you enjoy the party? Was it worth coming all this way to Greece for just the one evening?'

'Don't be silly! The party was just a small part of my holiday. To be able to come back and spend time with you and your lovely family has been very special, and I can't believe we've been here for over a week already. Do you need a hand with anything today? Put me to work, boss!'

'Oh no, you just take it easy. Normally, we'd now just be starting to get the hotel ready for the summer, but because of the party we started early and are basically ready to go. In just another couple of weeks the first guests will arrive and the season will officially be underway.'

'Yes, and you won't be here to greet them.'

'No, and I expect it will feel very odd for the first few days.'

'Odd in a good way or a bad way?'

'Just different. I think I need to grab that. Please excuse me,' she said, rushing off to answer the hotel's ringing telephone, and passing Helena in the doorway.

Paul and Helena greeted each other hesitantly and chatted about the party.

'I was just glad there were no dramas from any of the guests,' said Helena as Evangelina walked back with a coffee pot. 'Everything ok, Mum? Who was that on the phone?'

'To be honest, I'm not sure.' Evangelina shrugged. 'It was an elegant sounding woman wanting to know if we had a room for tonight. I explained we aren't yet open for the season and told her where she could find a room, and then she asked if Voula was still on the island and did I know how long she was staying. I'm not sure I should have told her, but I said tonight was her last night before going back to Rhodes.'

Helena suspected it would have something to do with Voula's renovation project; probably some top interior designer she'd hired wanting to get a head start on the redesign.

'Mum, you should be resting after all the excitement of last night. I'm going to have a tidy around today but that's easily handled.'

'I won't be resting. I need to go down into the harbour for a few things for tonight's family meal, and as for tidying, that can wait until tomorrow. Why don't you and Paul have a day out somewhere? I'm sure there's lots you need to talk about.'

'I don't know what you mean,' said Helena, keen to evade her mother's meddling.

'I don't mean anything in particular, I just thought it would be nice for you to wind down after last night.'

'That's a good idea, Evangelina,' said Paul. 'Shall we go for lunch? Throw caution to the wind and have wine with our meal, experience the excitement of Vekianos?' he asked Helena.

Helena had to admit that it would be a good opportunity to tell Paul what had happened, and her mum was right, everything else could wait.

Voula and Jenny arrived just then, so Helena

excused herself to go and get more coffee and another plate of pastries.

'Voula, a woman has called looking for you,' said Evangelina.

'If it's important she would probably try me on my mobile, and no one has messaged or called me yet today so I'm sure it's nothing to worry about.'

When Helena returned breakfast was a little subdued, all of them feeling the effects of the previous night's party.

'Helena and I are going out for a walk and then some lunch. Care to join us?' Paul asked his daughter.

'No, you're fine. I'm meeting Filippos to sort out dates for when I start on the boat, and then I'll need to look at booking my flight to come back from the UK.'

'Nadia mentioned you're going to live in the little studio in their garden,' said Voula.

Jenny nodded. 'Yes, I'm going to go have a look at it today. I think it'll be perfect for the summer.'

'Is there anything I can do to help you out today, Mum?' asked Voula.

'Nope. It's your last day so enjoy some rest. Dinner will be at eight tonight.'

Plans made, they all headed off in their separate directions.

Helena took one last look in the mirror before going across the courtyard to the hotel to meet Paul. She was looking forward to their day out but not looking forward to telling him about her spoiled plans for the hotel. She was anxious about the possibility of disappointing him, and worried that he might have no interest in staying now that the hotel project was off the table, but she knew it had to be done.

'You look lovely,' said Paul, running his appreciative gaze over Helena. 'Where shall we go? I was thinking that as your mum's cooking a big meal tonight perhaps we should opt for just a light lunch.'

'Probably a good idea. We could go to the bakery and pick up a few things and then walk along the coastal path?'

'Lead the way!'

As they walked, Helena got the impression Paul was nervous, but she couldn't blame him. She had been odd with him over the last few days.

'What are you planning on having?' she asked as they approached the bakery. 'No, let me guess... Spinach pie and a vanilla slice? Am I right?'

'You know me too well! Or is it just that I'm predictable?'

Helena smiled but didn't answer. What she wanted to say was: 'I do know you well, but I want to know you a lot better', but she was too nervous. They stepped into the bakery, chatted to the lady behind the counter, picked up their bag of goodies, and then continued on their way.

As they got to the end of the sea wall, the pavement turned into a rough, well-worn path.

'Shall I tell you a secret that only Marios knows?' asked Helena as they continued on.

'Are you sure I can be trusted with it?' teased Paul.

'I think so.' She smiled. 'The rocks further on that we're headed for are my favourite part of the island. I come here to centre myself. It's like I plug myself into the rocks and I'm regenerated, a huge shot of energy shooting through me that gives me just what I need to face whatever problem or issue drove me to seek out the rocks in the first place. A bit stupid, don't you think?' She laughed nervously.

'Not at all! I think it's wonderful that you have somewhere you can go to be alone with your thoughts and work things through.'

'I do love it on this path, the peace that comes

from walking away from all the hustle and bustle of a busy harbour into a kind of silence, just the gentle sounds of the waves splashing the rocks below.'

They walked on and Helena asked Paul if he could spot her special rock.

'No pressure on me then? I'm guessing it will be big enough for two people if Marios knows about it. Hopefully you'll let me join you? I've really liked spending time with you this past week, Helena.'

'I have, too, but there's something I need to tell you. Let's find the rock so we can sit and talk.'

They headed further on and after a while Paul slowed down. Of course he had managed to spot her special place.

'I guess you win a prize.'

'Wonderful! What have I won?'

'A burst of energy, of course. Take a seat.'

As Paul sat on the rock he shook his body as if it had electricity going through it, which had them both in fits of laughter. A silence followed and for the first time all day an uncomfortable feeling permeated the air. Helena knew what she had to say, word for word, but try as she might, nothing was coming out.

Thankfully, Paul broke the silence.

'You know how I said you knew me too well earlier? It goes both ways. I know you, Helena, and something is wrong. Why don't you tell me what it is so we can talk it through.'

'You're right, there is something I need to tell you. I discovered that my mum doesn't actually want to move to Parga, and if I can convince her to stay and buy a place here instead, there will be no money for the refurbishment.'

'That's not an insurmountable problem though. Give it another few seasons and you'll have built your savings and can start doing it in stages, updating a set number of rooms per year rather than doing everything in one year.'

'Unfortunately, that isn't going to happen. I've told Voula she can take over the hotel in October when it closes for the winter, and she can have her swimming pool and all the razzmatazz that goes with a luxury retreat.'

A long silence followed and Helena wished Paul would say something – anything!

'What are you thinking, Paul? And please be honest with me. Don't just say what you think I'd like to hear.'

Paul looked thoughtful for a long while and all Helena could think was that they had a long walk back to the hotel and it was going to be a very uncomfortable one if they had to endure it in silence. Just as she was about to say they should head back he spoke.

'So, that means ... come October, you'll have some spare time on your hands? Or will you be staying on to work alongside your sister?'

'No, I'll be at a bit of a loose end.'

'That's fantastic news!' Paul nearly shouted, jumping up and surprising Helena. 'That means we'll have time to spend together – the time we should have had all those years ago. Helena, I wasn't considering staying because you offered me a job, I was considering staying because of you. Hotel or no hotel, I want to be with you.'

Helena felt her eyes well up, her heart warmed by his words.

'I hope those are happy tears,' Paul teased gently.

'Yes, very happy. You'll never know how much I regret not seeing what was right in front of me all those years ago. I'm ready to make up for lost time.'

'Me, too. We have a big, exciting future ahead of us. I love you, Helena, and this time around I'm staying so that I can show you just how much each and every day.'

And with that, Paul pulled Helena into a kiss, and it was a long time before they came up for air.

Chapter 40

The hotel was empty and as Voula had the place to herself for a few hours, she planned to head up to the family apartment to work out how it might be divided up for spa treatment rooms. She needed to get the best result for the square footage, and she knew that once walls and doors were blocked up, and new doors and a corridor created, there would be no going back.

She enjoyed one last coffee and flicked through her emails, glad to see that there was nothing that needed any urgent attention, and so could wait until she returned to Rhodes tomorrow evening. She was just heading up the stairs to her room to get her file of paperwork on the renovation when she heard a car pull up on the drive. Her first thought was that it could be Filippos and Nadia, but when she heard the main hotel door open, she knew it couldn't be them, as they always let themselves in through the side door. She turned around and walked back down the stairs feeling annoyed because this was her last opportunity on this visit to measure the apartment.

'Hello, can I help... Oh! Athena, what are you...? Sorry, what I meant was ... what brings you to Vekianos? But more than that, how did you find out about this hotel and my connection with it?'

'It was quite simple actually. It's only a small island so after just a few minutes on the internet my search led me here. Of course, I hope you don't mind my bit of detective work. I was just a little curious about this hotel and what your plans are for it.'

Voula narrowed her gaze at Athena. 'Really?' she asked, an eyebrow arched.

Athena laughed lightly. 'Ok, you've caught me.

I'm here to try and talk you out of pursuing your renovation so that you'll be free to come and work with me instead.'

'And if I say no? I almost think I should take advantage of the situation – you showing up here unannounced with a plan to throw a wrench into *my* plans – and pick your brains and see how you would turn this dated hotel into a luxury retreat.'

'Touché. How about we discuss it over a drink? I don't think it's too early for a glass of wine, do you? I'd also quite like to take in the view as I think that will be your starting point for the project.'

'The view is the best thing the place has going for it. After that, sadly, it's all downhill I'm afraid.'

'But that could be a good thing. A blank canvas can be a blessing, though speaking from experience, it's not for the faint hearted. My hotel nearly killed me.'

'But look at the result you achieved. It's magnificent.'

'Thank you, that's very kind. Now, lead the way to this phenomenal view you've promised.'

As Voula led Athena outside and across the terrace she was intrigued to hear what the older woman might say about her renovation plans. Having seen what she was capable of creating, Voula knew Athena was a genius when it came to design, and also a very clever businesswoman with a magic eye for detail.

'Take a seat, Athena, and take in the view while I fetch the wine. Red or white?'

'White, please. What a setting you have here. If I were to walk to the end of the garden, would I be able to see down into the harbour?'

'Yes. It really offers the best of all worlds.'

Voula put together a tray of nibbles to go with the wine, and as she walked back outside, she could see Athena stood at the bottom of the garden looking up at the hotel. Once she noticed Voula she made her way back to the table.

'So, what do you make of the old building?'

'It needs some work. I imagine you're planning on getting rid of the chunky columns on the balconies and replacing them with glass railings?' Voula nodded. 'Good, and if the building was rendered it would look lovely and fresh, very modern.'

'That's the plan. It will be a big job, but it needs to be done.'

'Oh yes. One question though: will the new look fit into the landscape with all the other buildings on this hill?'

'No, it will be the first of its kind, but that's a selling point as far as I'm concerned.' Voula paused as a thought hit her. 'Should I assume that it was *you* who phoned and talked to my mum earlier today?'

Athena smiled. 'Yes, that was me. I was in Corfu and as I was so close – just a short boat ride away – it seemed silly not to check and see if you were about. I found a little room for the night down in the harbour. Now, tell me about your plans for the infinity pool. It will likely be one of the most expensive parts of the project.'

'Yes, and the scariest. The cost will be significant and there's so much about it that's out of my control.'

'You'll be fine. Regarding the cost, you can save money on the bedrooms and bathrooms by using the existing pipework, and drainage and electricity points, and updates to the restaurant and public areas are usually just a matter of decoration and creating a breathtaking image...' She broke off and stared at Voula, who couldn't help but smile. 'Something funny?'

'Yes, you sound like my internal thoughts. I'm sure I have everything you just said written word for word in my initial planning notes.'

'I'll take that as a compliment. You also have an advantage over me: you're twenty plus years younger, which means you'll have more energy for the project. You also benefit from not having an uninterested son to keep geeing up.'

'And how is Dimitri? Has he gained any more enthusiasm for the hotel?'

'No, which is why I'm still so keen for you to accept my offer.'

At that moment there was a noise and Voula realised it must be Evangelina returning. She had to think quickly.

'I think that's my mum. Please don't mention any of my plans in front of her. I will explain why once she's gone.' Voula stood and rushed inside to greet her mum and escort her out to the terrace.

'Mum, this is Athena, a friend that has a hotel on Mykonos.'

'It's nice to meet you. Such a shame you didn't arrive yesterday as we had a big party to send me into my retirement.'

'How wonderful and exciting for you. No more guests to deal with and everything else that comes with running a hotel – a job with never-ending early mornings and late nights.'

'Yes, it will be different, and probably a little strange to begin with, but I'm sure I'll get used to it.'

'I really hope you do. I tried it but it didn't work for me. I ended up building a whole new business!' Athena laughed. 'Now that's done I'm looking for a better balance in life, focusing more on my retirement and decreasing my workload. I'll have to see how it pans out.'

'Is there a reason it didn't work the first time?' asked Evangelina, sounding genuinely curious.

'I think it was because I stopped working completely. It just left me with too much free time.

Instead, I should have gradually slowed down so that the change in pace wasn't so apparent.'

'I see. Well, I hope it works for you this time around. I have some things to be getting on with, so I'll leave you two to your catch-up. I hope you enjoy your stay on Vekianos, Athena.'

'Why don't we go for a walk?' suggested Athena, as though sensing Voula's hesitance about continuing their conversation now that Evangelina was back. 'You could show me the harbour and where your guests might spend their evenings. I can't wait to see what this charming island has to offer.'

Voula had never been a fan of the word 'charming', feeling that it made everything sound old and unfashionable, the opposite of what she always aimed for.

'I'd be happy to. We can walk down and perhaps have a drink.'

'That sound perfect. I have to enjoy my little holiday while I can.'

'As long as you agree knowing I'll be picking your brains for ideas about what to do and not do.'

'Fine by me, and I promise to be very honest with you. Could I just use the bathroom before we go?'

'Of course.' Voula showed her where it was then went downstairs to tell Evangelina what her plans were and to see if she needed any help in the kitchen later.

'Your friend seems very nice.'

'She isn't really a friend as such, just an acquaintance. She wants me to move to Mykonos to run her new hotel. She had hoped her son would want to run it for her, but sadly he hasn't any interest in it.'

'Well, she must really want you if she's gone so far out of her way to visit you here. It seems as though everything is happening all at once for you.'

'What do you mean?'

'Leaving the job you loved on Rhodes, the offer on Mykonos, and me retiring. All those changes create a lot of possibilities, but I'm sure you'll figure out where you need to be, whether that's Rhodes, Mykonos, or here running this hotel with your sister.'

'I know what I want but Helena won't work with me. She has one dream for this place, and I have another. And then there's you, Mum. I feel as though the closer you get to your moving day, the more your heart is telling you that going to Parga would be the wrong thing to do. Am I right?'

'Perhaps, but if I stayed and you came back, could you see me, you, Helena, and Nadia successfully working together? It would be a disaster! No, I need to go.'

'Mum, can I ask you something?'

'Of course.'

'If I had a plan for the hotel, something that would take it to another level and bring in lots of money without as much effort, would you be happy for me to pursue it?'

'My only real hope is that the hotel stays in the family. Of course, I'd love it if you and your sister could work in harmony together, but that's something only you two can sort out. I refuse to get involved.'

'Thank you for your honesty, Mum. I promise to do my best to make you proud.'

Chapter 41

As Jenny approached the boat, she saw Filippos on the jetty talking to a group of chaps. She paused for a moment, not sure if she should interrupt or just walk away and come back later, but it was too late; Filippos had spotted her and waved her over. He was chatting away to the group in Greek, and she heard her name before he turned to her and explained, 'I was just telling my chums here that you're my new crew member for the summer. Apparently, they think you would be better off working on their boats as I'm not a good boss.'

This made her smile, and she told Filippos, 'You need to explain they have it all wrong. I'm coming on board as your captain, and it's you who will be working for me!'

This declaration provoked lots of laughter and a few responses, and Filippos translated that they reckoned he wouldn't stand a chance now with Nadia ruling his life at home and Jenny at work. He'd have to watch his every step!

'But ignore these old men, Jenny, and come aboard. Let me show you your new office,' he said, waving goodbye to his friends.

Standing on the boat Jenny began to feel nervous. There were so many questions she wanted to ask but she didn't know what to ask first. She was lost.

'We always start the day off with a strong caffeine shot before the holiday makers board the boat,' said Filippos, as if sensing her conundrum and wanting to help ease her into things.

'That sounds perfect, thank you.' She smiled warmly. 'Before we start, I need to ask you something.'

'You can ask me anything you like,' said Filippos.

'Do you really think I'm the right person for the job? You aren't just giving it to me because you're friends with my dad, are you?'

'Don't be daft! You're perfect and the most important thing is you get on so well with me and Marios. The way we work, it's so important that we get on together as a team, and I just know we will. Now, let me get you that coffee. While I do that, you try and take that worried look off your face. I promise you're in for a fun, happy summer. And you never know, you might even find you want to come back year after year.'

She smiled but knew this would just be a temporary job, something to occupy her while she took a break from the real world. Looking around the boat she started to feel more comfortable, imagining what it would look like filled with visitors sat waiting in anticipation of going somewhere they hadn't been before.

'There you go,' said Filippos, handing her a mug.

'So, what happens next, once the caffeine has kicked in?'

'That's when we let the visitors on board. One of us will be on the jetty checking the tickets and making sure people haven't come on the wrong day. We don't want someone ending up on Paxos when they thought they were off to Parga! Also, it's very important to log how many people are on board when we set sail for health and safety reasons.'

'And in the evening, I'll be selling tickets?' she asked. Filippos nodded. 'I imagine the atmosphere here is great with all the other boats, everyone relaxed after a successful day out on the water.'

'Yes, and a lot of that is because we're a small island and everyone sails to different places so we're never competing for the same tourists. The most important thing is to make sure that the person is buying the right ticket. We don't want any disappointed customers and it's no loss for us to redirect people to one of the neighbouring boats because they'll be doing the same for us. But don't worry, it's not like we will be leaving you by yourself in the evenings. Both Marios and I will be on hand to help out, and something tells me my son will be here most of the time. Anything to get away from spending time with Natalia.'

Jenny wanted to ask more about that statement but that was personal and today was all about her job here on the boat. After talking about the ticket procedure Filippos walked her around the boat, showing her again where the drinks were, saying, 'We only offer water. There are boats that do sell alcohol, but we're primarily a big taxi for the visitors, not a party boat.' Then he spent time running through the first aid boxes, which carried a lot of antiseptic cream as the sea around Antipaxos had a lot of jellyfish, and stings were a common occurrence.

'So that's a day in the life of the boat and crew,' she said when they were done with the induction. 'All I need to know now is when I need to be back in Vekianos to set sail on my summer adventure.'

'You can come back anytime. The studio is ready for you to move into now. Looks like we have a visitor,' he said, looking over Jenny's shoulder and waving.

She turned to see Nadia carrying a bag from the bakery.

'Hello, you two! I'm on the way up to the hotel and I thought you might appreciate it if I called in at the bakery first and brought some treats over. How is the induction day going? Has he told you his favourite part of his job?'

'I'm not sure he has.'

'Very funny, Nadia. Please ignore my wife, Jenny, she's just having her little joke.'

'Who's joking? You'll see, Jenny, how when he gets to Paxos he becomes a teenager again, meeting up with his mates to sit in the harbour, looking at all the pretty women walking by, laughing and joking and having fun. He thinks I don't know, but I have eyes all over Greece.'

This caused a lot of laughter.

'I'm only teasing,' said Nadia, giving Filippos a hug. 'Can you take Jenny up and show her the studio? Marios has borrowed my car as he's taking Natalia to see an apartment over in Keriaphos. Apparently she needs to be out of the place she's currently staying before the season starts. And Filippos, don't be late for dinner tonight, or you'll have me to answer to.'

With a wave, Nadia hopped from the boat to the jetty and headed towards the hill up to the hotel.

'You both make me laugh so much. Marios is very lucky to have you as parents.'

'Yes, and we are very lucky to have him as a son. He's never given us a day's problems, though a lot of that is down to the time he spent with Helena and my parents. They helped us raise him.' Filippos smiled fondly, memories obviously catching up with him.

Coffee and treats devoured, they hopped in Filippos' van and headed to his and Nadia's home. It was a lovely, big house, and once parked Filippos led Jenny away from the house and down a path to her new home. The studio flat, which was almost more of a bungalow, was tucked out of the way with enough room outside the front door for several chairs. She was thrilled with it.

'There you go. The door's unlocked so feel free to take your time looking around, and if there's anything missing or anything you think you might need, just let me know. We can make sure to get it for you before you come back.'

As Filippos headed back to the main house she opened the door to find a modern space with separate areas for living, sleeping and eating, with a bathroom through a door in the far corner. It was compact but had everything she'd need, and she knew she'd be spending most of her free time outdoors anyway, either in the sunshine or in the shade of the tree.

She couldn't wait to show her dad.

She walked back up to the main house to find Filippos. 'It's perfect,' she gushed. 'Thank you so much! It has everything I need and more, but I have to warn you that after the season is over, I might not want to leave.'

'That's fine by me. It just means you'll have to work on the boat again next year, which I'm all for. Shall I drop you back at the hotel?'

'No, that's fine, thanks. I want some exercise so I'll walk. Thank you again for the job and the fabulous new home. I'll see you later.'

It only took a few minutes to get back to the harbour, and looking at the time she saw that there was no need for her to hurry back to the hotel just yet. She was glad to have some quiet time by herself to take in everything that had happened today. She stopped at a little restaurant and ordered a drink. She had a job and a home, but most importantly, a whole summer on a Greek island. How lucky was she?

As she was smiling to herself, she spotted Marios and Natalia walking along the opposite sidewalk. They hadn't spotted her so she quickly picked up the menu to hide her face. Peeking out a moment later, she saw that they'd stopped and gone into a restaurant a few buildings away. They sat at one of the outside tables and she could see Natalia stroke

Marios' head and kiss him on the forehead. She decided it was time to head back to the hotel.

As she walked, she thought about what she had just seen. If she was honest, a large part of her excitement about the job and the studio stemmed from the fact that they would keep her close to Marios, but it was clear now that whatever attraction had been simmering between them was long gone – on his side, at least. Perhaps the perfect summer that she was so excited about wouldn't be as perfect as she had been hoping.

Chapter 42

'I love a little adventure,' said Athena as she and Voula headed down into the harbour. 'I suspect this is going to take me right back to the Greek islands I grew up on, back to the days when foreign visitors really started to discover the islands and the locals realised there were opportunities for them opening up. They were good times. No internet or mobile phones, just a towel and an umbrella on the beach, and at the end of the day, a visit to a little tucked away taverna serving beautiful food.'

'Life was a lot simpler then, but I'd argue it's only gotten better as you still have the same beaches and traditional food, but now with added chic.'

'But do the tourists who visit Vekianos want chic? I know you'll likely think the question is odd coming from me, someone who owns one of the most glamorous hotels in the Greek islands, but I have to be honest with you. I don't know if it will fly here.'

'This is where most of the little shops are for the tourists,' said Voula as they reached the main road near the seafront. 'There aren't as many here as other bigger islands, but there are a few nice clothes and handbag shops, and gift shops with souvenirs for the holiday makers to take back.'

They continued on and eventually came to the bend in the road that turned towards the sea wall.

'This is beautiful. This is the Greece I personally love so much. It's real, and there are no bright lights and flashness, just good old tradition.'

'Shall we stop for a drink?'

'That would be nice, but first let's walk a little further.'

Once they reached the sea wall Athena walked

over and rested her handbag on it before turning and looking up at the view behind them.

'It's stunning from both ways, and I don't think putting the new glass balconies in would spoil the view from here because the actual building will still look charming.'

There was that word again. Voula wanted it to look chic, not charming!

They walked back to an open restaurant and after a greeting from the owner, who talked about last night's party and said how sad it would be to see Evangelina leaving Vekianos, they ordered a carafe of red wine.

'You must be tired, Athena. You've had a long day travelling and now all this walking.'

'Strangely, I'm feeling quite buzzy. Last night I was feeling the atmosphere of Corfu town and now I've slowed down to this tranquil pace of paradise. It's a welcome reset before going back to the sharpness of Mykonos.'

'But you must be so proud of what you've created there.'

'Oh I am. Don't get me wrong, my hotel is the one of the things I'm most proud of creating in all my seventy years on this earth. I savour every moment I spend there, and to get to see my guests enjoying what I've created is just wonderful. But it's also nice to slow down and try a different pace of life every so often.'

'I was thinking you do seem very switched off and relaxed. Is that because when you're at your hotel you're always on duty making sure everything is running like clockwork?'

'Yes, exactly. But I have to say I enjoy both being "off-duty Athena" and "boss Athena", and dressing the part for each role. Why are you smiling?'

'Because that's me on Rhodes. Before I even close my front door my shoes are kicked off and the bag is thrown on a chair. I have a shower and wash off the makeup and I become someone else completely.'

In what felt like no time at all the last of the wine was poured and it was now late afternoon. Voula knew she should probably start to think about walking back up to the hotel to see if her mum needed any help with dinner, though no doubt Nadia would have arrived early to pitch in.

'I think I'd best start to think about making a move,' said Voula.

'Before you go, shall I give you my thoughts on your project? I did say I would be honest and tell you what I really think.'

'I would appreciate it. It would be so useful to get input from someone on the outside who is looking at it all with fresh eyes, especially someone who has no emotional connection to the hotel and so can be honest about exactly what is needed.'

'Good. Now, where do I start? The hotel is in a fabulous position, the view is to die for, the terrace and the garden are magnificent, and the infinity pool will be stunning. The bedrooms and bathrooms are a brilliant size, and with the design you've mocked up they will look so glamorous and very chic. You also have a wonderful space to create something very special and unique with the restaurant and bar.'

Voula was pleased with that feedback, but then she could see Athena's face change. Something else was coming and she wasn't sure if she was ready for it. What didn't she like about the project?

'There's something else though, and I'm so sorry to have to say it. Your dream hotel, and all the fabulous things you want to create with it, just do not fit on this island. The island is far too small and doesn't have the kind of high-end amenities and experiences the type of clientele you're marketing to look for. The customers that stay at my hotel want a choice of chic boutiques and high-end jewellers, they want flashy cocktail bars where they can live that Instagram life. Here on Vekianos there are no exclusive bars and restaurants, or high-end nightclubs where they can go and parade their wealth. I truly believe you can achieve your vision for the hotel, but it just doesn't work in the context of this island.'

Voula was stunned into silence. Her head felt ready to explode with frustration and her body was alive with tension, but before she could say anything Athena had called the waiter over and ordered two large gin and tonics, which appeared in what felt like seconds.

'I am so sorry to have to be blunt, Voula, and you need to remember that this is just my opinion, and I could be wrong, but you are such a clever woman, and I know that you'll be able to see that there are some serious shortcomings when it comes to what's on offer to your guests once they leave the hotel grounds. What you have planned will cost an awful lot of money, and I want you to not only be able to make back every cent you invest, but also make a significant profit, so you really need to think hard about this. If you're willing to scale back your vision you could certainly give the hotel an update, and I know you hate the word "charm" – don't think I haven't noticed the way it makes you flinch! – but that's where the success of your family business comes from – its charm. Are you sure you want to destroy that?'

Voula didn't know what to say. She was struggling to take it all in and she wanted to run up the hill and lock herself in her room.

'I've given you lots to think about so perhaps this is a good time for us to say goodbye. I hope it won't be forever though. It's been many years since I've been in the company of someone so like me, and I really have had a lovely day today. Thank you for showing me a little bit of this very special island.'

'Thank you for being honest with me,' Voula managed to say. 'You're right, it's not what I wanted to hear, but it's probably exactly what I needed to hear. Sorry, does that make sense?'

'It does completely, and please don't think I have intentionally put a damper on your plans just to get you to come and work for me. I'm just saying it as I see it.'

'I know you are, and I promise I didn't think that for a single moment.'

'But it's worth repeating that the job is there if you want it.' Athena smiled cheekily and Voula had to laugh at her persistence.

'Thank you. I'd best head back now. Goodbye, Athena.'

With that they hugged, and she walked back up the hill, but the last thing Voula needed was to be talking to her mum right now, or anyone else really. She needed some quiet time to stop and analyse the whole situation.

She poked her head into the kitchen to offer help anyway, but thankfully, was turned away by Evangelina and Nadia, who said they had dinner well in hand.

As she closed the bedroom door behind her, Voula felt depressed. As much as she hated to admit it, she knew Athena was probably right. But how could she walk away from her dream?

She had a while before dinner so she had a shower and sat out on the balcony. Her phone pinged with an email from the company sending her the quote for the swimming pool and she was pleasantly surprised to find that the cost was much less than she'd expected. Before she could think through what that meant for her plans, the phone went again, another email from the pool company coming through, this one apologising for not attaching the quote for the groundwork preparation that would be needed before the pool was put in place.

As she opened the attachment, her jaw dropped.

'I could build a whole new hotel for that amount of money!' she said out loud before putting her phone down and dropping her head into her hands. It looked as though her visit to Vekianos wouldn't be ending in the triumphant and promising way she'd thought it would.

Hearing someone giggling she glanced over the balcony railing to see Helena and Paul walking over to the end of the garden. Seeing the way her sister and Paul were looking at each other, she felt envious of Helena for the first time in her life. Voula had always hoped to find that level of contentment and happiness, but it seemed that content was something she was never destined to be.

Chapter 43

Helena took one last look in the mirror before heading over to the hotel. She couldn't remember feeling this happy ever before, and she couldn't get over the fact that she barely recognised the joyful face looking back at her. The day she had just had with Paul had been so special, and for the first time in her life she felt she was genuinely in love. She was so looking forward to spending the summer with Paul and when it came time for Voula to take over in October, Helena and Paul would decide – together – what their future should look like.

As she went to pick up her phone there was a knock at the door. 'It's open... Is everything ok?' she asked Voula, immediately concerned by the distress on her sister's face.

'Yes, I was just wondering if you have a belt I can borrow for tonight?'

The request was odd and it was clear something else was going on, but Helena wasn't sure yet what it could be.

'Yes of course.'

'I love this top but the skirt I have to go with it is just a bit too big. I thought if I hid a belt underneath, I could get away with it.'

'It's a lovely top, and very different for you.'

'Different how?' asked Voula, sounding a bit sharp.

'Sorry, I didn't mean to offend you. I just meant that it's more casual than what you usually wear.'

'Oh, thanks.'

Voula looked around the room.

'I really can't remember the last time I was in here. It has to be years ago now, maybe even decades. It looks lovely and is a lot bigger than I remember. Are you still happy living here?'

'Yes, I've always been happy here. It's a great size for me and near enough to the hotel to go back and forth easily.'

'But also far enough away that you can cut yourself off from work if needed.'

'I suppose so. I've not really thought of it like that before.'

'We'd best go over and see if we're needed.'

'Ok,' said Helena, still trying to figure out what was happening here.

'Look, before we go there's something I just want to say.'

Helena suspected she knew what was coming. It would be another speech from her sister about how wonderful it would be if she agreed to be part of this big renovation project, but Helena wasn't willing to listen to that tonight.

'Actually, I think we should chat tomorrow before you leave. We're running late as it is.'

Before Voula could protest, Helena was out the door and heading across the courtyard.

'Voula and I are here to help,' announced Helena as they entered the kitchen moments later. 'What do you want us to do?'

'Nothing. Everything is under control so why don't you both go out and chat to the guests?'

'Ok, but please shout if you want us to do anything,' said Voula.

Jenny knew it was time to go down but she felt oddly nervous, and really wasn't in the mood to be pleasant to Natalia if she showed up.

As she got to the lounge door, she saw her dad walking towards her.

'Hi, Dad, everything ok?'

'Yes, darling, everything is perfect. I've had a

lovely day and I'm happy to tell you that I'm definitely going to be staying here for the summer and helping Helena with whatever I can.'

'That's great! But what happens when October arrives and Voula starts making all the changes?'

'Helena and I have decided to cross that bridge when we come to it. For now, we'll be enjoying the season and taking things day by day. By the way, Filippos told me he showed you the studio. Are you happy with everything?'

'I am, and like you, I'm going to be focusing on the next six months, nothing after that.'

'Sounds like a great plan. Shall we go and join everyone?'

'Of course! No Marios and Natalia yet?' asked Jenny as they crossed the terrace.

'Not yet. Nadia said he wouldn't let his grandmother down by not being here, so I suspect they'll appear at some point.'

'Yes. Actually, you know what?' Jenny stopped walking and her dad swung back around to face her, looking concerned. 'I'm going to take a minute, if that's ok? I just need a little air.'

'Take all the time you need,' said Paul, putting a supportive hand on Jenny's arm and giving her an affectionate squeeze.

Jenny made her way across the garden to take in the view down into the harbour. She took several deep breaths and as she turned to walk back, she spotted Filippos waving to her.

'Come on, Jenny, we need to celebrate you being my new employee! Let's get you a drink.'

'But should I be drinking and socialising with my boss?' she joked, making everyone laugh.

Nadia's phone beeped and she looked at the screen. 'It's Marios. He's on his way and says he shouldn't be more than ten minutes. I'll let Evangelina know we can start to bring the food out.'

Jenny's stomach gave a jump but before she could start spiralling her gaze caught on Voula. Marios' aunt was standing on the other side of the terrace, and she was wiping her eyes and looking upset. As Jenny watched on, Voula got her phone out and called someone. The conversation didn't last long and as she hung up it was as if a switch was being turned off, and she was back to her normal self. Jenny wasn't the only one to notice this though, and she watched as Helena walked towards Voula.

Jenny edged closer to try and hear what they were saying.

Helena spoke first. 'Are you ok? Was that bad news on the phone?'

'No, it was actually very happy news. The perfect outcome, if I'm honest. We should sit down before Mum scolds us,' said Voula, rushing away from her sister.

'Come on, take a seat everyone. We can't wait any longer for my grandson; the food will spoil. Let's dive in.'

As everyone passed plates and laughed and chatted it hit Voula how special this was, the family all sat around the table, and she realised that perhaps now was as good a time as any to make her announcement.

'I have some news,' she said, abruptly. 'A friend came to see me today and has convinced me to take her up on a job offer. I'm going to run her hotel on Mykonos and I'm really excited about it.'

Before anyone could respond Marios walked in. By himself.

'Sorry I'm late, Gran.'

'It's not a problem, your father hasn't even put any bottles of water on the table yet.'

'Sorry, Mum, I'll get some.' Filippos started to rise from his seat but Evangelina waved him back down.

'No, it's ok. Marios is on his feet so he can fetch them. And perhaps you could give him a hand, Jenny?'

Jenny didn't need asking twice, aware of Evangelina's blatantly clear intentions. She jumped out of her chair and followed Marios inside as the rest of the gathered family started asking Voula all about her new job.

'Where's Natalia?' she asked quietly.

'She's gone. Jenny, I need to say how sorry I am. I should have put a stop to all this nonsense the minute she arrived. Being with you made it abundantly clear that I've been letting Natalia walk all over me, and showed me that I don't want to be with her. I told her we didn't have a future together and asked her to leave.'

'Wow. I don't suppose she was happy to hear that.'

'She wasn't, but it was better I was honest with her now. Please forgive me for being an idiot. I'm so sorry.'

Jenny smiled. 'Marios, stop babbling and just kiss me already!'

As they embraced the world around them disappeared ... until they could hear Filippos shouting.

'How long does it take to fetch water, you two? Come on, the food is getting cold!'

Evangelina jumped in and said, 'Oh, Filippos, leave them be. The food can wait.'

They headed right back with the water and everyone got stuck into the meal.

Voula was happy that everyone was so pleased about her news about her new job, but the future of the hotel was still up in the air, and she knew she needed to say something.

Voula took a large sip of wine before she spoke.

'I think we're missing a huge opportunity here at the hotel and it wasn't until I went over to Helena's bungalow to borrow a belt that it occurred to me.'

Everyone stopped eating and looked at her as she continued.

'Mum, I think you should move into the bungalow. That way you could stay here on Vekianos but have more privacy in a space away from the hotel. As Helena will be running the business, it would be better for her to be up in the family apartment so she can be on hand for her guests, and of course, as it's so much bigger, it would give her and Paul a lot more space. I really can't think why none of us have thought of it before. It's such a simple solution.'

There were tears in a lot of eyes as everyone processed Voula's suggestion, realising it solved all the problems that had seemed insurmountable just hours ago. For once, words weren't necessary because everyone's smiles and the sense of relief that settled over the group spoke volumes.

Helena was shocked at the turnaround of the last half an hour. Voula was off to Mykonos, Evangelina was staying on Vekianos, and Helena was back in charge of the family hotel. She knew how hard it would have been for her sister to give up on her dream, but something told her that Voula's life was never meant to be back here on Vekianos, and that she'd be able to accomplish so much more – and hopefully find the happiness she deserved – on Mykonos.

Jenny's heart was all of a flutter as she looked at Marios. His smile was to die for and she wanted to burst out singing, she was that happy.

'Well, Dad, it looks like our little two-week holiday is going to be a lot longer,' she whispered to Paul.

'Yes, darling, and do you know something else? We are going to be able to create some very special Greek island memories this coming summer, and that makes me very happy.'

THE END

Printed in Great Britain
by Amazon